CHASING
THE
DEVIL

CHASING THE DEVIL

Agata Stanford

A JENEVACRIS PRESS PUBLICATION

CHASING THE DEVIL
A Dorothy Parker Mystery / November 2010

Published by
Jenevacris Press
New York

This is a work of fiction. Names, characters, places, and incidents either are the product of the author's imagination or are used fictitiously. Any resemblance to actual persons, living or dead, events, or locales is entirely coincidental.

All rights reserved
Copyright © 2010 by Agata Stanford
Edited by Shelley Flannery
Typesetting & Cover Design by Eric Conover

ISBN 978-0-9827542-2-1

Printed in the United States of America

www.dorothyparkermysteries.com

for Mary Rose

Also by Agata Stanford

The Dorothy Parker Mystery Series:
The Broadway Murders
Chasing the Devil

Acknowledgments

Some writers say that their profession is a lonely one. But I've been lucky to have the companionship of an assemblage of fascinating real-life characters with me at all times, including the emotional support and encouragement of my family and friends, the artistic skills of Eric Conover, without whose design talents my books would not look nearly so good, and the editing expertise of Shelley Flannery, copyeditor and historian, who shows me the errors of my ways.

Contents

Cast of Characters ... ... *Page xi*

Chapter One ... ... *Page 1*

Chapter Two ... ... *Page 15*

Chapter Three ... ... *Page 55*

Chapter Four ... ... *Page 73*

Chapter Five ... ... *Page 95*

Chapter Six ... ... *Page 117*

Chapter Seven ... ... *Page 159*

Chapter Eight ... ... *Page 195*

Chapter Nine ... ... *Page 229*

Chapter Ten ... ... *Page 257*

Chapter Eleven ... ... *Page 279*

The Final Chapter ... ... *Page 313*

Poetic License ... ... *Page 323*

About the Author ... ... *Page 327*

Who's Who in the Cast of Dorothy Parker Mysteries

The Algonquin Round Table was the famous assemblage of writers, artists, actors, musicians, newspaper and magazine reporters, columnists, and critics who met for luncheon at 1:00 P.M. most days, for a period of about ten years, starting in 1919, in the Rose Room of the Algonquin Hotel on West 44th Street in Manhattan. The unwritten test for membership was wit, brilliance, and likeability. It was an informal gathering ranging from ten to fifteen regulars, although many peripheral characters who arrived for lunch only once might later claim they were part of the "Vicious Circle," broadening the number to thirty, forty, and more. Once taken into the fold, one was expected to indulge in witty repartee and humorous observations during the meal, and then follow along to the Theatre, or a speakeasy, or Harlem for a night of jazz. Gertrude Stein dubbed the Round Tablers "The Lost Generation." The joyous, if sardonic, reply that rose with a laugh from Dorothy Parker was, "*Wheeee! We're lost!*"

Dorothy Parker set the style and attitude for modern women of America to emulate during the 1920s and 1930s. Through her pointed poetry, cutting theatrical reviews, brilliant commentary, bittersweet short stories, and much-quoted rejoinders, Mrs. Parker was the embodiment of the soulful pathos of the "Ain't We Got Fun" generation of the Roaring Twenties.

Robert Benchley: Writer, humorist, boulevardier, and bon vivant, editor of *Vanity Fair* and *Life Magazine,* and drama critic of *The New Yorker,* he may accidentally have been the very first standup comedian. His original and skewered sense of humor made him a star on Broadway, and later, in the movies. What man didn't want to *be* Bob Benchley?

Alexander Woollcott was the most famous man in America—or so he said. As drama critic for the *New York Times,* he was the star-maker, discovering and promoting the careers of Helen Hayes, Katherine Cornell, Alfred Lunt and Lynn Fontanne, and the Marx Brothers, to name but a few. Larger than life and possessing a rapier wit, he was a force to be reckoned with. When someone asked a friend of his to describe Woollcott, the answer was, "Improbable."

Frank Pierce Adams (FPA) was a self-proclaimed modern-day Samuel Pepys, whose newspaper column, "The Conning Tower," was a widely read daily diary of how, where, and with whom he spent his days while gallivanting about New York City. Thanks to him, every witty retort, clever comment, and one-liner uttered by the Round Tablers at luncheon was in print the next day for millions of readers to chuckle over at the breakfast table.

Harold Ross wrote for *Stars and Stripes* during the War, where he first met fellow newspapermen Woollcott and Adams. The rumpled, "clipped woodchuck" (as described by Edna Ferber) was one of the most brilliant editors of his time. His magazine, *The New Yorker*, which he started in 1925, has enriched the lives of everyone who has ever had a subscription. His hypochondria was legendary, and his the-world-is-out-to-get-me outlook was often comical.

Jane Grant married Harold Ross but kept her maiden name, cut her hair shorter than her husband's, and viewed domesticity with disdain. A society columnist for the *New York Times*, Jane was the very chic model of modernity during the 1920s. Having worked hard for women's suffrage, Jane continued in her cause while serving meals and emptying ashtrays during all-night sessions of the Thanatopsis Literary and Inside Straight Club.

Heywood Broun began his career at numerous newspapers throughout the country before landing a spot on the *World*. Sportswriter and Harlem Renaissance jazz fiend, he was to become the social conscience of America during the 1920s and beyond through his column, "As I See It." His insight and commentary made him a champion of the labor movement, as did his fight for justice during and after the seven years of the Sacco and Vanzetti trials and execution.

Edmund "Bunny" Wilson: Writer, editor, and critic of American literature, he first came to work at *Vanity Fair* after Mrs. Parker pulled his short story out from under the slush-pile and found it interesting.

Robert E. Sherwood came to work on the editorial staff at *Vanity Fair* alongside Parker and Benchley. The six-foot-six Sherwood was often tormented by the dwarfs performing—whatever it was they did—at the Hippodrome on his way to and from work at the magazine's 44th Street offices, but that didn't stop him from becoming one of the twentieth-century Theatre's greatest playwrights.

Marc Connelly began his career as a reporter but found his true calling as a playwright. Short and bald, he co-authored his first hit play with the tall and pompadoured **George S. Kaufman**.

Edna Ferber racked up Pulitzer Prizes by writing bestselling potboilers set against America's sweeping vistas, most notably, *So Big, Showboat, Cimarron,* and *Giant*. She, too, collaborated with George S. on several successful Broadway shows. A spinster, she was a formidable personality and wit and a much-coveted member of the Algonquin Round Table.

John Barrymore was a member of the Royal Family of the American Stage, which included **John Drew** and

Ethel and ***Lionel Barrymore***. John Barrymore was famous not only for his stage portrayals, but for his majestic profile, which was captured in all its splendor on celluloid.

The Marx Brothers: First there were five, then there were four, then there were three Marx Brothers—*awww, heck,* if you don't know who these crazy, zany men are, it's time to hit the video store or tune into Turner Classic Movies!

Also mentioned: ***Neysa McMein,*** artist and illustrator, whose studio door was open all hours of the day and night for anyone who wished to pay a call; ***Grace Moore***, Broadway and opera star, and later a movie star; Broadway and radio star ***Fanny Brice***—think Streisand in *Funny Girl*; ***Noel Coward,*** English star and playwright who took America by storm with his classy comedies and bright musical offerings; ***Condé Nast,*** publisher of numerous magazines including *Vogue*, *Vanity Fair,* and *House and Garden;* ***Florenz Zeigfeld***—of *"Follies"* fame—big-time producer of the extravaganza stage revue; ***The Lunts***, husband-and-wife stars of the London and Broadway stages, individually known as Alfred Lunt and Lynn Fontanne; ***Tallulah Bankhead***—irreverent, though beautiful, southern-born actress with the foghorn drawl, who later made a successful transition from the stage to film—the life of any party, she often perked up the waning festivities performing cartwheels sans bloomers; ***Irving Berlin, George Gershwin,*** and ***Jascha Heifetz***—famous for "God Bless America" and hundreds more hit songs; composer of *Rhapsody in Blue* and *Porgy and Bess* and many more great works; and the violin virtuoso, respectively.

CHASING
THE
DEVIL

Chapter One

"I'mfreezzenmabalsov, frkrissake!" spat out Ross. "'Sfknkoloutere," he continued, a scowl furrowing his brow. The bristle-brush head was jammed tightly inside a brown woolen stocking cap. As his bulbous nose and hooded eyes retreated into his upturned collar, he looked not unlike a critter receding into the underbrush.

"Your language is simply atrocious, Ross," said his wife, Jane Grant. "Children can hear you."

We stood among the masses of New Yorkers lining the sidewalks of Seventh Avenue near Herald Square in the icy morning sunshine. It was Thanksgiving Day, and all New York had come to watch the spectacle.

For weeks, Herbert Straus, president of R.H. Macy's department store on Herald Square and 34th Street, had been advertising in all the dailies the "promise of a surprise New York will never forget." Four hundred employees of the store, mostly immigrants missing the Christmas holiday celebrations of their homelands, asked Straus if he would sponsor a special event marking the beginning of the Christmas season. Given the go-ahead, they devised floats depicting their national customs, hired bands, acquired animals from the Central Park Zoo, and appealed to Broadway celebrities to march in the parade along with hundreds of clowns and circus acts. And bringing up the rear, a float carrying Santa Claus.

The R.H. Macy's Christmas Parade started uptown on 145th Street and Convent Avenue, made its way across 110th Street at Central Park's northernmost border, and marched down Broadway to Seventh Avenue, culminating at the department store. Thousands of families turned out, and the fanfare and laughter and excitement of the children warmed even the chilliest of hearts, except, perhaps, that of my friend Harold Ross, who hated crowds and lived in constant fear of contracting the germ that would kill him.

And here they were, runny-nosed little monsters in abundance, bundled-up in hats with earflaps, leggings, woolen coats, and mittens, and lifted upon the shoulders of fathers to better see the floats and zoo animals, the marching bands, and the big balloons.

The Felix the Cat balloon loomed huge in the distance, tethered to walkers along the parade route. Squeals of laughter floated up like bubbles in the air with the youngsters' delight at seeing their cartoon hero in giant form. The black rubber cat, as tall as the buildings along the parade corridor, moved with the cumbersome drag of a sloth; the band's horn section pounded out "Alexander's Ragtime Band" with an insistent drumbeat and the repeated prodding crash of cymbals.

"What fun!" I said to Woodrow Wilson, my Boston terrier, whom I had dressed in his new red-plush coat to fend off the cold from his short-haired little black-and-white body. He shivered in my arms, so I nuzzled him closer against the fur of my collar as I stood perched upon a footstool. At my diminutive stature, the extra six inches raised us up just high enough to peek between the bobbing heads of average spectators.

"Crakinzak!" mumbled Ross, who stood between me and Jane, bobbing from one foot to the other, more in a show of impatience than in any effort to ward off the cold.

I turned in the direction of an exasperated *"hurrumph"* to face a gaping-mouthed fellow, a child hoisted upon his shoulder. His expression of distaste at Ross's rather colorful, if not terribly original, exclamations, prompted me to say, "Do forgive his unfortunate choice of words. He cannot help himself. It is a medical condition."

"Tourettes?" he asked, lifting his scarf to meet his fedora against the chill wind from off the Hudson.

"Oh, no, thank you, I've quit," I replied.

"Sonovbitch, can'feelmetos!, 'M goin' 'ome."

"Too bad his lips aren't frozen," I said to Jane.

"You can't go home," said Jane. "We're going to

Edna's. Go stand in that doorway, out of the wind, and try to behave yourself." Jane turned her pretty face toward me. "What are you laughing about, Dottie?"

"Your husband," I said, shaking my head.

"You mean my petulant six-year-old!"

She threw a mean glance toward the man huddled in the doorway, watching as he unscrewed the cap of a flask, a cigarette dangling from his chapped lips. Ross could be easily mistaken for a Skid-Row-bum-come-uptown.

Our friend, writer Edna Ferber, upon first meeting Ross at a fancy dinner party several years ago, mistook the sullen fellow as a vagrant brought home by the hostess as a practical joke on her well-shod dinner guests. That hostess was my good friend, Jane Grant, society and women's columnist at the *New York Times*, suffragette, and fierce opponent of housekeeping, marriage, and childbearing. The "vagrant" was my friend Harold Ross, newspaper reporter, Round Table member, and now publisher of a new magazine, *The New Yorker*, which debuted this past February of 1925.

When Jane married Harold (who was best described by Edna Ferber as "a clipped woodchuck" because of his bristly head of hair, overbite, and beady eyes), she retained her maiden name and violently cut off her hair, combing what was left into a dashing "man's cut." The effect was delightful, as Jane attained a modern, sleek look, which was accentuated by an exceptionally fine, slim figure and smashing wardrobe.

As much as I liked Ross, who was a notorious paranoid hypochondriac, I wondered how long this marriage would last. Jane was beginning to view all the troubles through the ages that sat upon the soft shoulders of her sex as having been Ross's fault. Where Jane usually viewed the world as a glass half full, Ross's world was a vessel that had been drained dry by all those who were out to get him.

"I thought you said Aleck was going to meet us on this corner," I said, a shiver warbling my voice. "What's the holdup, I wonder?"

"He had to go uptown this morning," said Jane. "He's probably stuck in traffic."

"Ah, there're the boys," I said, when the band broke into the intro of "Yes, We Have No Bananas!," calling our attention up the street where Harpo, Zeppo, Chico, and Groucho, dressed in costumes as the Four Musketeers, waved to the crowd while skipping and frolicking down Broadway. Their new Broadway show, *The Cocoanuts*, was set to open in a couple of weeks.

The Marx Brothers had become quite famous this past year, thanks to Alexander Woollcott, who discovered them when he reviewed their show, *I'll Say She Is*, last season. Aleck was the only first-string critic of a major newspaper to see the show when it opened, as all of the other newspaper reviewers believed the Brothers' show to be just another Vaudeville act unworthy of their papers' reviews. The opening night of the play Aleck was set to review that fateful evening was canceled, so, already dressed in evening clothes and his famous opera cape and scarf, he decided to make an evening of it anyway by seeing the show that no one else wanted to review. Alexander Woollcott's reputation was that of a star maker: Helen Hayes; Katherine Cornell; the husband-and-wife acting team, Alfred Lunt and Lynn Fontanne, are only a few of his many discoveries. In his review of the Brothers' show he raved about the hilarity and inventiveness of the four comedians, and literally overnight *I'll Say She Is* became the hottest ticket on Broadway.

As the boys continued their antics toward the newly expanded Macy's department store, I turned at the sound of the Devil himself. Aleck stood beside me, and for once, thanks to my stepstool, we stood eye-to-eye.

"You have on very high heels or very short stilts, Dottie, dear."

I smiled at the pudgy, triple-chinned, bespectacled face of the man I loved so dearly. "Such *élan*," I thought, as I looked him over. His wavy brown hair was covered by a wide-brimmed, black felt hat; a long, red cashmere scarf circled his lower two chins, and an oversized otter-lined black greatcoat tented his impressive body. As he leaned on his favorite ivory-headed walking stick, I thought that only Alexander Woollcott could carry off so flamboyant a costume that teetered just at the edge of where Style met the Ridiculous. But, of course, Aleck was flamboyant, he was stylish, and he was, at times, ridiculous.

"You're late, missed most of the parade. What have you been up to?"

"Had to do a favor for a friend."

"Oh, yeah? Who'd you have to bail out of jail? Your bootlegger?"

"That'd be the day!" he chuckled. "No, my dear Dorothy, my friend is actually the fellow one calls when one needs bailing. Now, tell me why, Dottie, dearest, why do they call this a Christmas Parade, that's what I want to know?"

"Because of Santa Claus, I suppose."

"But today is Thanksgiving Day. Christmas is a month away."

"How the hell do I know why it's called the Christmas Parade!"

"I'll have to send a wire to Straus and tell him he needs to change the name of the parade if he plans on doing it again next year. Christmas is Christmas and Thanksgiving is Thanksgiving, don't you agree?" said Aleck, as if there could be no argument.

"Shit, yes! The man's an ass, what can I say?"

The man in the fedora caught my eye. The child on his shoulder giggled.

"You're almost as bad as Ross over there, Dottie," chided Jane.

"Well, I've been badly influenced. I keep bad company. Perhaps I should go stand in the doorway corner with him," I said, stepping down from my stool. My feet were freezing and my kid-leather gloves were of little use against the cold. I lifted the silver fox collar of my coat to better shield my face, and buried my nose in Woodrow Wilson's warm body. "I could use a drink to warm up," I said. "Maybe I will join Ross. He's got the hooch."

"Shall we stop in at Freddy O'Malley's for a shot? Or do you want to wait to see Santa?" asked Aleck.

"Hell, no! Santa's not coming to my place this year!" I said testily. "I'm Jewish and, anyway, I've been a naughty girl."

"Then come along, my naughty little yenta."

Aleck folded in the legs of the stepstool and popped it into the old carpetbag Woodrow Wilson likes to sleep in. I told Jane we'd be at Freddy's on 38th Street if she and Ross wanted to stop in for fortification before heading up to Edna Ferber's apartment and the Thanksgiving feast.

We had started on our way when there was a sudden roar from the crowd, and I turned to follow Aleck's gaze up into the sky. The huge elephant balloon had been released and was rising up quickly over the buildings along Herald Square. Children were pointing and waving and laughing at the sight of the gigantic flying elephant.

We watched, transfixed, and after a few moments the Toy Soldier was released to the stratosphere. As the brightly colored figure began its rapid ascent into the blue, so, too, rose the sound of chattering children, not unlike the hysterical cawing of thousands of blackbirds descending upon crops of dogwood berries in Central Park this time of year. Soon cheers and whistles burst forth from thousands of onlookers. Just as Aleck and I were about to make our way from the crowd-lined street, a procession of midgets, from the current show at the Hippodrome and dressed as Santa's Elves, guided Santa's sleigh with the accompanying jingle of sleigh bells. Another roar of delight sprang from the spectators as a rotund, jovial, cherry-cheeked Santa came into view, *Ho-Ho-Ho*-ing as he waved to his little fans.

The noise proved too much for the Central Park Zoo's lion, immediately preceding Santa's float, nervously pacing in its cage. It answered the roar of the crowd with a startling one of its own, sending the children closest to the street into screaming fits of terror! And as if that wasn't enough to put an end to the morning's festivities, the giant gas-filled elephant exploded to smithereens above our heads, the horror of which was only compounded when the Toy Soldier, so grotesquely human, followed suit!

It was too late for Felix, I'm afraid, because moments before the elephant defied the laws of gravity and the toy soldier-boy waved his deathly farewell while soaring "over the top," the big cat, too, had been sent on his final journey. The sudden realization of the fate awaiting Felix struck every last soul on the street, and there fell a sudden hush upon the onlookers; Santa's waving hand froze in position, the jingle bells stopped jingling, and even the lion's roar was reduced to a shameful growl as all held their collective breaths for the dreaded, but imminent explosion.

It was not a pretty sight when it happened; the children, who'd whined and whimpered as their parents tried to shield their innocent young eyes and ears from the inevitable, let loose bloodcurdling, ear-shattering screams when the blast rang out.

Black-and-white rubber rained down from the sky to land like flattened carrion on the street.

"I'll have to mention the slaughter, too, in my letter to Straus," said Aleck, as we shuffled past the pathetic, mourning families, coping with loss and the death of fantasy.

The crowds seemed to press closer as we edged our way toward the side street off Seventh Avenue. I held Woodrow Wilson close to my chest as Aleck guided us toward an opening in the crowd.

There was pressure at my back and I began to stumble forward, but a grasp at the shoulder righted my balance. Aleck no longer had hold of my hand, and for a moment I panicked when hands gripped my shoulders. I was literally pivoted around to come face-to-face with a startling figure.

Light, almost white hair, wildly swept atop a pale head, a beard of several days' growth, speckled with spittle, and eyes! What eyes! A lizard's eyes! The strange ice-blue orbs bore into mine with an expression so crazed that I was struck motionless where I stood. Had Woodrow Wilson not whimpered in fear, I'd have thought I was overreacting, but my dog's whine only confirmed my own sense of peril.

As quickly as I'd been seized, I was released.

I was recovering, trying to pull myself together, both figuratively as well as literally, for my hat was askew and my scarf yanked from inside my coat in the shuffle, when I looked around for Aleck, and called out his name.

A few feet ahead a commotion: I glimpsed Aleck's familiar ivory-headed cane as it rose in the air. The crowd pressed in closer, alarmingly, but I forced my way through toward my friend.

With the flash of sunlight on steel, I glimpsed the blade of a dagger.

I screamed.

Voices raised up all around me. A scuffle further along sent people staggering and shouting. I pushed through the crush, searching frantically for Aleck. But by now people were in a panic, rushing, pushing toward me, away from danger, and it was all I could do to move onward in my search. I glimpsed the wild shock of light hair as the man with the startling face pressed forward in escape.

Finding my friend at last, I was relieved to see that he was unharmed. But in his hand he held a bloodied dagger, and another man lay prone at his feet!

Police whistles sounded along the street.

Aleck dropped the dagger and kneeled to assess the victim's injuries. He loosened the man's scarf and there, revealed, was a clerical collar. His overcoat was unbuttoned; blood oozed from his chest. Aleck was speaking frantically to the wounded man.

"Stop him!" I heard the man say with a fervent hiss. Aleck moved in closer to better hear.

"Who?" asked Aleck. "Stop whom?"

". . . save him . . ."

"Tell me his name! Who did this to you?"

"Save him . . . ."

But it was too late. Just as a policeman arrived at the scene, the man fell dead in Aleck's arms.

When pigs fly

Marching to oblivion

In memoriam

Jane and Ross

Chapter Two

I hate happy people.

Perhaps I should rephrase that statement.

I am suspicious of people who wear a smile all the time—people who laugh when nothing humorous has been said. The glass-is-half-full-look-on-the-bright-side-everything's-going-to-be-all-right-it-could-be-worse-God-doesn't-give-you-anything-you-can't-handle-when-a-door-closes-a-window-opens Pollyannas make me puke.

On what planet are they living? What do they know that I don't know? More to the point: *What they are hiding?*

Are these people blind to the tragedies of this world? Or are they so self-involved that they simply cannot see the inequities and torments that plague the human condition? Sometimes everything *isn't* going to be all right. Sometimes things can't be worse, and sometimes God, if one entertains the possibility of His existence, crushes a person, and they die because they can't handle what He's meted out. As the sky falls in on those smiling idiots, do they bother to run for cover? You bet!

I admire people who've suffered, yet move forward with courage. But always putting a brave face on misfortune is dishonest; it proves only that you don't trust your friends with your very real concerns, or that you believe they might think less of you for your failings. Such people reek of pride; so superior to others that they won't admit disappointments, losses, and tragedies. Who wants to be friends with an automaton? Who wants to be friends with a person who refuses to see your sadness, who goes around pitching platitudes like "When a door closes a window opens"? Sometimes when a door closes you're trapped, and you just yearn for a sympathetic shoulder to cry on.

Edna Ferber is a happy woman.

I have struggled; therefore, we are only fair-weather friends.

Edna writes big, fat, overblown potboilers. I imagine she types away at the speed of light, so content in her characters' miserable circumstances that her fingers fly along the keys, with frequent breaks for rubbing palms together in diabolical delight of the schemes in which she has ensnared them.

Like a spider spinning her web.

And as if her wretched tale is not enough, she wraps up the whole thing with an improbable, sappy, happy ending! In life, there are no happy endings — just temporary reprieves. And for the lie of the happy ending, she wins the *Pulitzer*!

I don't hate Edna Ferber; in many ways, I marvel at her success. She tolerates me because Aleck and FPA (Frank Pierce Adams) are her friends and they adore me. She knows that I know that she knows that her novels are nothing more than cash-cows that pay for her beautiful furnishings in her Central Park West apartment at the Prasada. I, by contrast, who have never cared much for acquiring things, and wish only to create works of literary art, view her prolificacy as prolixity. And so, I find her good humor difficult to stomach for very long.

When Aleck and I arrived at Edna's for Thanksgiving dinner several hours late, we were greeted warmly, handed martinis, and immediately seated at the dining room table. As I'd telephoned from the police station earlier to tell Edna we had encountered "a problem," and were being interrogated at the precinct, she'd graciously offered to send her lawyer over to post bail for my release, certain I had committed some crime. She didn't quite get the remark I'd hissed into the receiver, and came back with, "I beg your pardon?"

She'd wanted to serve dinner soon, and we were holding things up: "The gravy is congealing and the turkey toughening, you see," and it was all she could do to keep the stuffing from drying up.

"Stuff it, Edna."

"The bird *is* stuffed," she said.

She couldn't see me roll my eyes.

"Oh, put a sock in it."

"A sock?"

"*Awwwhhh*, crap! Put a wet rag on it, would ya, Edna?"

"Oh, all right," she said.

She must have taken me literally, because between the numerous questions posed by the dinner guests to Aleck, who held court as usual, we dined on the most succulent fowl, drowned with the richest gravy and the most divine chestnut stuffing I'd ever tasted in my life. The guests *ooh*ed and *ahh*ed their compliments on the fine fare through indistinguishable grunts.

A voracious school of piranhas had descended upon the fixings in their usual Round Table feeding frenzy, sloshing gravy (Ross and Heywood Broun), spilling the Riesling (Groucho and Zeppo), flinging globs of cranberry sauce onto the crisp white linen tablecloth (Ross, Heywood, Groucho, Chico and Bunny Wilson), knocking over water glasses (Aleck and Frank), and gnawing and sucking the carcass clean in no time (all of the abovementioned). I began to think that Harpo might be the only male to leave the beautifully appointed table unsullied, until, while waving his spoon to make a point in the conversation, it flung from his fingers and splashed into the pumpkin pudding, sending an orangey dollop into the eye of our hostess.

Edna was, if annoyingly buoyant, a terrific cook, and despite her sudden expression of despair, a good sport to our faces (although I doubted she'd ever invite us *en masse* to dinner again). To her surprise, Woodrow Wilson displayed the best table manners of the whole lot; he quietly ate all the lovely turkey and potatoes on the plate she had presented to him and licked the plate clean, leaving not a spot on the parquet, before curling up to sleep beside the fire.

"What is your secret?" asked Jane Grant. "This has to be the best turkey I've ever tasted."

"I told Edna to stuff it," I chimed in.

"But, of course, I'd already done that, you see . . ."

"So I told her to put a wet rag on it."

"Yes, well," replied Edna, nervously watching a fine crystal wineglass teeter toward extinction. "Sometimes your suggestions are very clever, Dorothy," said Edna, oblivious to the true meaning of my words.

"What's this about a rag?" asked Jane.

"Never mind that," said Frank, sometimes referred to by his initials, FPA. "I want to know more about what happened this morning."

"I'll tell you what happened! A couple-hundred-thousand kids watched Felix bust a gut right before their eyes," said Ross.

"I wasn't asking you, Dopey!" said the newspaper columnist. "I was talking to Aleck and Dottie about the murder."

"What do you call what happened to the Toy Soldier, Frank? A ride in the country?" said Zeppo, taking Ross's side.

"*Awww*, stuff it, Zeppo!"

"Yeah, stuff it!" said Harpo.

"Throw a wet rag on it!" said Chico.

When it dawned on her at last, Edna shot me a burning glance that a wet rag would not extinguish.

"Why're you all picking on me?" whined Ross, in his most pathetic victim's voice.

"The turkey's picked clean, Ross, and what better carcass to pick on than yours?" said Aleck.

Harold Ross has always been the butt of Aleck's acid tongue. It had been the case since they met during the War as writers for *Stars and Stripes*.

Aleck had introduced himself as "dramatic critic for the *New York Times*." The image of the pudgy, puffed-up, and pretentiously pompous Woollcott reporting about prancing, dancing chorines for a military newspaper produced a hearty laugh.

"What kind of sissy-boy job is that?" Ross had asked.

Not to be belittled, Aleck had haughtily scrutinized the gawky, disheveled figure before him and replied gaily, "You know, you remind me a great deal of my grandfather's coachman."

It was the beginning of their love–hate relationship.

Later, while in Paris, Aleck introduced Ross to Jane Grant, a society reporter for the *Times*. Ross was immediately smitten, and although he never intended to live in New York after the War, he did so to be near Jane. Stateside once more, Ross and Aleck resumed their rather odd, rather deprecating friendship. Ross was editing *The Home Sector*, but dreamed about publishing his own magazine someday. Last winter he did just that when *The New Yorker* debuted to less-than-rave reviews. Harold Ross may look like a tramp, but under those rags is an exacting and excellent editor. But as it appears now, it's doubtful the magazine will see another year of publication, even though lots of us have been contributing to the weekly in hopes that it will eventually find its readership.

"All of you behave yourselves," said Edna, knowing her remonstration held little impact on the men.

"Aleck picked up the dagger," I said. "That's why we were dragged down to police headquarters."

"Outrageous, really, that the police would think that I'd stab a good man of God with a stiletto!"

"A stiletto was the next logical step up, I suppose, after shooting all those bad actors with your vitriol," I said, trying to lighten his dark mood.

"Once the police looked me over they knew I couldn't have thrown the dagger."

"Because you throw like a girl?" asked Ross.

The table shuddered and the crystal clinked as Jane kicked Ross in the shin under the cloth. He flashed a frown at her smiling face.

Aleck pointed a beaky nose at Ross. "Thank you, Jane, for my retort!"

"What 'good-God-man' was murdered?" asked Harpo.

"A priest!" said Aleck. "Father John O' Hara from some little town down South."

"A priest! But why?" asked Edna. "Why would anyone kill a priest?"

"He couldn't find a rabbi?" said Heywood Broun.

"Was the stabbing random? Some act of a madman wielding a knife in a crowd?"

"I don't know, Edna," I said. "But Father O'Hara spoke to Aleck before he died, and it appears the priest may have known his killer."

All eyes turned toward Aleck, who paused, a fork of pumpkin pie hovering midway off his plate. "He said, 'stop him; save him.'" Aleck looked genuinely shaken as he uttered the words, but immediately found comfort in the forkful of pie.

"So he wanted you to stop his killer and then save him," said Jane. "A final act of forgiveness . . ."

"He was a priest! Salvation was the commodity he sold, for crissake!" said Ross.

"Looks like he made an exit while trying to make a sale," said Groucho.

"Have they caught his killer?" asked FPA.

"Not yet. Dottie's description of a man she saw fleeing the scene wasn't exactly what the police had in mind when they asked her what he looked like," said Aleck. "What was it you told the detective?" He didn't wait for me to reply: "'He was a tortured soul with eyes like drowning pools.'"

"Well, yes," I interjected. "It was a God-awful, frightening face."

"And she knows a God-awful frightening face

when she sees one," said Groucho, and everyone turned on cue to stare at him. "I wasn't referring to myself."

Everyone turned to stare at Heywood Broun.

"Actually," said Groucho, "I was referring to Ross, you nincompoops, but the majority rules: Heywood's got him topped, I'd say." (I remembered the time a few years back, when Heywood stood outside the Gonk after lunch, cap in hand, waiting for Aleck to join him. A woman passerby stopped, looked over the bedraggled, unkempt creature, and placed a dime in his cap so that he could "have a good meal.")

Aleck took the moment to shovel in a forkful of pecan pie.

"They hadn't the faintest idea what she was talking about," he continued after a gulp of coffee, "so she said he looked like the figure in Munch's *The Scream*, but that didn't help, so she offered to draw a picture."

"Oh, Lord, I can only imagine. I've seen a few of your sketches, my dear Dorothy," said Bunny, chuckling.

"Yes, Munch-ish, and I don't mean Benedictine!" said FPA.

"Well, borrowing Mary Shelley's description of Frankenstein seems farfetched, so I thought a good pictorial rendition might work," I said. "Wait! Where's my purse?"

I pushed aside items inside my pocketbook: pressed-powder compact, reading glasses, lipstick, comb, hair pins, pencil stub, and loose change. Paper money floated like debris atop an unfathomable ocean of long-forgotten days and nights. I pulled out a circular, grainy item that left a gritty mess on my fingers. It took a moment, but after a sniff I identified the cookie I'd stashed away during an afternoon tea I'd attended last month. Eventually, I found the folded sheet of paper I was looking for. "Here's my sketch," I said, handing it to Bunny.

"Just as I thought," he said, bursting out with laughter.

"Don't be a critic, Edmund Wilson, you're no good at it!" I said.

"You have to admit, Bunny," said Edna, "that there is a 'Munch-ish' quality about it." She gurgled when she laughed, and for a moment I did hate her.

"I'd say the artist is influenced by the cubists: Braque, Picasso . . .," said Groucho.

"I see more a melding of the surrealists with the cubists, don'chathink?" added Zeppo.

"Dada, no?" said Chico.

"Dada, no," said Harpo, shaking his head.

"Dali, no?" said Groucho.

"Dali, yes!" said Harpo, nodding.

"Shut up," I said, and they all fell silent. "It's his expression that I was trying to—well, express."

"Expressionism!" yelled FPA, jumping up from his chair.

"Laugh if you like, but if you saw the monster, you'd be hard-pressed to describe him in any ordinary way."

"Dottie's, right," said Aleck. "He did have a crazed look about him, and Dottie saw his face clearly. I did not; only saw the back of him as he fled. So she will have to identify whomever the police bring in as suspect."

"In the morning, a police artist will try to make sense of what I've been saying."

Later, we all lounged around Edna's overly decorated "cranberry-red-and-buttercup-yellow" (her description!) salon: lots of *frou-frou* ruffles, sumptuous velvet and silk over down-filled upholstery.

Again, I sound wretched, but the truth be known, I am happy in my rooms at the Algonquin Hotel—all right, perhaps not exactly *happy*, but it suits me fine. I can tumble out of bed at noon, fall into the elevator, and roll through to the dining room for our Round Table luncheon each day. If while there I've had too much to drink, I'm a few steps from the elevator and my rooms. At the Algonquin I need not pay for a telephone answering service, or a maid. I have room service and dog-walking service, so the ice bucket is kept full and the dog is regularly emptied. With all those benefits, Edna can keep the *frou-frou*.

We played word games, and then a rather rambunctious round of charades, which woke up Woodrow Wilson. He barked and ran circles around the boisterous team members before settling on my lap.

After the splendid dinner (much of which landed off the table), Edna appeared less nervous about Woodrow soiling her thick white carpet. It was more likely that one of the boys would knock over the coffee pot, or the decanter of crème de menthe brought over from the bar. With friends like ours, it's best to hold your parties in a gymnasium.

Ira Gershwin arrived with his tall, lean brother, George, in tow. Although I see Ira occasionally at the Gonk at our one o'clock luncheons, I hardly ever see Gorgeous George. George looked marvelous in his pin-striped, double-breasted navy-blue suit, rose-colored silk tie, and immaculate white spats. He greeted the ladies with a big smile and pecked our cheeks and shook hands with the men. Aleck, stretched out on a divan with the air of a Renoir nude, but looking more like a fat frog in heat lying on a lily pad, looked up admiringly at George through his thick, round eyeglasses.

"How's the new show going, George, my boy?"

"Working with Oscar Hammerstein—well, he's a good lyricist, all right, but I'll be glad when the show opens on December Thirtieth. The show looks as good as any show looks the month before opening, I guess."

"What he means," said Ira, "is whatever the show looks like now is no indication of what it will look like on opening night."

"How true," said Aleck.

"Act Two was scrapped last week, and I wrote three new numbers for Act Three."

"What title did they decide on?" asked Edna.

"*Song of the Flame*, with a title song by that name."

George made a beeline to the grand piano. Groucho and Harpo made like bookends.

"Got a new song for the second act."

"For heaven's sake, George, play it," said Edna.

"Thought you'd never ask."

George's fingers ran over the keyboard for the intro of *Midnight Bells*. Groucho and Harpo sat quietly as George played, proving that music soothes the savage breast. When the song had been sung, George said, "Ira and I are working on a show for next fall." He tinkled the keys as he spoke.

"Gertie Lawrence and Victor Moore are set to star. It's called *Oh, Kay!*" said Ira. "George, play them one of the songs we wrote."

"*Do, Do, Do?*"

"No, no, no."

"Please, please, please?" mimicked Groucho.

"Sure, sure, sure," said Harpo.

Ignoring the Brothers, Ira walked to the piano and turned to face his audience. "George, key of G!"

George whipped off a string of notes in the key of G.

They broke into an up-tempo tune that raised our spirits from out of our postprandial stupor. *Clap Yo' Hands* had us all singing the chorus; Harpo and

Chico became dance partners; Groucho grabbed me for a twirl about the room, and Zeppo, Jane.

Edna refilled glasses, and watched us from the bar.

Aleck bobbed a dangling foot.

Heywood observed, puffing his cigar.

Ross picked his teeth.

Frank sat smiling, tapping his feet, and I knew he was planning how best to describe the scene in his famous daily column, "The Conning Tower," for his paper's morning edition.

George's music was so reminiscent of Negro church spirituals I'd heard in Harlem. "Clap yo' hands, stomp yo' feet, *alleluia, alleluia!*" I said as much when he'd finished the number with a flourish and everyone fell back into chairs, breathless, laughing and exhilarated.

"*You* get it, don't you, Dottie!" said George. "It's the Negro prayer, born in the colored man's church." He beamed that beautiful smile at me, and in an instant I wished he loved me!

Ever since George teamed with lyricist Buddy Da Silva to write the score of *George White's Scandals of 1922* to include a short Negro opera called *Blue Monday*, which was cut after opening night, George became obsessed with the Negro influence of jazz on popular music. Although *Blue Monday* was what I and most critics thought a failure because it was presented in outdated blackface, with a story that was boorishly melodramatic and frankly demeaning of colored people, the musical style and the dramatic possibilities it promised were evident. In other words, the idea was sound; its execution, wanting.

Only a year earlier, a musical derived from the Harlem production, *Shuffle Along*, had made a hit with white audiences when it was moved to Broadway. But *Blue Monday* proved only a sad attempt by the producers to cash in on that popular Negro musical. George was brilliantly original, but the book was trite.

Even though the short opera failed, it brought a young, unknown Negro composer named Wil Vodery into George's life. It was he who wrote the orchestral arrangements of the failed opera, and he and George became fast friends. George, who is always genuinely interested in the works of other composers, admires and has learned much from Wil. Paul Whiteman, who was orchestra conductor of the *Scandals* production, saw something unique in George's talent. Although George's "I'll Build a Stairway to Paradise" became one of the biggest hits of the day (White and Ziegfeld and other producers liked "stairs" so they could get all the show's chorus members onstage and make a big finale number), it was the jazzy *Blue Monday* that prompted Paul Whiteman to ask George to write a jazz symphony for a concert he was planning the following year. And what a piece George composed! *Rhapsody in Blue* is more than just a jazzy modern symphony: It is the sound of New York, and when a blind man hears it, the city appears in sharp focus!

"You need to write another Negro opera,

George," I said. "But next time you need a story as good as the music you write."

"And with colored singers, no whites in blackface," said Aleck. "Leave that to Jolson." Then, as a thought popped into his head, he looked up over his spectacles and said with a frown, "There's a colored actor who sings mighty good, George. Name's Robeson. Dottie, remember that young man we saw? Real stage presence..."

"Paul Robeson. He sure can act and sing. Aleck's right, you know. Blackface is just plain silly. You need a colored cast."

"I have a story for you to consider, George," said Aleck. "It's a true story, and it is so current that you'll not be able to write the ending until the trial is over."

"Oh?"

"A man, a doctor, buys a house where he and his wife hope to raise their children and live the fulfillment of 'The American Dream.' Problem is, the doctor is a colored man, and the house he's bought is in a white neighborhood."

"And why is there a trial?" I asked. "Just because he jumped to the other side of the tracks?"

"The doctor's father shoots a man when a mob storms his home—a white man. Because he defended his property and family, the old man is on trial for murder."

Ross piped in, "Yes, I read about the incident. An old friend of ours from *Stars and Stripes* days is covering the story for the *Detroit Herald*. You remember Harry Nash, Aleck?"

"Sure. I know a few of the principal players, too."

"Elaborate, will you?" said Jane.

"Arthur Garfield Hays is a friend of mine."

"Oh, the lawyer . . ."

"Not just any old lawyer. He sat second chair to Clarence Darrow during the Scopes Trial."

"The 'Monkey Trial'?" asked George.

"Yes, that's right."

"Darrow hasn't exactly been on a winning streak," said Ross. "The young men he defended, those kid murderers, Leopold and Loeb, were found guilty, anyway, and as far as the Scopes Trial, he lost again; they say the trial and what Darrow put William Jennings Bryan through killed the statesman."

"Nonsense!" yelled Heywood. "Darrow saved the young killers from death sentences, and the Scopes decision is on appeal so that the law banning the teaching of science can be reckoned with. Darrow knows what he's doing. He knows how best to lose a case, how to get it the most attention, too, in order to get the country talking seriously about important issues."

Aleck waved his hand, a gesture of disregard for Ross's comment. "Where was I?"

"You were talking about the Negro doctor's father who shot a white man when—the Detroit case," offered Heywood.

"Yes, yes, before I was rudely interrupted. Darrow has been asked to defend the case against the doctor's father."

"A controversial subject."

"Political dynamite, yes it is, George."

George thought for a moment about the idea of creating an opera around a politically volatile subject. "After what *Birth of a Nation* did to rile-up the Ku Klux Klan ten years ago, maybe it's time to face our disgraces," he said after a moment's consideration.

Edna was smiling an unusual, rather secret smile as she listened to the conversation. The homely face shone with a light that made her almost beautiful. Aleck noticed and commented, "That Cheshire Cat over there has something up her sleeve!"

"You're mixing your metaphors, for crissake!" said Ross.

"Oh, be quiet or I'll mix up your face," said Aleck. "Edna, dear?"

"*Humm?*" said Edna, drawn back into the room from her distant travels. "Just thinking . . . ."

"Don't be coy, Edna dear," I said, admittedly losing patience. "Share what little dust motes are floating around in that little brain of yours."

"It's just that racial prejudice is a theme in my new book."

"You've been working on that tome for centuries, darling," said Aleck.

"Yes, well, *Slowpoke* is finally finished. It's done, out of my hair, out of my hands at last. The publication date is sometime next year."

"*Slowpoke?*" I said. "What-in-fresh-hell kind of name is *that* for a book?" I said. "Is *Slowpoke* the name of some poor antebellum slave boy? Like "Step'nfetchit"? How shameful."

Edna laughed, and made me look like the idiot I was. "My name for *Showboat*. It just took me *forever* to write."

Yeah, sure, I thought, a sour taste in my mouth. She just cranks them out like pork sausage links. "Oh, the Mississippi tugboat story you were writing," I said.

Another doorstopper, I thought, *and goddammit, another Pulitzer, no doubt!*

I, who have trouble writing the shortest of short stories, hoped the green hue rising along my jaw might be mistaken for gangrene. "Great," I said, hoping my envy didn't bleed through. "Good for you," I said, trying again, pretending heartfelt wonder, but hearing only the strident tone of my revolting resentment.

"It's a love story and a tragedy, and a tale of struggle and survival."

"Sounds like a fun read," I said, trying to lighten up. I caught Aleck looking at me; I was transparent to him, if not to everyone else in the room, except Edna.

"Well, it's timely, anyway," continued Edna. "A story about what happens when a light-skinned Negro tries to pass for white. What Dottie calls a 'potboiler.'"

Forget the green, my cheeks were *red*. I knew

the woman hadn't read my thoughts, yet she knew my sentiments, and that the little bird who'd told on me was not so little after all, but the fat man posed like a diva on the divan. *Serves me right*, I thought—*never tell Aleck anything you don't want coming back to haunt you.*

"What did you say, Dorothy, about my book, *So Big?*" asked Edna, referring to her Pulitzer Prize–winning novel of the year. "Something like, 'It's not a novel to toss aside lightly; it must be thrown across the room with great force?'"

"That was Benito Mussolini's book, actually. I said your book was . . ." I continued on sheepishly at first. Then, realizing I was digging myself into a deeper hole, "Now, don't gloat, Edna. It makes you look bloated."

I can be unconscionable.

"Not everybody can be like you, Dorothy."

"Oh, God, I hope not," I said, looking around the room for a rock to crawl under.

"Most people actually have to write something to be called a 'famous writer.'"

"*Touché*, Edna dear," I relented, hoping this was my chance at redemption. She was right, of course; it was always a great strain for me to write anything. And yet, I was famous for my *bon mots*, a few poems and short stories. Edna had invited me to dinner and had fed me the most divine meal imaginable. I needed to rein in my bitch-let-loose.

I said, "My fame is my potential, you see, dear. It might be years before I deliver on projected profits.

That I should have all this one day," I said, indicating the splendid room with a wave of my hand, "is what keeps me going. Let's retract our claws, whaddayasay?"

Edna laughed, and refilled my glass.

It's hard to dislike happy people, but I keep on trying.

Eight stories below, the view of Central Park had darkened to black. Balls of light from lamps along the walkways threw an ethereal glow that floated up from beneath the building. Earlier in the afternoon we had marveled at the sight of scores of wild turkeys fluttering alongside sheep that grazed the park's Sheep Meadow, marveling that they had escaped the ax on this, their execution day.

Looking around the beautifully appointed salon, I noted that the reds and yellows of the fabrics couldn't have been prettier and more intense in the daylight than they were now. Firelight and soft pools from table lamps warmed the elegant space. The ebony piano shimmered from reflected light, and George's swarthy complexion was striking against his black hair and rich brown eyes. The Marx Brothers circling Edna as she danced awkwardly was surreal, and to see Aleck beaming in reclining splendor—well, for a moment I had the odd impression that there was something very special about this gathering.

George switched tempo and startled us with a simple little melody, with lyrics by Ira, that brought tears to my eyes. It is not often that that happens!

Animals make me teary; the sight of a tired hack-horse stops me in my tracks; I'm an easy mark for strays. Whether it was because I'd had too much whiskey, or because autumn days were growing colder, shorter, and darker, or because I had no man to hold me close at night, the lyrics George sang, "Someone to Watch Over Me," tore at my heart. I truly felt like "a little lamb who's lost in the wood/I know I could always be good to one who'll watch over me."

Ira is a brilliant lyricist who touched on the need in all of us to be loved, and with George's soulful, haunting melody, it is a song that will endure a hundred years, I am sure. I think what I like most about the song is its lack of cynicism. For a woman famous for mistrust in matters of the heart, this is big.

By the time George picked up the pace with "Fascinatin' Rhythm," I was back to my dry-eyed self. The jazziness of the tune, with its musical hesitations, prompted me to ask if anyone wanted to take a ride up to Harlem to hit a couple of clubs.

Before I received an answer, Irving Berlin walked into the room, talking a blue streak as usual, in lieu of a normal greeting. As is often the case with him, it was more as if we had suddenly moved into his space, while he was in the middle of his dialogue with whomever happened to wander across his path.

"What'd I tell you, George?" said Irving, slapping George on the back. The older man looked at the rest of the party and said, "Ain't these boys the best you've ever heard!" referring to the Gershwin brothers. "This young man," he said, indicating George, "came to me a few years ago, and he wanted work from me as a pianist. I asked him to play me something he'd written, and he did, and I said to him, 'Whatta ya wanna work for me for, kid? You're so good, you gotta work for yourself!'" Irving turned back to us and asked, "Was I right or what?" The National Treasure rumpled the black hair of the prodigy.

There was lots of joking about the new show, *The Cocoanuts*, music by Irving and book by George S. Kaufman and starring the Marx Brothers. It was due to open after successful tryouts in Boston and Philly.

Irving pretended to crack the whip, and George relinquished his seat at the piano when Edna begged a number from the show. Groucho leapt up and sang his big number from *The Cocoanuts*, entitled, "Why Am I a Hit With the Ladies?," with the boys taking on the roles of the chorus girls backing him up.

Edna hugged our mutual friend, handed him a scotch, and asked if he had another song for us.

"Sure I do, but Fran Williams ain't here to do it justice," he said, looking at Groucho, who feigned a hurt expression. (Frances Williams is in the show, too.) He sat down on the sofa next to me and asked, "Did I hear you say something about heading up to Harlem?"

"I haven't seen the new show at the Cotton Club, and George was just playing a new tune that reminded me of Negro spirituals, so I thought...."

An hour later, George, Ira, Aleck, FPA, Heywood, and I were sitting pretty at a table amid the lush jungle décor at the Cotton Club, watching the floorshow. Woodrow Wilson slept alongside me on the banquette. Jane and Ross begged off as the magazine's deadline loomed over their heads and the night must be spent working. Edna wanted a quiet night at home, probably to recover from the task of playing nursemaid all day to a schoolroom of overgrown children. The Brothers left to join their mother, Minnie, for a second Thanksgiving feast, and Irving's latest *Music Box Revue* had an 8:40 p.m. curtain.

Aleck was a bit down-in-the-mouth, and it was no wonder, as the full import of the events of the morning began to weigh on his spirits. A man had died in his arms, he'd been questioned for several hours at the police station, and he'd eaten enough potatoes at Edna's to have saved a small Irish village from famine. He'd been getting quarrelsome, too, from the time we'd left Edna's, during the cab ride uptown, and the wait to be seated at the club.

His irritability waned when the orchestra ended its jazzy rendition of "When My Sugar Walks Down the Street," and a brisk musical intro brought a dozen long-limbed mulatto beauties scantily dressed in silver halters and tap pants onto the stage.

Andrew Peer conducted his ten-man Cotton Club Orchestra; the Chicagoan musicians squeezed the blue notes from a variety of brass. The fever of expectation thrilled through from the banquettes, across the dance floor, over the gleaming horseshoe bar and up onto the multileveled stage, egged-on by the cool, insistent heartbeat of percussion.

The all-white audience purred with joy as the bevy of beauties parted ranks, and Earl "Snakehips" Tucker slid out onto the stage. His astonishing dance contortions sent waves of applause over the footlights.

Dan Healy, the new director of the Cotton Club show, had outdone every production before him. The orchestra was finely pitched to meet its match in the precision choreography, as the tall, handsome Snakehips, dressed in snug-fitting trousers, cummerbund, and open-collared silk shirt, lithely gyrated with sophisticated grace before turning to welcome the beautiful, long-limbed Evelyn Welch onto the stage to partner the routine, her brief costume's red fringe flirting along her glorious thighs, moving at counterpoint to the beat.

You couldn't help but feel the excitement course through you; that uplifting kick that comes with awe and mirth and admiration for the brilliant talents gathered onstage. Such fun! Such perfectly synchronized performance!

Here was artistic expression pitched at us white folks, screaming with more honesty and energy and humanity than any contrived *Ziegfeld Follies* extravaganza I'd ever seen. One's admiration is unsullied by the prejudices of race; art mixed with joy and as unpretentious as this transcends envy, suspicion, fear, and hatred. How can one feel anything but profound happiness when swept over by such pure exhilaration? Brass blared, percussion vibrated through the room, applause reverberated.

The world outside these doors should understand how simple it is for souls to connect, but we often need devices to make the connections. The graciousness and generosity of the performers inspires the connection, and through some irresistibly flowing force the audience returns the favor.

George was ecstatic; reveling in his musical element, he entered a different consciousness. His face wore an otherworldly glow as he absorbed the sights and sounds. It was as if he could smell the music, swim in the rhythms, so wholly absorbed was he. While the rest of us were emotionally driven, his connection was *visceral*.

White audiences flock to the black clubs not merely to be entertained or to be seen at a currently trendy nightclub. Say it's a call from God, a force, whatever, but here they find a kind of love springing forth through music and dance and voice and the riptide of blatant sexual allure that makes one grasp for some unspoken truth. Here the Negro is a superior race; even though he appears to serve the white clientele, he is really instructing them. The illusion of the jungle décor, the muted lights and the revealing costumes touch a deeper, primal yearning: life lived to the fullest with love, with raw, lusty, undiluted, unchecked emotion.

The rich white swells, the young white New York socialites, and the tourists from small towns let their hair down along with their defenses, abandoning propriety to experience the innate primeval dance long hidden in the dark places of the soul. They flock to the club on 143rd Street likes wolves to the call of the wild. It isn't slumming, for in fact the bar is raised. Perhaps they feel the urge, like children wanting to run away from their staid, secure homes to join the circus, to seek out carnie adventures alongside the flame thrower, the aerialist, the lion tamer. And here, too, they are witness to the dignity of a culture unbeknownst to them: a world so attractive and rich and unique that they can't help but desire to leave their poor and parsimonious existences for a time to go on a trip into fantasy.

In Harlem clubs the Negro is royalty. For the first time since leaving the African continent, the Negro is not looked upon as chattel, but revered as treasure. Here, for a few hours, the banker from Buffalo donning top hat and tails can contemplate the possibilities of his nature. For a few hours, the Park Avenue hostess might imagine a dreamed existence of abandoned responsibilities, even if she has never before been conscious of those deep desires.

Etiquette is maintained, of course, but the example is set by the Negro. The colored waiter is dressed to the hilt, his blindingly white linens crisply starched; the crease of his trouser leg, sharp; his tie, level. He smiles without the grimace of subservience, and speaks without deference, although always polite in approach. The white clientele is expected to refrain from loud, obnoxious behavior, especially during the floorshow, or the party is asked to leave the premises. It may be the only place in the world that a Negro can order a white man to quit his place of business!

    The condition of the Negro beyond these few precious blocks of Harlem is not enviable. Stripped of talent, muted-hued stage lights, glamour and exotic illusion, a harsh light glares upon him. The colored man becomes, once again, suspect. As the banker boards the train home to Buffalo, the colored redcaps, who can't sing and dance or torment his soul with the soaring refrains of jazz, revert to nonentities in his eyes. He views with indifference the indignities suffered by the Negro race and acknowledges no part or responsibility in society's injustices. The hostess from Park Avenue accepts no blame for the past and offers no help for the future of her dark-skinned sister scrubbing her marble floors or nursing her baby. Walk outside these doors, these few square blocks of real estate, and the struggle is ongoing.

    I loved the entertainment at the Cotton Club, and at Connie's Inn, but I don't like the idea that coloreds aren't allowed in their audiences. I heard tell that W.C. Handy, the Father of the Blues, was turned away by Frenchy, the doorman at the Cotton Club, even while the band was playing his own "St. Louis Blues"!

    Many clubs that adopt a white-only policy don't last long.

A new club opened last month with a dance floor the size of a football field painted blue and orange. It has a great band, and top-notch entertainment, and it's called Small's Paradise. At Small's the swells in cutaways and Poiret gowns dance alongside the shoeshine boys and kitchen maids from the neighborhood.

I prefer the less audacious, integrated places, the less salubrious joints where the patronage is mostly colored, the dance floors smaller, the jazz wilder, and the fried chicken crispier. But whites aren't really welcomed in those clubs; it's seen as blatantly disrespectful—*slumming*. A white face is conspicuous, intrusive. A sort of reverse lunch-counter discrimination, or how you might be made to feel showing up at a dinner party uninvited. Outright resentment is veiled but can't help but bleed through. I understand it, but I don't like it. Only people like George Gershwin and Heywood Broun can walk into those places and really feel welcomed.

We ordered a fifth of scotch for eighteen bucks under the table, and George bought me a bottle of champagne. By midnight we piled into a cab and headed downtown, dropping George and Ira at their apartments and FPA home to his wife, but Heywood wandered off to Small's Paradise with a young Negro poet we met on the street by the name of Langston Hughes. Aleck, subdued, if not a little depressed, didn't want to return to his apartment in the house he'd bought with Jane and Ross a couple of years ago on West 47th Street, so I invited him to my rooms at the Algonquin Hotel for a nightcap.

We got out of the taxi on Broadway and 44th, and walked Woodrow Wilson the two avenues east toward home. Whether it was the effect of the liquor, or the windless night, the air felt pleasant, less frigid than when we stood watching the parade that morning.

Then, abruptly, Aleck said, "Why does one murder a priest, Dottie?"

"Wish I knew," I said. "Maybe some disgruntled Catholic, for all we know."

"I got the strangest impression that the fellow knew me. The priest, that is, not the murderer."

"Who in hell doesn't know Alexander Woollcott? And, I should add, who on earth doesn't for that matter?"

He ignored my little joke. "The way he looked at me. He was trying to tell me something more."

"Like whom to stop and whom to save?"

"That's it, Dottie!" said Aleck, stopping in his tracks. He said, 'Stop him. Save him.' He wasn't telling me to stop his murderer so that I could save him from something. He was telling me to stop the murderer so I might save someone else."

"Oh, I see what you mean."

Aleck looked distressed again. His eyes narrowed and his brows lifted behind his spectacles. For the first time since we met back in '19 he appeared to be at a loss for words. And for a man known for his verbal prowess, I found this disturbing. "How am I supposed to do anything about that?" he finally said, and then the solution dawned. "Let's call Bob and—oh, I forgot. He's not in town."

Bob is Robert Benchley, famous writer, wit extraordinaire, critic for *Life* magazine, star of last year's *Music Box Revue*, and best of all, my closest friend and confidant. We met half a dozen years ago, when I was hired by *Vanity Fair* as theatre critic, where he was editor. A couple years later, when I was fired because I was, let's say, uncharitable to a Broadway star (Billie Burke) in my scathing review of her performance, disregarding the fact that her husband was not only one of Broadway's biggest producers (Florenz Ziegfeld) but a major advertiser in *Vanity*, Robert Benchley resigned his post in protest of my dismissal! No one had ever stood up for me before. He was not just a fair-weather friend with whom I shared good times. He became my champion.

With no job, but with a wife, children, and mortgage in the suburbs, Mr. Benchley decided to try freelance writing, so together we set up an office in a broom closet. Might as well have been a broom closet—a partitioned-off four-by-eight-foot end of a hallway in the Metropolitan Opera House studios close to Times Square for thirty dollars a month. With room for one desk, two chairs, one on either side, our typewriters butt-to-butt ("an inch smaller and it would have been adultery"), we set up shop. There was always some work to be had, for we were writers of note, but during the months we rented the broom closet we spent most of our time unproductively, lunching half the afternoon away with our Algonquin Round Table friends as had become our custom, then returning to our cubbyhole to play cards, watching and commenting on the traffic of pedestrians from the window, and generally joking around until five o'clock. Eventually we abandoned our pathetic enterprise.

Since shutting the door of that closet we spend much of our time together, lunching, going to the theatre, shooting the breeze, and gallivanting all over town. Mr. Benchley (who calls me "Mrs. Parker," as we were first introduced to each other at *Vanity*) keeps rooms at the Hotel Royalton, a bachelor residence across the street from the Algonquin, since appearing on Broadway last year; the commute to Scarsdale after the show each night didn't get him home until two in the morning. He's kept those rooms, however, since the show closed last summer, and returns home to the suburbs on the weekends. There's been lots of talk, lots of speculation about our relationship. Some people have insinuated we are lovers. We are *not*, and never have been. Mr. Benchley and I were married to other people when we met, and although I have been separated from my husband, Eddie, for over a year and feel free to seek out new relationships, Mr. Benchley is happily married. Happily enough to stay married, anyway, although of late he has been visiting Polly Adler's brothel with some regularity: "Mistresses break the monogamy, Mrs. Parker." He is my best friend in the whole world. We share a mutual admiration, and our "love" for each other transcends the romantic, and therefore holds great value for me. I sometimes think that if I had been born a man, I'd *be* Mr. Benchley.

"Mr. Benchley was having Thanksgiving with Gertrude and the boys."

"Let's call him from your room."

"Don't think Gertrude would appreciate a one-A.M. call, Aleck."

"Oh, bother."

We were passing a corner newsstand when Aleck stopped, turned, and walked over to pick up an evening paper. He grabbed a *New York Post* and a *Tribune*, too, and flipped a nickel to the newsy.

"Let's see if there is any mention of this morning's murder."

We stood for a moment as he perused the headlines on the first few pages of each paper. Woodrow Wilson tugged at his leash, so I followed his lead that he might investigate an unidentifiable dropping off the curb. I didn't like the looks of it, so I pulled my pup away and turned to look for Aleck, twenty paces back.

As I waited for the big man to catch up to us, my attention was called by a group of rowdy young men in evening clothes, decidedly "tight," staggering out of the Harvard Club. Several bent fellows stumbled off the curb, arms flailing, spitting out anemic whistles in ineffectual attempts at commandeering a cab to take them on to a brothel adventure, no doubt. A couple doors down at the New York Yacht Club, there emerged from its French Rococo façade and brightly lit bowed windows a doorman looking to see what the ruckus was about. Noting that the fuss was simply the breast-beating of healthy youth, the guard retreated back into the sanctuary of the club.

Fifty feet further along and across the street, the Hippodrome's marquee was dark at this late hour, the crowds having long since dispersed from the extravaganza that was currently playing there. The stately white limestone building directly across from my hotel, the New York Bar Association, dozed in dark shadows like sleeping royalty.

Aleck called out and was catching up to me, re-folding the newspapers, when something caught my eye and I turned back to look across at the Bar Association Building.

A man lurked in a doorway, his hat slouched over his eyes and casting a shadow across his face. Our eyes met, and he stepped back into the doorwell's dark recess. Even with all the millions of men in New York City dressed in nondescript overcoats and banded fedoras, I knew that underneath that hat would be revealed a shock of wild blond hair.

I ran back toward Aleck, Woodrow Wilson sprinting after me.

"Aleck!" I yelled, grabbing his arm and causing one of the newspapers to fall to the sidewalk. "The murderer! He's there!"

Aleck stopped, bent down to retrieve the paper,

and turned to look in the direction at which I pointed. "I don't see anyone."

"The man across the street," I said, as a truck passed, blocking our view. When it was gone, so was the man.

"There he is, walking toward Fifth Avenue," I said, watching him turn the corner. "He was waiting for us."

"Dottie, dearest, your nerves are shot. Your imagination is running away with you."

"No, Aleck, it was the man, the murderer!"

"But how can you know for sure? It's dark, the streetlights cast shadows, and he was just a fellow walking down the street."

"He was waiting for us, lurking in the doorway across from the Gonk."

"No, dear; if you are right about the fellow's identity, it was not *us* he was waiting for, but *you*. I don't live here, remember? He would have been watching your hotel, if I'm not mistaken. But, how likely is that, now? The fellow might have just stopped to light a cigarette out of the wind."

"There is no wind tonight."

"But, how can you be so sure he is the man? Did you see his face?"

"No, but it was he," I insisted. "Why else would he bolt when I looked his way?"

"All right, if you feel so certain, perhaps we should call in the police."

"And what would I tell them? I saw the murderer; he looks like every man on the street?"

Aleck took my arm. "Let's get inside and get that drink you promised me."

Peter, the Algonquin's night doorman, whom we referred to as "St. Peter" because he guarded our heavenly gates, greeted us as we entered, and once in the lobby I thought to ask if he'd seen the man, whom I described, lurking in the doorway of the Bar Association.

"I can't honestly say for sure, Mrs. Parker," said Peter. "Overcoat and fedora? I'm sorry, but there are so many—"

I stopped him in mid-sentence. "That's all right, Peter, never mind. But, if you notice anyone hanging around, watching the hotel, would you call up to my room?"

Peter, a tall Scotsman, leaned in to scrutinize at my face.

"This guy bothering you, Mrs. Parker?"

"I don't really know," I replied vaguely.

"You will let us know if you see anyone skulking about, won't you?" asked Aleck, more an order than a request.

"I will keep a vigilant eye on the street, Mr. Woollcott!" said the saint. "And I will make sure that Joseph is told to do so when he comes on in the morning." He straightened his epaulettes and touched his cap in affirmation.

I checked at the front desk for telephone messages and wires: My sister Helen called from Connecticut where she was on a short holiday to wish me a happy Thanksgiving, as did my friend and once-neighbor, artist Neysa McMein, to invite me up for drinks Friday at five. There was a wire from Scott and Zelda (Fitzgerald) from Cap d'Antibes where they were spending the holidays with Sara and Gerald Murphy, ex-pats living in France: "When was I sailing across the pond for a long visit with the Murphys?" they wanted to know.

Scott's latest novel, *The Great Gatsby,* had received scathing reviews and had flopped in sales since it came out last summer. I'd wired to him in Paris that I liked the book.

Some accuse Scott of being guilty of having set a standard for the mindless, sophomoric, devil-may-care philosophy of the wealthy, spoiled, upper-class fops of our generation: "Have fun before it's too late." The strict code of social behavioral ethics practiced by the Victorian parents of today's youth had brought their children into a war. "Let's abandon the rules," their children seem to say. "Be outrageous! *Carpe diem.* Tomorrow we all die." The rich can get away with anything, and in Scott's book, even murder. Scott acts the fool much of the time, indulging in too much booze and naughty behavior, but shallow he is not. He isn't encouraging any devil-may-care philosophy for living. He is simply showing in *Gatsby* that such a life of carelessness, purposelessness, and disloyalty has become glamorous, when in fact it masks betrayal and empty promises. Sophistication has less to do with education and culture and fortunes and poses, and more to do with the corruption and adulteration of longstanding mores. One has only to attend one of the extravagant soirees hosted by Herbert Bayard Swope and his wife at their Long Island estate to understand the point of his book, written with self-effacing, brutal honesty about his own life and his fascination with Zelda, but I doubt any of the reviewers had ever been invited to one of those parties, and therefore they have missed the point entirely.

My other messages were that the police sketch artist had called to ask if I would appear at the precinct house at 11:00 A.M. so that he might create a portrait of the culprit from my description.

And Mr. Benchley had called.

"It would be rude not to return his call, Dottie," Aleck said, rationalizing why I should ring up our friend. We'd gotten off the elevator and were walking toward my door.

"But be a good soul and let him sleep. You can tell him everything in the morning. Now, let's get settled with a scotch and soda."

Aleck resplendent

F. Scott Fitzgerald

Duke Ellington backing the Cotton Club Chorus

Snake Hips

Chapter Three

Mr. Benchley, having returned to Manhattan, arrived at my door with an offering of coffee and donut at the ungodly hour of ten A.M.

"What's this I hear about exploding cats and soldiers, murdered priests and Aleck reviewing jailhouse cuisine?" said Mr. Benchley, with a bit more zeal than I was used to so early in the day.

I tied my kimono, splashed cold water on my face, swallowed down a couple aspirins, and appraised my face in the bathroom mirror. It would be hours before I could face the world.

Taking the paper cup from my energetic friend who stood leaning at my bedroom doorframe, I staggered to the living room sofa, Woodrow Wilson at my heels. A bite of donut for me; the rest for Woodrow.

"I leave town for a couple of days and all hell breaks loose!" exclaimed my dapper Mr. Benchley. He took the chair across from me, lit a cigarette, and I wondered how, with the hectic life he led, he could look so pulled together: crisp collar, bright, smooth knotted silk tie, folded breast-pocket kerchief, charcoal double-breasted waistcoat, immaculate spats, groomed moustache, and center-parted Brilliantined hair.

"I hate you," I said. "You look like an advertisement for Brooks Brothers, all clean and shiny and new, and you smell good, too. *Yuck*."

"My thanks to you, Cinderella. Would that *that* could be said of you."

"It must be all that wholesome living in the wilds of . . . the Schenectady—"

"Scarsdale."

"Yes. All that fresh air and sunshine and that good home cooking of Gertrude's in your little cabin in the woods of the Saratoga—"

"Scarsdale."

"But what about the horses? I thought you had horses."

"That's Saratoga."

"That's what I said before, at your home in the horse country of Saratoga—"

"Scarsdale," he retorted, pulling out his pocket watch.

"Scarsdale, Schenectady, Sasquatchua; it's all so very far away . . . ."

"Why didn't you telephone me, then, if you needed to talk?" said Mr. Benchley, hearing the message beneath my cranky retorts.

"You need your sleep, even if you do disturb

mine, and what time is it, dawn?"

"Most of the day has passed you by, my dear Mrs. Parker. The early bird, and all that, has not only caught, but swallowed, digested, and shat the proverbial worm. Now, if you can manage to make something of yourself, perhaps I'll allow you to escort me to the offices of Messieurs—"

"Oh, shit!" I exclaimed, "What time is it?"

"Don't whine. It's ten-twenty-seven by my watch. Do I take it that you have—"

"*Shit-shit-shit!* I've got to get dressed and down to the precinct house by eleven."

"What, pray tell, Madame, for?"

"Come with me. No, not to the bedroom, idiot, but down to the jail."

"Oh, very well," said Mr. Benchley. "Whom are we bailing out?"

"Would you mind very much escorting Woodrow Wilson on his morning constitutional while I get ready? Oh, and put on his new red coat."

"I doubt it will fit me," he replied, "I've only two legs and this is not my best shade of red. Well, come along, my bewhiskered Commander-in-Chief; let us take a stroll around the rose garden."

The right hat can disguise an unkempt head of hair, so I pulled on a little chapeau bought at Bendel's last month. I've noticed that items attributed to the French designers always carry a higher price tag, and as this was a pricey little number, from the House of Madame Claire Beaumont, I refer to this piece of art from abroad as *chapeau*. Of course, it is entirely probable that it was made by a little old man in Hackensack, New Jersey, as there is nothing distinctly "French" about it.

Although it was cold outside, as I noted when I raised the window and stuck out my bare arm, it was also brightly sunny, so I slipped on hosiery and a new wool dress. I looked at myself in the standing mirror: no breasts, no waistline, just a straight fall from the shoulders of amusingly tailored fabrics. This was truly comfortable, but I did have a rather neat little waist, and I mourned that it would not be on view again for several seasons.

I pumped a cloud of Coty's Chypre *parfum* (notice the French spelling!), fetched gloves, purse, and jacket, and then rode down to the lobby and walked out into the street where I spied Mr. Benchley, halfway up the block having his shoes shined. Woodrow sat beside him, dizzily watching the buffing brush fly from side to side across the leather.

"Young Lincoln, may I introduce the famous Mrs. Parker," said Mr. Benchley to the young Negro boy who was down on one knee, buffing away.

"Yes, Ma'am, how'd you do?" said the boy.

"Pleasure, I'm sure . . . ."

"Lincoln, here, is Washington Douglas's eldest son," said Mr. Benchley.

"Filling in for your father, Lincoln?"

"Yes, Ma'am."

"Mr. Douglas had a bit of an accident last week,

you see, so Lincoln's taking over for a while."

"What kind of an accident?"

The boy, who couldn't have been older than twelve, did not look up from his work, although I noticed a hesitation in the circular application of the shoe polish. Head down and close to the shoe, he picked up speed, throwing me a side glance. "Fell off the trolley, Ma'am."

"Is he badly hurt?"

Bored with the show—or hypnotized—Woodrow curled down to nap.

"He'll be just fine, soon. Thank you, Ma'am. Jus' fillin' in."

The boy put his whole heart into buffing in the polish with the woolen brush; his discomfort was palpable. Mr. Benchley shot me a look that silenced the questions forming on my lips.

"Well, that's just swell, then. I'm glad to hear he's recovering."

Mr. Benchley rose from the bench, and riffled through his pockets for change. Finding none, he took out his billfold and handed the boy a dollar.

"Thank you, young fellow. Why, I can comb my hair in these," he said, staring down at his shoes. He handed me Woodrow's leash and we started to walk toward the Algonquin. I followed, dragging my lazy pooch.

"Your change, Mr. Benchley!"

"Oh, no, that's all right, Lincoln. Keep the change, and regards to your father."

"What's this? Joseph informed me about a stalker in the neighborhood." said Mr. Benchley as we entered a cab hailed by the aforementioned doorman.

St. Pete, our night doorman, had been true to his word, having alerted Joseph to watch for suspicious activity. I elaborated on the events of the evening before.

"It's a good thing that my rooms are across and facing the street from yours, so that I, too, can keep an eye peeled for the monster."

"That would be a reassuring comfort if it weren't for the fact that you are almost never home."

The police station was busy this morning, with officers milling about with the previous evening's catch of criminals. The NYPD had for some time turned a blind eye to violators of the Volstead Act, as thousands of speakeasies and bootleggers operated throughout the city. An occasional raid might be conducted of the most troublesome establishments to appease the Feds, but if the prohibition law were to be enforced, most everyone would be in jail, the providers and the imbibers, or they would have left the city to live in the obscure, but "wet," regions of the Canadian Rockies. So the job was left to federal agents to make a show of enforcement with arrests and convictions. But as of 1925, no-one's heart is really in it, anymore.

Today the majority of offenders awaiting booking, alongside the usual disorderly drunks and burglars, were a handful of Thanksgiving-night vandals and a dozen young men from the Columbia University student body, identified by way of their beanies and jerseys, brought in for having released several hundred live turkeys onto Central Park's Sheep Meadow. The birds were destined for the chopping block and stolen from trucks on the way to Delmonico's last Tuesday night. That accounted for the birds we spied from Edna's window yesterday afternoon grazing with the sheep in Central Park.

Aleck's cousin, Joe Woollcott, is desk sergeant at the precinct, but was far too busy this morning to doggie-sit Woodrow Wilson and tend to our inquiries. After a few pointers in answer to our queries from several policemen, we managed to find the sketch artist assigned to draw a likeness from my description of the murderer of Father John O'Hara.

It was not a pleasant hour, with Mr. Benchley commenting on what he considered my "obtuse" observations, but we did, in the end, come up with a rather uncannily accurate drawing of the man. Of course, few people walked about town with such a crazed expression plastered on their faces, but as I did not see the man smiling or in an *unemotional* state, it would have to do as facsimile.

"The artist appears disposed to take to his bed," noted Mr. Benchley as we departed. "If there is such a creature as you've described, Mrs. Parker, he will not get far without a disguise."

"Let's hope not and that they catch him soon."

It was a lovely noontime in the city, and the traffic was thick with autos and pedestrians enjoying the long holiday weekend for shopping, sightseeing, lunching, and, for some, business as usual. There was a disproportionate number of children about on the sidewalks accompanied by adults marveling at the skyscrapers built during the past half-decade. One can easily tell the tourists from the city's residents, without taking into account their costumes, as the tourists' heads are always in the clouds, while we who live in Manhattan rarely look up. We are a jaded lot, having quickly taken for granted the miraculous engineering feats around us; also, looking up while walking the crowded streets of the city could get you run over.

We decided to walk the dozen blocks back to the Gonk, heading south on Fifth Avenue, for our one o'clock luncheon in the Rose Room. As we made our way, children would spot Woodrow Wilson leading us along and stop to ask to pet him. As if anyone had to ask: Woodrow Wilson is a very socially adept creature, who basks in the light of praise and affection. A child would offer a hand for him to sniff and stoop down to pet his well-groomed fur, and in a few seconds another child, and then a third and fourth would materialize proclaiming his various attributes. My little man would raise his princely head high, as well as his tail, and bear the acclaim with regal dignity before being forced to move on to accommodate the burgeoning crowds.

Our daily luncheon at the Algonquin has been

taking place at one o'clock in the dining room of the hotel since 1919. The "attendees" of the daily fare have varied slightly over the years, and there are around thirty notables claiming membership. The regulars are the famous newspaper and magazine journalists—reporters, columnists, art reviewers, editors, and publishers—as well as actors, musical geniuses, playwrights, novelists, and poets. Aleck presides. The regulars include myself, Mr. Benchley, FPA (Frank Pierce Adams), George S. Kaufman, Harold Ross, Heywood Broun, the Gershwins, Marc Connolly, Robert Sherwood, any or all of the Marx Brothers, Edna Ferber, Irving Berlin, Alfred Lunt and Lynn Fontanne, Noel Coward when he's in town, Jascha Heifitz when he's in town, and many others who like to drop in when they are in town.

 We gather around a huge round table that the hotel manager, Frank Case, set up for us years ago, so our daily luncheons have become known as the "Round Table Luncheons"; we are often referred to as "Round Tablers." But, privately, we call ourselves "The Vicious Circle." The conversation is rapid-fire, rapier sharp, and quoted in the papers, most often in FPA's daily column, "The Conning Tower." I have become famous for many of the one-liners, but much of what I say is unprintable in publications distributed to the general public. I have to hold my own in a room full of sharp-witted men, after all, and although I am treated tenderly by the big oafs, and my company sought out, it is because I have never allowed any of them to intimidate me or out-wit me in terms of the humorous.

Tourists pop their heads in through the entrance of the dining room to peek at us. Frank Case has positioned our table for advantageous viewing, so the curious can see which famous (or infamous) persons are dining on any given day (if you can call it "dining"; it's more like feeding time at the zoo).

To be truthful, my dinner gang appears not to be so distantly related to the primates in the zoo. I'd given it quite a bit of thought last summer, the day I was reading about the Scopes Monkey Trial and the Tennessee Anti-Evolution Law. *Shit!* I thought, looking around the table at lunchtime, watching Marc Connolly fight Harpo for the last popover in the breadbasket, and wishing Ross's soup-slurping and Broun's lip-smacking would end sometime soon. In school down South a teacher talks to his students about Darwin's theory and it all winds up in a courtroom with William Jennings Bryan quoting from the Bible! Had Bryan only had the chance to observe my Round Table friends at lunch there would have been no question that Man is recently descended from apes!

Today there were only a handful of us present, as the holiday weekend had claimed the familial commitments of many. Mr. Benchley and I were first to arrive. Bunny Wilson came in with FPA, followed by Marc Connolly with Robert Sherwood. Aleck walked in last and in an agitated state. Without Harold Ross present to provide fodder for Aleck's angst, the mood was anything but effervescent. In fact, Aleck's mood cast a pall over the dinner table, and our efforts at congenial conversation proved more difficult than sucking pâté through a straw.

At Mr. Benchley's prompting, Bunny told us of the latest Condé Nast indiscretion, real meat for our lion, but the story of our much-hated publisher at *Vanity Fair* held little interest for Aleck. I felt his forehead, as he'd left food on his plate and ordered only one, rather than multiple, desserts, and determined that as he was not feverish he was simply displaying residual remorse from yesterday's brush with death. It was obvious to me, if not the others, that there was an elephant in the room blocking out all light, and until we acknowledged its presence it would not depart and there would remain a dark, gloomy shadow over the table. We had to face the beast head-on.

"Any news about the motive for the murder, Aleck?" I asked. "Cousin Joe was too busy to speak with us this morning."

"Nothing," he replied, and then drained his coffee cup.

FPA chewed his cigar and said, "The afternoon editions will say that Father John O'Hara arrived in town last Saturday, and was staying at the rectory of St. Agatha's Church on East Forty-third Street. No motive for the knifing, but the police believe it was probably a random attack."

Aleck slammed his coffee cup down with such force that it shattered. He pointed an index finger at

FPA, the cup's looped handle still dangling on it, and with all his chins in perfect alignment, his lips set in a straight line, his hazel eyes flashing through the thick lenses, and all color drained from his face, he said, "Random, my pretty little ass!"

"Why, your ass isn't pretty at all," said Mr. Benchley. "Come to think of it, it's not so little, either."

"Course it's not!" stormed Aleck, "That's my point!"

"Whatever are you trying to say, Aleck?" I said, flashing Mr. Benchley a withering glare. I answered my own question with another. "Do you believe that the priest was marked for murder?"

"Why would anyone want to kill the poor old fellow?" asked Marc Connolly.

Aleck turned his head toward Marc, an owl appraising his dinner mouse. The playwright ran a hand over the few blond hairs remaining on his head in a gesture of nervous habit from years gone by. For all of Marc Connolly's accomplishments over the past couple of years, he still found Aleck's glare daunting.

"You are missing the point, you imbecilic knucklehead!" said Aleck slowly and calmly, and I thought that had he only chosen words with the letter *r* to be rolled, his insult might have proved more powerful, more worthy of him. He was certainly off his mark today.

"The murderer was not out to kill the priest!" he said.

"But, you said just now that it was as random as your pretty little ass," said Mr. Benchley, refusing to play into Aleck's game of bullying the college graduates. "We agreed, did we not, that your ass is *not* little and presumably not pretty? Although I can't attest to its aesthetics myself, as I have never had the life-altering experience of viewing that humongous phenomenon, we shall assume it is appalling; pompous, perhaps—no!—for *sure,* pompous. This leads me to say, I believe what you meant by your self-denigrating exclamation was that the murder was not random, and that the priest *was* the killer's mark. So, please, Mr. Woollcott, make yourself clear as to the meaning!"

"Oh, for God's sake, Bob, shut up!" hissed Aleck. "He was after me!" Then, in a hushed tone, as the attention of a few luncheon stragglers had been directed at our table, he hissed, "The murderer was after me!"

I was alarmed that the idea had been torturing my friend all this time and no one had come to even think of the possibility that Aleck might have been the intended victim. Of course he was out-of-sorts; he was scared to death!

Mr. Benchley's concern was evident by the very fact that he would not permit Aleck to wallow in paralyzing fear, if Aleck might wallow more productively in active anger. "Now, why would anyone go out of his way to kill you, Aleck? Makes no sense at all."

"Why, lots of people want to kill me."

"You say that with a certain amount of macabre

pride, like it's some sort of badge of honor, old boy," said Sherry, with a chuckle. He rose from his seat to tower over the table. "Got to get back to work: deadline," he said, throwing two dollar bills on the table. Bunny Wilson settled his bill and tip with a dollar and fifty cents tossed onto the cloth and bid us adieu.

"See you later at Neysa's place," said Sherry. "And don't worry about yourself, Aleck. It'd be Dottie the killer is after."

"What do you mean?" asked Aleck, brightening a bit.

"Well, she's the only one who can identify him. She saw his face clearly. You only caught a glimpse of his back as he escaped through the crowd."

Marc turned to Robert Sherwood: "You're right, Sherry, the killer may have had designs on killing Aleck, but now that he's killed a priest, he'd want to get rid of Dottie, and then get out of town."

"It is I who should be afraid. He was lurking around last night," I said, and a shiver ran through me. "I saw him."

"It'd be bad for him if he were caught," said FPA. "He killed a man of God, of all people!"

"Wait a minute! Is killing a priest worse than killing me?" howled Aleck, eyebrows raised to his hairline.

"Certainly," said Mr. Benchley. "You are a critic. Everyone knows that the world would be a better place with fewer critics. Pawn of the Devil you are,

Aleck, you know that: one of the evil, little, mean men spreading venom."

"Hey!" I objected. "All right, evil, little, mean *women*, too. Is that better?"

"That's better," I said. "But remember you are a member of the club, as well," I said to *Life* magazine's theatre critic.

"Yes, but I never say anything really mean in my reviews."

"He botched it up, the killer that is. Is that what you're suggesting?" FPA asked Marc.

"I'm *saying*, not suggesting," said Marc, putting on his coat and hat. "I'll see you tomorrow. Mother awaits." And the journalist-turned-Pulitzer-Prize-winning playwright who still lived with his mother left the dining room.

"I'm off, too. *Vanity Fair* and the entire Condé Nast empire await my final approval," said Sherry with pompous deliberation.

"Shit." I said.

Sherry laughed and pecked my cheek, "*You*, Mrs. Parker, be very careful."

"I'll put Woodrow Wilson on red alert."

I threw off the glib retort, but in my stomach my lunch was being tossed about like clothes in an automatic washing machine. And then I felt my guts squeezing through the wringer.

As I was at my place of residence, I didn't have to go out onto the streets and expose myself to a madman who wanted to do me in. I could just take the elevator up to my room and hide under the bedcovers. I could have meals sent up from room service, have the bellboy walk Woodrow Wilson as needed, continue to have guests up for drinks at dusk, and get a lot of writing done, too, while I waited it out until the man was caught.

That seemed a good idea for a minute, until I realized that it was only a temporary measure against the inevitable. I had plays to review, publishers' offices to visit, and several important engagements over the next few days. No money equals no hotel room sanctuary.

"Well," I said, turning toward the others with a smile plastered on my face, "I can't lock myself away in my rooms and wait like a sitting duck for the killer to climb in through my window and murder me. I'm going to have to find him myself and bring him to justice."

"Very big of you, Mrs. Parker," said Mr. Benchley, "for such a tiny woman."

"I don't see an alternative plan, do you?" I replied, all the while hoping he had one, the cool bravado in my voice cracking like thin ice.

"We. *We* will find him and bring him to justice, my dear."

"What do you mean, *we*?" said Aleck, alarm quivering his voice.

"All of us, Alexander! Frank, here, can keep his eyes open and his ears tuned to police reports about the murder case. And he can check through his sources into the background of Father John to see if he was up to anything that might have made someone want to kill him."

"And what do you expect me to do?"

"You will go about your business as usual."

"But, what if it is me he was after?" asked Aleck.

"I'll bet my life he wasn't after you."

"That's easy for you to say, Bob."

"If you're so worried, why don't you just stay close to Mrs. Parker and me? She'll protect you."

"That's easy for you to say," I said.

"Yes, we established that," said Mr. Benchley. "Let's go."

"Where're we going?" asked Aleck.

"A house of prayer."

My partner in crime-solving, Mr. Benchley

Lincoln's father, Washington Douglas, before "the accident"

Chapter Four

Against the flow of Aleck's complaints about exposing himself as target for the killer, Mr. Benchley, Woodrow Wilson, and I walked the two avenues over to St. Agatha's Church on 43rd Street without incident.

We entered the lovely gothic church tucked into the north side of the street, and once in through the doors, marveled at the beautiful stained-glass windows that threw beams of sunlight in colored hues across the pews and altars.

The central aisle was being mopped by an elderly woman, who directed us to the rectory, a limestone building connected to the church, but accessed by the public from the street. There we would find Father Michael Murphy, she said.

The bell was answered by another elderly woman, and after identifying ourselves and requesting to speak with the rector we were ushered into a marble-floored hall, where we took seats on an intricately carved red-velvet Belter sofa from the previous century. A grand, flying staircase curved to our left, and a pair of tall doors loomed to our right. An ornate demi-lune console table graced the wall, on which stood an arrangement of chrysanthemums and above which hung a portrait of the Pope staring down benignly at us.

It took barely a minute for the housekeeper to appear through the walnut pocket doors and bid us enter into the rector's office, a spacious room carpeted with intricate Persian designs under a massive desk, chairs, sofas, and gleaming mahogany tables. With the walnut wainscoting and the bookcases that held hundreds of leather-bound editions, the papered walls bearing the portraits of past churchmen of note, dozens of framed landscape paintings of the Hudson River School, and the moss-colored, bullion-fringed damask drapery hanging heavily like drooping eyelids against the sunlight, it was like stepping into a salon from one of Edith Wharton's Gilded Age novels.

Father Michael Murphy walked around his desk to greet us and, as we introduced ourselves, shook our hands with the enthusiasm of reunion with long-lost friends. The round little man of fifty years, his protruding belly evidence that the priest enjoyed the privileges of his surroundings, who had never missed a hearty meal, or denied himself the pleasure of tobacco (as the heavenly smoke that rose from his pipe attested), knew who we were by reputation as writers. There was a knowing twinkle in his eye, and I wondered if he knew all about our disreputable escapades as well.

"Come and sit by the fire," he urged us, guiding us toward a grouping of chairs facing the fireplace. "And if Mrs. Daniels would be so kind as to bring a tray with tea?" He raised an eyebrow above his half-lenses, and with a wicked little tilted grin and giggle, added, with the thick brogue of his Northern Ireland, "or would the gentlemen prefer something 'medicinal'?"

"This lady takes her medicine, too, without too much fuss," I said, slipping onto the settee next to Mr. Benchley.

Aleck took the big wingchair opposite Father Michael's, stretched out his legs, and beamed as he accepted the tumbler of Irish whiskey from Mrs. Daniels. The grave expression he'd been wearing dissolved as he savored the fine liquor. With Father Michael's potbelly protruding in the chair opposite, the two were a mirror-image of each other, in form, if not in costume.

Father Michael smiled at each of us in turn, waiting patiently for one of us to speak. Finally, Woodrow broke the ice, walking from my side at the sofa to lean his head on the priest's knee, waiting to be petted with appreciation. Father Michael complied and asked the Boston terrier's name.

"*Ahh*. A fine name you've given him. A fine name. I had many pups when I was a boy in Ireland. Herders. They were working dogs—couldn't herd sheep without them, of course."

"Woodrow Wilson is a working dog, too, of sorts," I said, trying to play up my canine's dilettante credentials. "One can't easily catch a taxi in Manhattan without him."

Father Michael smiled and nodded as if I made perfect sense—or perhaps he was weighing my degree of sanity. How was he to know that what I spoke was the truth, that with the help of Mr. Benchley and FPA a couple of years ago I had trained Woodrow, after several sessions, to zigzag between and around the feet of the unfortunate competitor, nipping at the cuffs of each alternate trouser leg on the command, "Woodrow! Hail a cab!" Put into practical use on any New York City street at rush-hour, Woodrow would cause enough diversion with his figure-eights to momentarily distract the mark from securing entry into the taxi. Before the gentleman figured out the dodge, we'd be pulling away from the curb. So he *was* a working dog; he worked for me, herding away the city's big men who would otherwise trample over little Dorothy Parker for a cab in the rain.

"Father Murphy," began Mr. Benchley, "we are here not just to enjoy your very fine libations, but to inquire about Father O'Hara."

A solemn look settled over his ruddy complexion, draining his high color. Shaking his head he said, "It is a sad time. He had only arrived a few days ago. I had not seen him since we graduated from seminary college back in ought-two. Of course, we kept in touch through letters...."

He came out of reflection, his eyebrows rising as he studied us over his spectacles. "You wish to write about him for your publications, is that why you've come? Well, there is little I can tell you that I haven't already told the police, or that hasn't been in all the papers this morning. And I know that Mr. Woollcott was with him when he died. Did you know John very well, Sir?"

"Oh, no," said Aleck, "we'd never met. You see, I was in the crowd when he was—killed. I was standing closest to him and he fell into my arms before he died."

"I am mistaken, then. But the newspapers gave the impression that you had been accompanying Father John at the time."

I looked over at Aleck and read his thoughts. If the papers promoted the idea that Aleck was not just a disinterested bystander witnessing the incident, that he had been on friendly terms with the priest, then the murderer probably thought so, too. In short, Father John O'Hara could have told Aleck the name of his assassin before he kicked the bucket. It suddenly did not seem so outrageous for Aleck to believe he might be the killer's next victim.

I'm certain that Mr. Benchley understood the gravity of the situation, but from his expression, he would not let Aleck see his concern, nor would he burden Father Michael with our dreaded conclusions about Aleck's safety. Mr. Benchley didn't deny or confirm our interests in writing about the dead priest; he simply pursued a line of questioning that any journalist might employ for a story.

"Why did Father John come to New York?" he asked.

"He called me the night before his arrival asking if he could stay with me. He very much wanted to see me. He'd been able to take some time off and wanted to visit before the Christmas season. He said that he hadn't gone anywhere since he'd been assigned the church in Tennessee eight years ago. I was surprised, actually, that after so many years . . ."

"I thought he came to the city from Detroit?"

"Well, he said he'd been to Michigan to visit with his godson, Timothy Morgan, in Grosse Pointe, before coming here. He said he'd never seen a Broadway show, you know."

"How long was he planning to stay?"

"He didn't say. But he did speak as though he'd planned to return to Tennessee after the weekend, as there is much to do at Christmastime."

"Would you know if he had other friends in New York, other people he may have met with?"

"I wouldn't know, because he mentioned no one. I saw so little of John. He was out the door early in the morning, and would return late at night, except on Wednesday night when he did not return. The last time anyone here saw Father John was on Tuesday morning, as I told the police."

"Did he tell anyone where he was going?"

"No, and that didn't concern me at first, until

my housekeeper noticed that his bed hadn't been slept in Tuesday night."

"Weren't you worried that something might have befallen him when you'd no word from him after two days?"

"Why, yes, of course I was worried, and was about to telephone the authorities, but he'd sent a wire Wednesday afternoon stating he'd had pressing business but hoped to be here in time for Thanksgiving dinner."

"And he didn't mention what that pressing business was all about or where he was staying, if he was still in the city? Do you still have the telegram?"

"I do," he said, getting up and walking over to his desk where he retrieved the yellowish rectangle from its Western Union envelope. He unfolded the paper and handed it to Mr. Benchley. I leaned in to read:

> EXCUSE ABSENCE STOP UNEXPECTED BUSINESS STOP HOME FOR THURSDAY DINNER STOP JOHNNY.

Mr. Benchley handed the telegram to Aleck, who, after a cursory glance, gave it back to him.

"Father Murphy," began Mr. Benchley, "may I keep this for a few days?"

A questioning look flashed over the priest's face, and was gone. "Yes, you may have it, if you want."

And before the priest could question why he

wanted the wire, Mr. Benchley launched into his next question: "Was there anything unusual about Father O'Hara's behavior?"

"Odd that you should ask such a thing," said the priest, his demeanor suddenly guarded, eyes to the floor, brows knitting furiously. He resumed his seat by the fire, Woodrow Wilson jumping up on his lap. "Father John O'Hara was a fine man, and I'm certain—"

"Oh, we don't doubt he was," I said. "We just want to know of his whereabouts over the past few days. Perhaps he was doing good works, aiding a mission in the Bowery . . . ?"

If Father John had been killed because of a crime he'd witnessed or a secret he'd chanced upon while sightseeing, or if he had been kidnapped or abused in some way, and if he'd already shared that secret with his old friend, Father Michael's life could be in danger, too, should the murderer deduce as much. It would be premature, if not downright cruel, to alarm the priest with our suspicions that Father John was not the victim of a random attack by a madman, but the quarry of an assassin.

Father Michael Murphy nodded and his face relaxed into a smile. "No doubt, Mrs. Parker, John O'Hara was the kind of good Christian who followed Christ's examples. If he saw suffering or injustice, he would act to end it."

"Yes, as Mrs. Parker said, there's no doubt," reiterated Mr. Benchley. He weighed the wisdom of speaking more frankly, and decided to share with the priest the little we knew. "Before he passed on, Father O'Hara spoke to Mr. Woollcott."

Aleck picked up the cue: "He said, 'Stop him. Save him.' Do you know what he could have meant by those words?"

"I suppose it to mean that our Lord Jesus Christ offers salvation to any man, saint or sinner, upon the asking. Perhaps Father John was not speaking directly to Mr. Woollcott, but rather to our Lord as he was about to leave this world. It would be like John to consider the state of the soul of his transgressor." The priest's eyes glistened with moisture as he considered the character of his longtime friend. He nodded and said, "John O'Hara was the embodiment of Christ-like compassion."

We three sat quietly for a long moment, observing the priest, each of us trying to decide how best to continue the interview. It was Father Michael who rallied with, "There *was* something that weighed heavily on his soul. I could see that, when he arrived here last Saturday."

"Did he talk to you about it?"

"I sensed that was the urgency behind his visit to me. I tried that first day to give him the opportunity to share with me whatever was on his mind. But he said nothing. I did not hear his confession. I offered to hear it. Although he came all that distance to see me, we spent very little time in each other's company after dinner the day he arrived. I sensed from his nervousness, his mental distraction when we did speak, that there was something, some dilemma with which he wrestled."

"What did he talk about that made you concerned?"

"He spoke about the condition of mankind, the increasing violence and corruption in the government, and the poverty and ignorance that existed in his seemingly idyllic rural town in Tennessee. The Ku Klux Klan was a powerful force, and their intolerance and blatant hatred upset him. And then there was the Scopes Trial. He respected William Jennings Bryan, you know, and when Bryan suddenly fell over dead, a week after defending the faith from the trouncing he took on the witness stand from Clarence Darrow's questioning, well, a lot of people found that troubling. Heresy. An omen of sorts. I suspect that the atmosphere down there greatly affected him."

"Was he having a crisis of faith?"

"Perhaps he was. Bryan's death begged the question."

"Why would Bryan's death cause a crisis of faith in Father John?"

"Evolution. Science challenging Genesis. Six days for the Lord to make the world, the moon and the stars . . . oh, there are lots of people, good people, very pious, who saw it as a sign."

"David versus Goliath, but Goliath wins?" I said.

"Something like that, yes."

"An End-Time scenario?" asked Mr. Benchley.

"Do some people see Darrow as 'the Beast'?" asked I.

"Many blame him for the death of William Jennings Bryan."

"Darrow has said that blaming him for the statesman's death is nonsense," I said (recalling Ross, with wicked delight, warning Aleck that Bryan died soon after gorging himself all day at a banquet). "Darrow claimed that he died of a busted belly."

"I would think Darrow's comment would not be well received among Bryan's admirers," said Mr. Benchley.

"Sure and it's unreasonable to think the lawyer was to blame," said Father Michael with a smile. "But lots of people take the Bible literally, you know."

"Do you?" I asked brazenly.

"I do. One's faith is tested when it's difficult to believe, you know. I take the New Testament literally, and the Old with a grain or two of salt, I must admit."

"I'm sorry, Father," I said. "It's none of my business—"

"That's all right, really," he said and laughed. He had a nice smile, good teeth, and I liked the way his eyes crinkled. "That's been my crisis of faith, you see."

"And you can think of nothing he said, thinking back on those times you spent with him, that might lend some insight as to why he was . . . troubled?"

"Mr. Benchley, the life of a priest is often fraught with opportunities that challenge our way of life. Some people call them temptations; I see only opportunities, opportunities for tests of faith. I can't presume to say why or about what Father John was conflicted, as he did not take me into his confidence, and while here, made no confession. Had he asked me to be his confessor, I could not speak of it, you understand? But whatever the challenge, the conflict, Father John would have found his way with the help of his faith. Of that I am certain."

Mr. Benchley nodded. "We would like to speak to people who knew him well, and those from his parish church who might shed some light on what may have been troubling him, and whether he suspected he was in danger."

"You aren't saying that you believe someone actually murdered him with malice aforethought?"

His choice of the legal term for premeditated murder struck an almost-comical note of high melodrama coming from the holy man's mouth. There was a sinister bent to the expression that sent a shiver down from the nape of my neck.

"It's a possibility," I said.

Malice aforethought.

Aleck, his whiskey gone and his calm evaporated, stiffened his back. "I believe the murderer intended to kill me."

"But, the police said—"

"Yes, that it was random," said Aleck, nodding

slowly, his voice low, expression grave. "Alas, no! I believe I was the intended victim!"

"But Mr. Woollcott, who would want to murder you?" asked Father Michael, his voice raised an octave, his expression, incredulous disbelief.

"You'd be surprised," I said, not quite under my breath.

Aleck flashed me the Evil Eye.

Woodrow Wilson whined.

Mr. Benchley said, "On the chance that Father O'Hara was in fact trying to warn someone, trying to protect someone from violence, Mr. Woollcott even, would you be so kind as to telephone should you remember anything, anything at all, that he might have said that may give a clue as to why he may have been in danger?" He handed the priest his card.

"Yes, of course, whatever I can do," said Father Michael, as Mr. Benchley and then Aleck rose from their chairs. Woodrow Wilson leapt from the priest's lap.

"We'll want to speak with the godson, Timothy . . . ?"

"Yes, Timothy Morgan. I'll ask him to telephone you when he gets in."

"He's here, in New York?"

"He's arriving today from Michigan. Perhaps he can tell you more about his godfather's state of mind."

The degree of Aleck's upset was evident from the fact that he did not ask Father Michael to refill his glass, and when we departed the rectory, he insisted on taking a taxi home instead of suggesting a stop at Tony Soma's speakeasy for a cocktail. It was only a bit after four o'clock, but the afternoon sun had dipped low into the horizon as twilight fell over the city. The short November days gave in without a fight to endless nights, as the winter solstice encroached with cold indifference upon the lives of Manhattanites, egged on with the stiff competing gusts of wind off the rivers that bordered the island east and west.

I've always watched dusk, the time of day that the French call *l'heure bleue*, with a sense of trepidation. I don't know why it affects me so, but that hour of the day saddens me. Profoundly. I'm sure some student of Dr. Freud could tell you I'm afraid of change, or of the dark, or that the hour signals a time in my childhood when I felt unloved or unwanted or endured suffering. But, I'm not afraid of change, really, as I've little to lose, or of the dark; and what child hasn't at some time or another felt bad about something or other?

And it seems that, just before the arrival of this time of the day, when I need to light a lamp to chase off the creeping gloom, I seem to have forgotten; I suffer amnesia of sorts, forgetting the experience of the previous day's melancholy. I don't anticipate the moment, so it always takes me by surprise and dismay. Others must feel as I do, for as if to battle the gray that cloaks the city at dusk, thousands of lights come on to brighten the shadowy spaces, to chase away the baleful blues, and soon the atmosphere changes in aspect from dreaded dreary to deliberate and determined celebration.

With each new light comes another beam of hope.

My spirits revive. How could I have forgotten that I am not alone?

Because that is what I fear: walking through the shadows alone.

I suppose, then, that with each lamp lit I am made aware that I am not alone in this city of seven million people, even though in most respects I *am* alone in this world. My parents are dead, my brother disappeared mysteriously a decade ago, my aunts and uncles have gone to their graves, and my husband home to his snooty mother in New Haven. There is only my sister, Helen; at least there is she. And Woodrow Wilson.

So, in this great city at dusk, at this hour of mourning for all that has been lost, for all that has not yet been accomplished, with each lamp lit there is human solidarity against the approaching darkness. It is better to make the night gay, we all seem to agree, as we await the dawn together.

Tell Dr. Freud I figured it out. (My friends pay big bucks to lie on divans in Park Avenue offices talking to bewhiskered alienists. Being broke like me proves mighty thrifty.)

Aleck slammed the door of his taxi, gave the order to the cabbie, and without even a "Good evening" to Mr. Benchley and me was off to his West Side flat.

It was unlike Aleck not to offer to share a cab, so we knew how badly affected he'd been by the events of the past two days.

Mr. Benchley and I looked inquisitively at each other; Woodrow Wilson waited patiently at our feet, looking from one to the other of us for direction.

"Neysa's?" I asked Mr. Benchley. We'd been invited to our friend Neysa Mc Mein's for cocktails at five.

"We'll arrive quite early. Very well, shall we taxi uptown?"

The street was relatively free of pedestrian traffic this far east on 43rd, a side street off the busy avenues, which we attributed to the long holiday weekend making for a subdued rush hour. Woodrow Wilson need not be employed for taxi roundup.

Mr. Benchley stepped to the curb, stuck two fingers in his mouth, and let out a blood-curdling whistle in the direction of Second Avenue. Arm raised, he hailed a cab coming around the corner.

I stooped down to lift Woodrow Wilson into my arms, and was rising with my little fellow tucked under my elbow when I heard a car backfire and the ping of metal. Woodrow yelped and struggled to be set free. He is easily disturbed by lightning and thunder or a knock on the door; any sound piercing the calm will set him off yapping and jumping and circling frantically. As I had not yet straightened up when he leaped from my arms, his leash tangled round my arm and I fell hard to the sidewalk. Just then, the taxi drove up to the curb.

Mr. Benchley was kneeling at my side. "Are you hurt?"

I shook my head, and that was cue enough for him to open the taxi's passenger door and lift me onto the seat. He told the cabbie to drive around the block and to wait for him on the avenue. Taking Woodrow's leash in hand he bolted down the sidewalk.

But when another report pierced the gray-blue hour and set the hanging sign of a podiatrist's office out front of the building next door to the church to swaying, I had trouble believing a backfire had produced such a result. The cabbie and I ducked down in our seats. I heard Woodrow Wilson's fervent barking, so I rose up to look through the back windshield as my pup turned suddenly, head up, sniffing at the wind, and with a violent yank gave chase along the sidewalk with Mr. Benchley in tow.

The cabbie was pulling out into the street when I shrieked, "*Stop!*"

He stomped on the brake so suddenly that I was sent sliding off the leather seat and onto the floor. Cursing under his breath, he flashed a visual sentiment at me through his rearview mirror. I pulled myself up by the window strap to kneel on the seat, facing out the back window. Mr. Benchley dodged the steady flow of traffic on the avenue as he followed my bloodhound. "Follow them," I ordered the cabbie.

Another shot sounded; people screamed; then the shrill screech of car brakes. Pedestrians dispersed, rushing for cover. Police whistles sounded with insistent repetition. And with the sound of sirens the crowd reassembled to rush forward once more to witness the cause of the commotion. From where I sat, there was little I could see other than heads bobbing over the black hoods of automobiles. I opened the door and got out of the taxi, much to the objection of the cabbie. I fished out a dime from my coat pocket and handed the coin to him before I fled up the street. A police whistle cut through the jumble of excited voices.

All I could think about were the fates of my beloved Mr. Benchley and my most precious puppy. Again the police whistles cut through the cacophony of car and truck horns, the *cling-clang* of the trolley jiggling along its tracks, and the booming rumble of the el train passing over the avenue. A siren ululated in the distance, its whirring whine ricocheting against the taller buildings of Midtown. The smell of gunpowder mingled with the smell of onions frying at a restaurant on the corner and the belching musty coal smoke of furnaces. Funny how one notices mundane details at times of intense experience: the black cat diving through the overflowing trashcan in an alley, the street cleaner's impressive moustache, the election bill still posted on a brick wall weeks after election day, the spidery pattern of shattered glass on the windshield of the auto parked at the curb; smells and sounds and sights bombarding the senses.

After zigzagging around curved steel, chrome

headlights, and running boards, I finally poked through the tightly knit crowd gathered on the corner. Automobiles honking like frightened geese or the *hee-haw* of donkeys reached an ear-splitting crescendo as scores of impatient rush-hour drivers, unaware of the incident, sounded their horns. The noise faded with the throbbing beat of my own pulse in my ears. The rush of adrenalin burned like hot embers on my eyeballs, my stomach and chest were gripped with the paralyzing pressure of panic at the thought of what I might discover just beyond the last wall of topcoats.

"Fred!" I screamed, tears blurring my vision, as I pushed on, forcing breaks in the mass of bodies with insistent fists.

And then I heard the metal clinking of Woodrow's collar and tags, and his yipping response to my voice! My brown-eyed treasure broke through and under and around the legs of the hulking bystanders, his leash trailing, to leap up into my waiting arms. As his tongue windshield-wiped the tears from my face, I was only half relieved of my anxiety. I was sick to my stomach with fear.

"Fred!" I yelled hoarsely with no response, clutching my dog to me as I elbowed through the wall of bystanders.

"*Fred . . .*" I whispered, now, the affectionate name I sometimes used for Mr. Benchley, my voice breaking like heartache.

"He's dead," I heard a man's voice ring out clearly over the rumble of noise.

I clutched Woodrow closer, my face searching for solace in the plush of his winter coat. I felt my world dropping out beneath my feet; I was reeling in space and would have fallen to the ground had I not been propped up by the pressing crowd.

Woodrow whimpered. A constant shiver wracked his small body, and through my tears I could discern one large brown puppy-eye regarding me fiercely as he wiggled for relief from my stronghold. I loosened my grip, and with what I'd attribute as gratitude, he once again licked the tears streaming down my cheeks.

I couldn't face the horrible scene of my dead Fred lying out on the street before me, and yet, I could not leave my place in the crowd as long as he remained there—beyond the tall, unrelenting onlookers blocking my view. How could I go on without my friend, my best friend? What would my world be like now that he was gone? "Oh, Fred!" I cried out weakly, and the anguish I heard in my own voice brought a new knowledge to me. Mr. Benchley had been the only person in the world, other than my sister Helen, whom I deeply loved. And now, he, too, had been taken from me!

"Dottie?" The sound of his voice was only inches away, and then the hand appeared to guide me to him. My relief was so complete as I was clutched in an embrace. I leaned in to feel the soft cashmere fabric of his overcoat against my inflamed cheek. I'd lost my hat in the scuffle, and his warm hand patted my head like a reassuring parent's.

A coat button pressed painfully into my forehead; Woodrow Wilson fought for air. I pulled away to look up into the smiling face of my best friend.

"You're all right?" I asked, looking him over; all was good with the world!

"Why, Mrs. Parker, what made you think I wasn't?" he said, leading me away. "Are you all right, my dear?"

I turned to look back from whence he'd appeared, as the circle of spectators closed in. "I am now. I thought you were—but, you're not."

With a reassuring arm around my shoulder, Mr. Benchley led me to the sidewalk. "As much cannot be said for the murderer, I'm afraid, the man who shot at you, Mrs. Parker. He ran in front of a truck just over there."

"Is he . . . ?"

As he had no clean handkerchief, Mr. Benchley took the purse from my wrist and opened the latch. Finding a clean lace hankie, he proceeded to wipe the devastation from my face as he spoke. "Dead, yes. From your description of the fellow you saw kill Father O'Hara, I'd say you and Aleck have nothing to fear any longer, my dear."

For a change, I was speechless. And so very, very happy. I allowed Mr. Benchley the belief that it was for my own safety that I smiled.

Father John and Father Michael when young seminarians

Chapter Five

After we were questioned for a couple of exhausting hours at the police station, and having given our sworn statements, we were given leave to go home.

Mr. Benchley delivered me to my rooms at the Algonquin, ran a steaming hot bath for me, and called room service to send up White Rock and ice. While I soaked in the comfort of bath salts, listening to the *drip-drip-drip* of the faucet, he telephoned Neysa with regrets for missing the cocktail hour, and then Aleck to tell him the news.

When I reentered the living room, robed in my favorite terry wrapper, my dear Mr. Benchley handed me a scotch on ice.

"Aleck is coming over. Are you up to having a bite to eat downstairs, or should I call room service?"

"Oh, dear Fred, I'm just fine and dandy, all right. Any more pampering and I'll be spoiled rotten, you know."

I took a hearty slug of the burning booze from the glass that was frosting icily in my hand. Rolling the tumbler along my cheeks and the insides of my wrists, I closed my eyes, enjoying the contrast of hot and cold.

And then I remembered.

"*Ohhhhh, sssshhhiiiittt . . .*" I whined.

"Yes?"

"I've a show to review tonight."

"Noel's new play?"

"Yes, *Hay Fever. Ohhhhh, crap-crap-crap!*"

"Perhaps it will be good-good-good, after all," said Mr. Benchley, emptying his glass and then rising to his feet. He took his coat from a chair and threw it over his arm. "I'm off across the street to change. Shall we meet downstairs in an hour, or shall I come up to fetch you?"

I smiled at his kind consideration. "You're grand, and far too good to me. I think I can ride down the elevator on my own, my dear."

My Mr. Benchley is known for his kindness and consideration. With formal Victorian manners he expresses his very genuine concern for the welfare of the women in his life. There is something engaging about the man. It is not simply his clean, well-groomed good looks, or his vast knowledge, which he downplays so as not to appear superior to anyone (even though he is, in my book, anyway), or his unique sense of humor, which provokes unbridled laughter from even the most staid matrons and grim bankers. There exists beneath the attractive surface and proper social countenance a deep and abiding respect for his fellow human beings, and a touching sort of empathy for the human condition that is rarely seen in the circles we frequent.

He patted my head and was gone.

Forty minutes later I was sitting at the bar with Aleck when Mr. Benchley, resplendent in white tie and tails, the reflected light of the chandelier shimmering from his top hat to his patent leather evening shoes, walked in through the arch from the lobby. After checking his coat, silver-headed cane, and hat, he came over to greet us and together we walked into the more intimate Oak Room just off the lobby. Here we could discuss the day's events with more privacy than we'd be afforded in the Rose Room, where we regularly lunched.

We ordered a very light supper. We would be dining again at midnight, as was our custom on opening nights. Later still, we'd be off to make an appearance at the new play's opening-night party, where cast and creative crew, and their friends and family, awaited the arrival of the late-night and morning editions of the dozen New York papers. Inside were published the notices, the reviews of the play, by the most important critics of the day. Raves or criticism or bland remarks could make or break a show; a good review could keep it running for months, even years. Great notices, and the theatre's box office would be stormed the next morning; but if the show were panned by too many of the influential men, it would close even before the second performance.

After tonight's play, Aleck will leave the theatre before the curtain calls and race to the room he keeps at the Gonk, with several fellow reporters, to write his review. (Mr. Benchley and I can wait a day or two for submissions as our critiques are published in weekly and monthly publications.) With unbridled praise and flowery prose Aleck will bestow his blessing, or, with hatchet in hand, he will make mincemeat of the show. After telephoning his review to his desk at the *Herald*, he'll ride down the elevator to the dining room for a late, expanded supper before his grand, if terrifying, appearance at the opening-night party. I say "terrifying" because as he enters the room a hundred or more heads turn in his direction. The expressions are questioning, the conversations halted, and the greetings tentative. They do not have his review in hand yet, and he obviously relishes the power he wields by his very presence.

This is where Aleck smiles and nods his hellos, never giving any indication of his opinion, always royally gracious to his admirers. Will their sentences be commuted? Or will they be sent to the gallows? Will Judge Alexander Woollcott be merciful or vengeful?

As we partook in a preshow meal we tried to make sense of the events of the afternoon. Aleck ordered a small dinner of Cornish hens, fried potatoes, broccoli-and-cheese casserole, apple fritters, and cornbread stuffing, to be served after a dozen Blue Point oysters, crab-stuffed mushrooms, two baskets of buttered popovers, cheese biscuits, a variety of muffins, and cream-of-mushroom soup, and to be washed down with two bottles of crispy, chilled Chablis and a pleasant Riesling, all followed by only two items from the dessert cart, several shots of twelve-year-old Martel, and four cups of coffee served with heavy cream.

This should hold him until midnight.

I ordered a cheese sandwich; Mr. Benchley, lamb chops.

The most pressing business seen to, Aleck handed the menu to our waiter and then turned a critical eye toward Mr. Benchley.

"So you caught and killed the priest-killer, did you, Bob? Tell me all about it."

"Certainly not!" said Mr. Benchley, his reaction one of appalled horror. "He ran into traffic. I was simply trying to catch the maniac after he shot at our Mrs. Parker."

"Really Aleck," I said with a *tsk*. "Mr. Benchley saved my life, and would have yours, had you not left in such a huff, and you accuse him of—"

"All right, all right! Of course he didn't deliberately kill the man, as you say, if the fellow ran into traffic." He slathered butter on his second biscuit.

"Did he say anything before he died?"

"Aleck," began Mr. Benchley, "It's been a long day, and it appears it will be a long evening. A man is dead, and I take no pleasure in rehashing my role in his fate."

"Oh, very well," said Aleck. "I am grateful that I need not fear walking the streets once again, is all."

"If you'd just stop pissing on people all the time, you'd have no enemies to fear," I chided.

"We know it's impossible for a man of such great proportions as Aleck not to piss on a great proportion of the populace," said Mr. Benchley.

Aleck's tongue was rendered mute for it was occupied with slurping out an oyster from its magnificently convoluted shell; he had no time to invent, or blithely deliver, a stinging retort.

Mr. Benchley continued: "A man of such great proportions of sophistication, taste, and influence will always have to watch his back."

"Calling me fat, Benchley?" he managed to gurgle out.

"*Moi?* I'm saying you are a man of, *ahh-hum, great stature.*"

"Right."

"With a big mouth."

Aleck swallowed the slithery thing with a great gulp. He considered his friend for a long moment.

Then, "You've had a trying afternoon, Bobby, so I will let that go. Please pass the salt, Dottie."

Aleck salted the stuffed mushrooms, and spoke with somber expression. "I am sorry I left you both in such a huff this afternoon, left you to fend off that villain on your own. Our Dorothy almost killed, and my pain-in-the-ass best friend tackling the demon. Alone. I commend you!"

"Mr. Benchley tackles demons every day at one o'clock, like Dante spiraling down the eight circles of Hell!" I said, referring to the Round Tablers.

"True enough," agreed Aleck.

"Well, it's not me you need thank," said Mr. Benchley, his lamb chops having arrived.

"Whaddayamean?"

"I didn't tackle the man. I never got my hands on him. He was running away before I even spotted him," said Mr. Benchley. "A passerby on the street saw him fire the gun and pointed out to me the direction the killer was running. It seemed odd, really."

"Why odd?"

"There were so many places to hide, so many buildings, doorways through which to escape. But, he just sort of put himself out there, like he wanted me to chase him."

"That's odd all right, but odd only in your thinking."

"I suppose so. Even after hours with the police, we don't appear to know much about why the man killed the priest, or even the name of the murderer! Everything happened so fast. First the shot, and it missed Dottie by an inch! And then Woodrow and I are chasing the devil. And then gunshots, but the police never found his gun. I even thought for a second that he, the killer, was actually leading me somewhere, like he wanted me to chase him. But, of course, that makes no sense at all. And then, after he was struck down and—well, he stared up at me with that crazed look in his eyes that Dottie described—the poor girl had to identify the man as well!"

Oh, my God! I thought; *Mr. Benchley is very upset from the events of the afternoon, more so than I, for he only refers to me as "Dottie" when in his cups or protesting an injustice!*

"And I could see—" he said, stopping midsentence. His face went blank except for the rapid movement of his eyes as he stared down at the plate before him. He wasn't seeing lamb chops; no, he was elsewhere, reliving the moment before the fellow died. Then, face serious—I could actually read his thoughts!—he flashed a look across at Aleck.

Our fat friend appeared oblivious to Mr. Benchley's mental turmoil, for he was fully engaged in the dissection of one of the Cornish game hens.

"Go on, Bob," he said when he noticed the prolonged silence. He looked up from the sad twin bird carcasses and shrewdly appraised his friend over his spectacles. "Here, have an oyster," he said. "You're right. There is nothing about the events of this afternoon to take any pleasure in, Bob."

"All I can say is, thank God it's all over." I said. "I don't know why that man killed the priest. It's one mystery that may never be solved, but he's dead now, and you and I, Aleck, have nothing more to fear."

I'd had enough of death for one week; I'd been badly shaken these past couple of days. I didn't want to think or talk about it anymore. Going to the Theatre this evening was a welcomed distraction.

———

Curtain time for the new Noel Coward play, *Hay Fever*, was 8:40. We'd finished supper a little before eight o'clock, and Aleck excused himself. He was headed uptown to pick up the young actress, Helen Hayes, from the apartment she shared with her mother, to accompany him to the show. He'd see us at our seats, he said, knowing Mr. Benchley and I would be sitting directly behind him in the orchestra section's critics' circle, our usual place on opening nights. So Mr. Benchley and I lingered over a last cocktail before taxiing to Maxine Elliott's Theatre. It was an opportunity for me to ask him why he had not told us of the revelation he'd had earlier while gazing deeply into his plate of chops.

"Nothing, really," he said. "No revelation or

word from God or anything. I was just observing that Aleck had suddenly regained his appetite. Had this fellow not been . . . stopped . . . Alexander might have trimmed down substantially."

Heywood Broun caught a glimpse of us as he passed through the lobby, and he came over to our table, sat down, ordered a drink, and begged for details of the events of the afternoon. A minute later, FPA walked into the Oak Room, sat down, ordered a drink, and we had to tell the tale from the beginning.

When Bunny Wilson appeared with Sherry through the arched entryway and made a beeline for our table, Mr. Benchley turned to me and said, "'Hell is empty; all the devils are here.'"

Ten minutes later, after raucous arguments (supposedly reminiscent of Mr. Benchley's dormitory days, from whence that quote had originated)—Mr. Benchley refusing to disclose the author or source—we six critics-at-large piled into a taxi in time to make it to our seats for the play's curtain.

Hay Fever was Noel Coward's second play to open in the 1925 season. A few months earlier, Noel had crossed the pond from England to star in *The Vortex,* to great acclaim. So, now, *Hay Fever*, which Noel co-directed and for which he'd received rave reviews in its London production, was eagerly anticipated, especially as Noel boasted to having written the play in just three days.

At 12:15 A.M., after barely a half-hour spent writing his review of the show, Aleck emerged from the second-floor room of the Gonk to join Mr. Benchley, FPA, Helen, and me at the bar where we sat waiting for him to join us for a late supper.

He walked toward us with determination, a look of distaste in his mouth and brushing off the sleeves of his coat. In answer to our querying looks he said: "Just wiping off the blood."

We then all proceeded to the Rose Room where our supper was laid out, after which we piled into a taxi, dropped Helen home to her mother, and proceeded uptown to the play's opening-night party.

The party was in full swing by the time we'd arrived at the apartment Noel Coward had leased from Ziegfeld Follies star Mae Murray at the Hotel des Artistes on 67th Street and Central Park West.

It was like an epidemic these days, a current fad, for stars of Broadway and Hollywood to choose husbands from European nobility. Pola Negri and Gloria Swanson had picked a count and a marquis, respectively. But Mae Murray trumped them when she fetched herself a little old Russian prince, David Mdivani. Off honeymooning indefinitely, she leased her fabulous digs to the visiting British star.

The Hotel des Artistes is a triumphant expression of the new modern Art Deco design. Aleck puffed up as we entered the lobby with its sleek décor. With his beaky nose and huge round spectacles he'd often reminded me of a barn owl, but never more so than now as he squared his shoulders under his massive cape like a big bird ruffling his feathers. There was something about the place, its spare but richly appointed glamour, which prompted one to straighten one's spine, to stand taller, as if to make the grade. *No riffraff allowed entrance here*, the glossy walls announced in beautifully enunciated, hushed tones.

Off the elevator, we were met with the bright, up-tempo musical strains of piano, bass, and violins as we walked into a great, marbled entry hall, into which the overflow of personages from the magnificent apartment spilled. Aleck, like an icebreaker ship, cut through the sea of people and into the foyer overlooking the grand two-story living room, its glass wall affording an outstanding view of Central Park. Competing with the view, a stained-glass mural depicting a ship at sea dominated the entire north wall of the room. The furniture was sleek, boxy, and curved; the upholstery, lush silks and velvets; the wood tones, blond with inlaid geometric designs; mirrors reflecting the brilliantly lit chandeliers and sconces; the carpet, white and thick; the statuettes, figurative and slim. And filling the space were scores of impeccably tailored gents in evening clothes escorting beautifully coiffed and begowned gals resonating with the excitement of frolic and booze. The place was aglitter with sleekly draped contours covered with sequins and bugle beads, satin and organza, trimmed out with mink, fox, and marabou, and evocative of Manhattan's sparkling skyline at night.

Mr. Benchley took my fur-trimmed evening coat, and I smoothed the hips of my blue satin Lanvin gown, inconspicuously realigned my bosom into its proper location, and checked my face and the position of my feathered cloche in the giant mirror gracing an entire wall of the entry hall. All in place, I stepped between Aleck and Mr. Benchley, with FPA bringing up the rear, and stood ready for our descent of the sweeping staircase.

Looking down from the landing there could be seen a gracefully curved bar, at which waiters and bartenders in crisp attire attended to the constant pouring and serving of champagne. A table was laden with mounds of food: roasts of beef, ham, turkey, and lamb, imported cheeses, caviar and molded aspic, lobster, oysters, shrimp and eel, breads and soufflés, and cakes and puddings.

Aleck's eyes lit up as he caught the aroma of ripe, runny English Stilton rising through waves of Chanel No. 5, Bal au Versailles, and My Sin.

Like the Red Sea parting for Moses and his tribe, the crowd sprang away for our descent down the flight of stairs. A murmur swept across the multitudes, and, as in a mass hypnosis, faces turned one by one to look up at Aleck—Moses sans tablets. He swept off his top hat with the flourish that Cyrano de Bergerac did his plumed chapeau, and then, with a dramatic twirl, whipped off his black, red-satin-lined cape.

The music trailed to a discordant stop, and a

hush descended with us.

Noel, sitting on the arm of a sofa, rose stiffly to his feet, put out his cigarette, and moved like a Haitian Zombie to the foot of the stairs, where tall wrought-iron gates marked the entry into the salon. (I always feel like part of "the delegation" at times like these, but as my review of the evening's fare would not be read for another week or so, I felt quite safe, even had I not been swaddled between the men.)

Holding their collective breaths, a hundred pairs of eyes watched as Aleck, with slow deliberation, handed his garments and ivory-headed cane to the butler, who'd presented himself for the task. Then, turning with opened arms and smiling large, Aleck pushed open the elaborate gates to stand before the playwright. (Actually, it was Noel who stood before Aleck, if you really want to know. Another simile comes to mind: a sinner facing St. Pete at the Gate. Poor Noel.)

"Dear Noel," said Aleck, smiling beneficently at the wiry star.

"Aleck?" His voice cracked; eyes wide, expectant. Noel shuffled from one foot to the other.

Poor Noel. Poor, *dear* Noel.

This is what was said:

"Magnificent!" said Aleck.

"The play?"

"No, this apartment!"

"But, what about *Hay Fever?*"

Aleck put an arm around the slump-shouldered lad. "My *dear* boy," he began with paternal patronization, "you should have taken two or three more days to tinker with that play."

"Didn't you like it at all?"

I thought the boy would burst out in tears.

"I wrote perfectly dreadful things about all you terribly talented people," pronounced Aleck with jovial fanfare.

"Calamity!"

"Nonsense!" chided Aleck, and then, with magnanimous reassurance, "That's what they said about me, at my very beginning: '*Calamity!*' Look at me tonight—bursting with good fellowship!"

Mr. Benchley was soon surrounded by a chorus of chorines, quite literally hanging off his sleeves. FPA ambled over to Marilyn Miller and Tallulah Bankhead, who were singing a duet of *Toddle Along*. A self-proclaimed twentieth-century Samuel Pepys, Frank would undoubtedly include mention of the actresses leading the new dance sensation, the *Toddle*, in his newspaper column tomorrow morning.

I headed straight for the bar and a glass of the bubbly. And that's where I saw it, the newspaper article.

"The Thanksgiving Murder," that's what the headline called it on the front page of the *Evening Star*.

A stock photo of Aleck, captioned THE INTENDED VICTIM, alongside one of Felix the Cat, moments before the feline's explosive demise, stared up at me from the bar. I had little time to read the copy before I turned to see an enraged Aleck at the center of a crush of gushing actors wanting to hear first-hand of his adventure fighting off the killer at the Christmas Parade. I could see his distress, but it seemed unfounded, really, in light of the events of that afternoon. The killer was dead, although that fact had not as yet hit the papers. Within hours, however, there might be a stock photo of me and Mr. Benchley on Page One of the morning papers. I had foolishly believed that because we were so entrenched among the most powerful reporters and editors of the day our names would not be revealed! Of course we didn't know every city editor, nor were we all on good terms with every reporter. A scoop was, after all, a scoop, and we'd been scooped, all right.

I worked my way through the throngs of beauties in shimmering glitter accosting Mr. Benchley, and managed to pull him aside to inform him of the situation. FPA appeared, and the men freed Aleck, while I found the butler, who fetched our coats.

"May I be of assistance?" asked the owner of a rich baritone voice. There was a trace of Midwestern casualness in the flat vowels. I turned to look up into the clean-shaven face of a man in his early forties with rich, light auburn hair and a complexion so fresh as to be reminiscent of chilled summer melon.

"Thank you, young man," said Aleck, even though there was little difference in their ages. As Mr. Benchley helped me on with my coat, the "young man" took the cape from the butler and placed it on the shoulders of the critic.

"I've got to get out of here," said Aleck. "It's not safe here."

"Has someone threatened you, Mr. Woollcott? You must tell me immediately, and I will see that the fellow is dealt with," said the impeccably suited fellow. There is nothing so attractive as a man who can carry the responsibility of evening attire. And he carried his burden divinely. I don't remember, but I must have stood there with my mouth open, and possibly my tongue dangling, because I was mesmerized by his compelling charisma—and promise of brute strength.

"Not yet, but the evening is still young. I've just panned their play and there are a hundred actors who'll want to wring my neck when they see the newspaper. Calamity!"

"Forgive me. I should introduce myself, Mr. Woollcott," he said, offering his hand to shake. "My name is Pinchus Seymour Pinkelton. My friends call me Pinny."

Can you ever forgive your parents? I said—in my head.

"And you are Dorothy Parker. I knew you the

instant you walked into the room from your photos in the magazines."

He took the ungloved hand I offered and kissed it.

"And I'm Bob Benchley, gadabout, man-about, and rarely sad about—anything, and this is Frank Pierce Adams, the newspaper columnist."

They shook hands all around.

"You're *not* an actor, are you?" asked Aleck, with suspicion.

"I can't walk across a stage without tripping," Pinny said with an amused twinkle in his eyes. "I tried once, I must admit, at Princeton, but the other actors on stage wanted to wring *my* neck, so I understand your feelings tonight."

The near-hysterical Aleck became suddenly still.

"They'll be coming now."

"Aleck?"

"All of them!"

"All of whom?"

"Every damned actor and playwright and director that I've buried," he said, his eyes wide, his body rigid, and a shiver coursing through his rotundity. "They'll be rising from the graves I put them in; it will be like the old Wild West: I'm Wyatt Earp, and every silly gunslinger I ever crossed will want to take me on!"

He looked like he might faint, collapse dead from apoplexy, he went so quickly from red-faced to white pallor.

Pinny asked the butler to fetch his overcoat, and once down the elevator to the lobby, he offered his car to transport us all home. I accepted before there could be any objections from the men.

As we waited for the doorman to fetch Pinny's chauffeur parked half a block away, we wandered out into the brisk night air. Central Park across the street sent over a sharp, invigorating fragrance of winter woods, and after the smoke-filled, perfume-drenched closeness of the apartment, it was refreshing. We lit cigarettes all around.

"*Extra! Extra!* Read all about it!" shouted the newsy that came from around the corner to stand under the building canopy, out of the icy sleet that had started to fall. "Woollcott cheats death, priest sacrifices life!"

"Oh, shit!"

"I couldn't agree with you more strongly, Mrs. Parker!"

FPA flipped the boy a nickel. "Keep the change, Kid," he said, and he began reading aloud: "'Famed theatre critic and star-maker, Alexander Woollcott, survived an attack on his life yesterday by a dagger-wielding fiend moments after the mid-air blast of

Felix the Cat. Woollcott, forty-three, was shielded by the selfless Roman Catholic priest from Tennessee who'd been on a sightseeing vacation at the time and had come to witness the spectacle of R.H. Macy's Christmas Parade...."

"We get the idea, Frank," I said.

"Take me home," cried Aleck, as we ushered him into the elegant, creamy-yellow Duesenberg.

"Don't worry, Aleck, I'll set things straight in my column tomorrow."

"That's what I'm afraid of, Frank!"

Pinny Pinkelton ordered his chauffeur to 412 West 47th Street, where we saw Aleck into his apartment. Pinny refused the offer of a drink, and said he'd been happy to be of service but had to return to the party where he'd left the woman he'd escorted to the theatre that evening.

I was disappointed, but recovered from my foolishness with the help of several shots of Jane's home-brewed gin.

Noel

This three-day play needed a couple more days of "tinkering"

Cast parties do get wild!

Joan Crawford (who came to the cast party) was waiting tables when she helped with clues to solve The Broadway Murders, *and a year later is on her way to stardom!*

Chapter Six

"Go away, Mr. Benchley."

I stuck my head under the pillow, ignoring the continued knocking at the door. Woodrow Wilson stood rooted at the foot of the bed sounding responding yaps, like a metronome, piercing through my veil of sleep. I huddled tightly under the blanket. Woodrow jumped on the bed and continued his rant.

"No!"

"*Yap!*"

"No!"

"*Yap!*"

New approach: blanket in teeth, pull and growl.

The blasted knocking began anew.

"It's the pound for you, Mr. President!"

"*Owwuouwww, yap!*"

"*Ohhhh*, for cryin'outloud," I whined, throwing off the covers and pushing up my eyeshades. Woodrow Wilson leaped off the bed, victorious, and led the way out of the bedroom and toward the door to the hall. Applying his herding skills, circling back and around my shuffling feet and barking encouragement at my slow progress, he led the way.

"What do you want, Mr. Benchley," I said, belting my kimono and throwing open the door. My eyes fell upon a pair of heavy-soled shoes, and traveled up to a rather pedestrian brown overcoat, and it dawned on me that Mr. Benchley was not standing across the threshold. But, why was my hat, my Aberdeen cloche with the ginger-colored feather and garnet crystal brooch, dangling before me?

I ventured a peek above the turtleneck. There was no going back now. Two blue eyes met my mascara-smeared squint.

"Mrs. Parker?"

"*Ahhh*, heck . . ."

"I'm Timothy Morgan."

I covered my face with one hand and waved him in with the other.

"Shit," I mumbled under my breath.

"Excuse me?"

"I said, 'sit.' Have a seat, sit."

By this time Woodrow Wilson had herded the

stranger to the sofa, leaped up, and growled for the fellow to sit, too. Woodrow prevailed.

"I'll be a few minutes," I said, taking the hat and returning to the bedroom. A trip to the bathroom to splash cold water on my swollen face, a quick tooth brushing, hair brushing, a touch of lipstick, a spray of cologne, and then to the closet to find a modest wrapper.

By the time I returned to the living room, Woodrow Wilson sat staring at me from his perch on the man's lap, enjoying the stroking of his shiny coat.

"Now, who are you, did'ya say?"

"Tim Morgan," said the ordinary-looking man of thirty or so years, as if I was supposed to know who he was.

"This is swell!" he said, facing my blank stare. "I can't believe I'm meeting you!"

"No, I suppose you can't."

There was a lovely lilt to his speech, betraying Southern charm. And charming he was, especially his smile, turning a plain face into an appealing one. Blond and blue-eyed, and probably not too bright: just what I look for in a man. I wondered if he was an actor I'd seen in a play, or might have met at Neysa's or somewhere, because there was something vaguely familiar about him.

"I found the hat on the street near the rectory."

"How'd you know it was mine?" I asked, calling down for room service to send up a pot of coffee, some rolls, and a couple of cups.

"Mrs. Daniels recognized it as yours."

"Who the hell is Mrs. Daniels?"

"Father Murphy, Michael Murphy's housekeeper?"

It took a few seconds, but the light dawned.

"I'm afraid I came at a bad time, Mrs. Parker."

"Was up 'til dawn, is all."

"Father Michael said that you and Mr. Benchley hoped to speak with me, but I've not been able to reach Mr. Benchley."

"That's because he's more ambitious in the morning than I. The 'man about town' is probably about town," I said, searching the icebox for a can of something to feed my pup. I shoveled the remains from an opened can into Woodrow's dish and filled his water bowl. Woodrow held his post. "Corned beef now, pâté for lunch, young man."

It didn't excite.

Jimmy the bellboy arrived and placed the tray on the coffee table. Woodrow Wilson jumped off the sofa, fetched his leash, and the two were off for a brisk walk.

"Ah, now I remember. You're the godchild," I said, pouring the coffee.

"Yes. John O'Hara was my godfather," he said, and I found the southern accent most endearing.

The telephone rang. Mr. Benchley was in the lobby; might he come up?

My friend had brought the morning papers. We were page-three news in the *Herald,* the *Tribune,* the *New York Times,* and the *World.* As soon as the men were introduced and seated we brought Timothy Morgan up to date on the events occurring immediately after our departure from the rectory last afternoon.

"You could identify him, Mrs. Parker. He wanted to get rid of his witness. Thank goodness you are all right!"

"I've never been *all right*, really," I said, but the blank look on his face told me I was being drolly self-deriding without effect.

"It must have been a random act of violence that killed my godfather," said Mr. Morgan. "He had no enemies that I knew of, unless he made one when he came to New York."

"That's easy enough to do—just hang around with me for a day or so—but whatever you've heard, New Yorkers don't go around wielding daggers, just dirty looks."

"Oh, Mrs. Parker, I didn't mean—"

Good God. I was being taken seriously.

Perhaps I was serious, after all. I don't like it when out-of-towners criticize my city. What do they expect? With seven million people living and working in close proximity to each other there are bound to be a few crazies. Doesn't every backwater hole-in-the-woods have its village idiot? Who else will pull the bell cord in the church steeple and serve as example to children of what happens when they neglect their school lessons? One idiot wouldn't be enough for a city the size of New York. We need thousands to do the job. No, I don't like tourists criticizing my New York. We like to do our own dirty work.

"Oh, don't mind me."

"That's right, Mr. Morgan, don't mind Mrs. Parker."

"Call me 'Dorothy,' please," I said, repentant—but not for long. "I reserve 'Mrs. Parker' for *intimate* friends," I said, and flashed a look at Mr. Benchley, who scolded me with a twitch of his moustache, "and we've not become intimate yet." I was feeling wicked today.

Timothy Morgan twitched in his seat. Was he really so naïve?

"Where were we?" I asked, giving up. The fellow was witless, but heck, he was cute.

"Oh, yes," I said, wanting to get my point across: "I'm not so sure that my witnessing had anything to do with the murderer wanting to kill me."

"What do you mean?"

"Perhaps he really had meant to target Aleck, but *accidentally* stabbed your godfather. And was after me, too. Perhaps he's some disgruntled actor Aleck and I panned in our reviews. I meant what I said, Mr. Morgan: Hang around me for a day, and at my heels will trail a dozen or so new enemies."

Mr. Benchley jumped in: "Mrs. Parker exaggerates, Mr. Morgan. I'm the only one trailing her heels, and I'm no enemy."

What was this country bumpkin to think?

"Anyway," continued Mr. Benchley, "I believe that had the killer been after Aleck and Mrs. Parker, he'd have taken the opportunity to 'do her in,' as they say, when he came face to face with her on Thanksgiving morning."

"I suppose you're right, Mr. Benchley," I conceded. "But, if he'd been worried about being identified, why didn't he leave town? I'd never have seen him again."

"There is that point, of course, unless he couldn't leave town for some reason. Family, perhaps? A job and kiddies?"

A thought struck me. It was something the police had never asked me about, and that I'd never before thought to add to my description of the killer when interviewed on Thanksgiving: Although the clothing the culprit was wearing when he killed Father

O'Hara was nondescript—jacket, hat, et cetera—it was most definitely the costume of a rural life.

"Remembering what he looked like and how he was dressed, I'd say he wasn't cosmopolitan at all."

We were all silent for a long moment.

"Yesterday, I saw that he was wearing boots," said Mr. Benchley. "I doubt he was an angry actor out to kill the critics and who left his spats at home, now that I think about it."

"He came to New York for a reason: surely not to intentionally kill my godfather? Is that what you've decided?"

"I honestly am unsure, Mr. Morgan. When Father O'Hara visited with you, did he say that anything or anyone was troubling him?"

"Not at all; he seemed just fine. We kept in touch through letters, of course, and he had planned to make his visit to me quite some time ago."

"What brought him to New York?"

"He wanted to make a long holiday of it. Wanted to visit his old friend, Father Michael."

"For how long did he visit with you?"

"Three days."

"And during that time, how did he spend his days?"

"I can't account for all of his time—we spent evenings together—because during the day I attended to my responsibilities. I just assumed he'd be returning straightaway to Tennessee. But he probably just wanted to make the best of the time he'd taken."

Again, he was digging into memory.

"You know, I remember that he didn't tell me *why*, but when I asked *what* he planned to do here, he was rather vague—church business, and to visit with his old friend Michael Murphy."

"Could your godfather been having a crisis of faith, Mr. Morgan?" asked Mr. Benchley. "Could he have wanted to leave the Church?"

"Oh, dear me, no! It couldn't have been that. It's not unusual for men of the Church to sometimes grapple with doubts, especially in these modern times when science is always presenting answers to what were once believed to be exclusively the miracles of God. John told me that when he was a young seminarian he'd wrestled with nagging doubts about the transubstantiation, the acceptance of it as the miracle that it is, and not as symbolic ritual."

I had no idea what he was talking about. A Jewish child educated at a Catholic academy for girls, I thought of biblical stories as no more than the fancies of old men in long robes, long beards, and longer hair. David and Goliath, multiplying fishes and loaves, parting seas, Jonah and the whale, Noah and his ark: all children's fairytales just like Hansel and Gretel. I couldn't deal with six-syllable words like *trans*—whatever-he-said.

"You've lost me," I said.

Mr. Benchley said, "Have you had a chance to go through your godfather's belongings, or do the police have them?"

"The police didn't have anything except his wallet, which they returned to me this morning. I was hoping that you knew something that could shed some light on why he was killed."

"Have you looked for any papers or notes that might indicate places he'd been while in New York?"

"I didn't think to do that."

"The room he stayed in—are his belongings still there?"

"Yes."

"Would it be all right with you if we—"

"Of course."

"Let's find out if there are any clues as to why he was murdered."

"Then, you believe it wasn't random. He was deliberately murdered!"

Our silence was response enough for Timothy Morgan.

"I'll only be a few minutes," I said, walking into the bedroom to dress.

Half an hour later, Mrs. Daniels bade us enter the rectory of St. Agatha's on 43rd Street.

"Good morning to you, Mrs. Parker, Mr. Benchley, Father Timothy."

"*Father* Timothy?" I blurted out loudly.

"Yes, that's right," said the priest, removing his scarf to display his clerical collar. "I thought you knew."

"We do now! Here we've been behaving all sacrilegious—"

"Speak for yourself, Mrs. Parker," interrupted Mr. Benchley.

"That's all right," said Father Timothy with a laugh. "We Jesuits are used to heresy."

Damn it! I had to discard my designs. After all, *Girls seldom make passes at men who say masses!* By the way Mrs. Daniels beamed dreamy-eyed at the young priest I surmised there were lots of repressed "church ladies" who might challenge my observation.

Father Michael was meeting with a church committee, Mrs. Daniels told us, and would not be free until the hour, which, by Mr. Benchley's pocket watch, gave us about fifteen minutes to examine the bedroom in which Father O'Hara had spent his last hours on earth.

Timothy Morgan led the way up the wide, carpeted stairs. My hand glided along the rail of the brilliantly polished dark-walnut banister to the second-floor landing, where, to left and right, wainscoted hallways led to rooms entered through paneled doors.

He opened the second door to the right and we walked into the sparsely decorated bedroom.

Weak winter sunlight shone through the diamond-shaped panes of leaded-glass casement windows; an armoire, bed frame, and bedside table were polished to a looking-glass shine; a stream of dust motes danced along the arrow of light that shot in from outside and onto the bed.

There was little to say as the three of us began opening drawers and doors. Timothy looked under the bed, Mr. Benchley peered into an empty trash bin, and I checked the pockets of a coat jacket that still hung in the armoire. I folded the jacket and laid it on a chair. Father Timothy opened a small leather valise.

Inside were articles of clothing: one shirt, two clerical collars, two each of socks, undergarments, a pair of trousers, along with a shaving kit containing razor, brush, toothbrush, manicuring scissors, hair comb, and a bottle of Carter's Little Pills.

There was nothing, absolutely *nothing* that gave us any clue as to where the priest had traveled and for what purpose during the days before his murder. But it was obvious from the sparse contents of the valise that he never intended an extended stay—not in Michigan, nor in New York City.

"We're fresh out of trash," stated Mr. Benchley, displaying the metal trash bin flipped upside down. Father Timothy's blank expression brought out Mr. Benchley's serious side. "Let's ask Mrs. Daniels if the trash has been collected. And, by any chance, do you have a recent photo of Father O'Hara?"

Father Timothy went to his room across the hallway and returned with a snapshot of his godfather, which he handed to Mr. Benchley, along with a parcel returned to him from the police containing clothing worn the day of his death. He placed the parcel on the bed and untied the string that held it together. Pulling away the flap of paper, we stared down at the bloodstained shirt, collar, undergarments, and socks and shoes. Beneath the neatly folded garments lay trousers, waistcoat, and overcoat, all black, and all marked with dried blood.

Mr. Benchley and I remained silent, watching as Timothy Morgan examined the clothing, gingerly running his hand along the fabric of the lapel of the waistcoat, and then carefully, lovingly, lifting the clerical collar between his fingers. From the pocket of the waistcoat he pulled a string of ebony wooden beads. Father John O'Hara's rosary. He turned to look at us, and I felt, as did Mr. Benchley, like we were intruders. Mourning is a personal experience and the young man's intimate connection with the deceased priest was profound.

"It's all right," he said, with a little smile of understanding, as if he'd read our thoughts. "These are of no importance any longer. Uncle John is in a better place, a place he'd prepared to go all of his earthly life. It's just me, you see. I will miss him."

Whatever I thought of religion and whatever I didn't believe in didn't matter much. Throughout my life, when I felt alone or had known despair, I never thought about God; never thought to ask for divine intervention. Prayers were just words said in churches and temples reassuring God that you loved Him. But, did He love us back? And if there is a guardian angel watching over me, I've never seen him. Every other little kid at the Academy had one for protection; at least, they said they had. None had been assigned to me; I was on my own. There was no life after this one pathetic condition, even with all the assurances of the nuns of the academy, of my stepmother, of the great poets and statesmen of centuries past and present. And as I was Jewish and not baptized, I was told that I would languish in limbo among the other unbaptized children and heathen peoples of the world, never to be admitted into Heaven. Of this I was assured by the nuns. I saw a picture, a pen-and-ink drawing, when I was little that depicted limbo. I envisioned myself among all the little children like me, the stains of Original Sin unbleached from their souls by fontal waters, roaming about some vast, cobra-infested jungle, searching for places to hide from grotesque deformed demons and from naked, painted, spear-carrying savages who were, undoubtedly, cannibals.

I was frightened at first. As I grew older, I saw the absurdity of it all.

I could not believe.

I didn't want there to be nothing. I didn't want to think I was alone. I didn't want to deny the existence of a God that I might lean on, appeal to, and eventually reunite with. *I didn't want to be left out.* But, I felt there was nothing for me; I was alone; there was no great Being to comfort me, to go to. I was left out.

In many ways I envied the faith that Timothy Morgan held close to his heart, as he now held the rosary beads to his chest. I wanted to have that kind of conviction held by people of faith, but I just couldn't wrap my mind around the irrational premise of it all. I wasn't an atheist, mind you; I knew of no absolutes. If, as Karl Marx stated in his *Manifesto*, "Religion is the opium of the masses," I can attest that opiates depress me, and I get depressed enough without any help. I prefer the effects of Johnny Walker and tobacco.

But, in that moment, too, a light of sorts did shine in on me, like the dust mote–filled shaft of sunlight warming my face: I have an undying, if irrational, faith in love. Strip away all the big and little conflicting interpretations of theological dogma, and the message, the only truth, remains: love. The message of Jesus spoken through His Beatitudes; Buddha, Mohammad, Abraham—all the same message: Love one another. Too bad the world is so hateful.

So what if I didn't follow an organized religion? Religion had been responsible for so much death and misery in the world. Christians killing Muslims, killing Jews: crusades, inquisitions, royal feuds. It's not an original idea, but just look around. I struggle every day with my own hatefulness.

I am a Jew, a half-Jew. I don't shout out the fact. Jews have been blamed for all the ills of the world, and for "half-baked" people like me, it's an ambiguous existence. I don't let it cripple me.

But perhaps it has crippled me. Even though I am separated from Eddie Parker merely by mutual agreement—he wasn't the same after fighting the War in Europe, and as hard as we tried after all the years apart, we never regained our tempo as a couple—I will, in the event we divorce, keep my married name. I became famous as Dorothy "Parker," and had I kept my maiden name, Dorothy *Rothschild*—not of the great-fortune Rothschilds, but of the sweatshop coat-manufacturing Rothschilds—I doubt I ever would have been permitted to become the model of style and sophistication for my generation. Religion is often worn like a nametag, and in our society determines whether love is offered or denied.

Love. I think that is all there is.

But, I regress.

"Where's his prayer book?" asked Father Timothy, pulling me out of my trance.

All the coat pockets checked, and finding no book, we left the room in search for Mrs. Daniels. Our inquiries as to its whereabouts proved useless. She'd not seen it anywhere about the house. Perhaps

Father Michael had it, she offered. As for the contents of the dustbin, she had discarded the few items from the receptacle. The trash was out back behind the kitchen; she'd not taken it to the incinerator as yet. Look for the brown paper bags she'd recovered from the bedrooms, she said. We went on a fishing expedition.

It's amazing how much you can learn about a household just by looking through its trash. Father Michael enjoyed Red Bordeaux and quite a bit of it from the number of bottles we encountered; had a propensity for indulging in Belgium chocolates, German pastry, custard pies, and Prince Albert pipe tobacco, as revealed by the merchants' cardboard and tin packaging; and paid for the consequences of those indulgences with stomach bitters and milk of magnesia.

After looking through several brown paper bags we found the one that was probably taken from the receptacle in Father O'Hara's room. We spread the contents on a worktable: train ticket stubs of his journeys from Tennessee to Detroit, and a one-way to New York. We'd found no ticket for his return home among his belongings, one that, for economy, he would have likely purchased upon leaving Tennessee. Strange, that; the Christmas season upon us, the busiest time of the year for any parish priest, and he up and leaves his flock without notice and without a date of return. Obviously, he was resigned to traveling wherever he had to go. To do *something*. My impression after talking with his godson and Father Murphy led me to believe Father O'Hara's sudden decision to hop a train for New York had nothing at all to do with the on-the-spot decision to visit his old seminary friend. Perhaps the murdered priest was not trying to rid himself of any inner spiritual turmoil at all, and he was not chasing rainbows, either, but rather, was running away from something.

He was running away from something!

He'd never had any intention of returning to Tennessee! Perhaps the visits to his godson and old friend Michael were attempts at escape.

He was *afraid*, not conflicted.

But, from what had he been fleeing? The Law? Had he run off with the church building fund, or the Sunday offering? Not that we knew. If so, where'd he hide the money? I'd have to get FPA to use his newspaper's resources to find out if the police in Tennessee were looking for a parish thief.

My imagination was running wild: Had he become involved in a love affair with a married woman? The church secretary, or a pretty member of the Rosary Society, or the beautiful wife of a wealthy parishioner whom he'd been counseling for kleptomania? Maybe he was innocent of any lascivious conduct, but a jealous husband nevertheless wanted to put out his lights?

We uncovered a box of matches from the Garden Café.

I asked Father Timothy if his godfather smoked. He did not. Was it taken as a souvenir of his trip to New York? Not if he was on the run.

Several candy wrappers, a Cooper Union schedule of lecture programs for the winter season, and a crumpled-up piece of stationery from the University Club.

I deduced the priest liked hard candy, was handed the lecture schedule by a street promoter as he walked around the city, and because the schedule had been trashed, he had no real interest in going to any lectures.

The matches and stationery? Although discarded, they could have been picked up anywhere for reasons of little importance. But from all of these seemingly inconsequential items light could be shed on his whereabouts during the days immediately preceding his murder. We had to follow up, retrace his steps, if we had any hope of understanding why he had been marked for death. Perhaps we might stumble upon a connection between the priest and his killer. I don't like loose ends. There have been too many loose ends left dangling during my life. And the one that haunted me the most was the mysterious disappearance of my brother, Harry, so many years ago.

Father Murphy welcomed us into his study.

I got right to the point: "Father O'Hara wasn't conflicted, wasn't fighting inner demons, was he?"

The look on Mr. Benchley's face was one of

wide-eyed surprise. "Did I miss something, Mrs. Parker? I thought we were looking for a prayer book."

"I doubt it is of any consequence whether we find it or not."

"I'm sorry?" asked Father Murphy, also wearing a look of surprise.

And in response, the godson's eyebrows raised up in astonishment. "It is of consequence to me," he said.

"Yes, of course it is," I said, trying to soothe his sudden indignation, which was so unexpected. "What I meant to say was that finding the book is of no consequence to solving the mystery of why Father O'Hara was murdered. The killer may be dead, but still the question remains: Why? What did Father O'Hara do that got him killed? The book is moot."

"Why are you so sure of that?" asked Mr. Benchley. "If he was in the habit of carrying his prayer book with him, he might have scribbled a clue, or inserted a receipt or some such thing between its pages."

Father Murphy responded to my friend with a chuckle. "No, Mr. Benchley. No! We men of God do not deface our prayer books or use them as wallets!"

He walked to his desk and from a stack of books lifted a small book. Handing it to Timothy Morgan, he said, "I found it the evening before he was killed, half-hidden beneath the console table in the hall. It must have fallen from his coat pocket when he left that final time. Only his name is inscribed on the frontispiece."

I wanted Father Murphy to address my question: "Was Father O'Hara in some sort of trouble? Was he running from someone or something?"

"John was an exemplary human being—"

"My godfather would never do anything that—"

"Oh, please!" I said over the two reproachful voices. "Let's try to be honest here! I didn't say he ran off with the church building fund—or did he?"

Expressions of disbelief registered on all three faces, as if I had said something sacrilegious, or worse, was suddenly stripped naked before them. I'd try a different tactic.

Mr. Benchley's jaw lifted off the floor and into a sly grin before I could continue. "Mrs. Parker, are you saying that you suspect the sort of trouble Father O'Hara may have found himself in might have been of a . . . personal nature rather than a criminal one?"

"What would I do without you, Fred?"

"How often I ask myself that very question," he murmured in an aside.

Fully clothed, I addressed the men: "Anything you can tell us might shed some light on the real reason he traveled across the country for the first time in so many years. It could also tell us why he was murdered.

Father Michael said, frustration cracking his voice: "I only wish I could."

Mr. Benchley handed Father Timothy his card, so that he might telephone should he learn anything more that might shed new light on why his uncle was murdered, and then we said our goodbyes, a piece of stationery from the University Club, a box of matches from the Garden Café, and a Cooper Union lecture schedule our only clues.

We left the priests and walked out into the cool daylight. Mr. Benchley took a paper from his inside coat pocket. It was the telegram Father O'Hara had sent to Father Murphy last Wednesday evening informing his host that pressing business would keep him away and that he would try to return to the rectory the following day for Thanksgiving dinner.

"Well, thanks to a friend at Western Union, I've been able to find out that the telegram was sent from a telegraph office on West Fifty-fourth Street, a couple doors down from the University Club and the Garden Café."

"So the business that needed his attention must have been at the café or the club."

"Presumably," said Mr. Benchley.

"I do dislike that term of speech, '*presumably.*' After all, who is doing the presuming, will you tell me that?"

"Inextricably?"

"That's even worse."

"Indubitably?"

"I'll just ignore you."

"Ineluctably!"

"Idiot!"

"*Ahhhh*, Imbecile-ic-ably?"

"Shut up."

"Indefatigably!"

"Quite!"

I'd had enough of trying to solve this puzzle. There was no real urgency, as there was no longer any threat to me or Aleck or anyone else since the murderer was dead. The day was bright, and I wanted a break from all the drama of the past few days. We left our "clues" on my desk for future review, and went down to join the others for our one o'clock luncheon, after which Jane and I spent the rest of the afternoon shopping at B. Altman's and Lord & Taylor's on Fifth Avenue. I was anxious to try on a fox-trimmed embroidered coat I'd seen advertised at Stewart & Company on 37th Street.

As it was the Saturday of a holiday weekend the stores were mobbed with out-of-towners from the suburbs getting a jump on their holiday shopping. The store windows were decorated with fairyland and winter-countryside scenes with mechanically driven figures of ice skaters circling a frozen pond, dogs romping about, horse-drawn sleighs winding along snow-covered lanes, children sledding down hills before forests of snow-blanketed evergreens. There was a wonderful Santa's Workshop, a window bright with elves at workbenches, hammering and wrenching together the body parts of toy soldiers, jack-in-the-boxes, and life-sized dolls. A family decorating a sparklingly lit tree with scores of brightly wrapped presents at its base; the father on a tall ladder, shining star in hand at the tree's top, mother adding tinsel, daughter placing an ornament on a lower branch, son peeking at a gift box through a tear in the paper (reading American BB gun), small dog pulling the seat of the son's pants between his teeth, tail wagging. A happy change from the usual fare of slinky manikins draped in fashionable attire.

Runny noses and sticky fingers pressed against plate glass with wide-eyed wonder as the holiday music played and the sleigh bells jingled along carrying the beat. Shoppers, laden with stacks of boxes, maneuvered through revolving doors, in and out of taxis, onto and off of streetcars, dodging the perils of traffic and the sea of humanity. Furs flying open, hats pushed back, gloves dropped, scarves pocketed, knee socks slipping to ankles. Then, time to take a break at Schrafft's.

Inside the stores, too, were the wonderlands: thousands of icicles draped down from the ceilings, tinsel-like snowflakes bobbing above the expansive floors; silver and white and gold and sparkle everywhere. The countertops offered an array of glittering goods, jewelry, perfumes, holiday accessories, feathered and bejeweled chapeaus, delectable candies—marzipan stacked into images of Christmas trees—candy canes galore! The stores were glowingly lit, inside and out, lending an atmosphere of warmth and cheer.

Between the two stores, I purchased a bright silk-screened shawl for Neysa, a sky-blue Chinese tunic embroidered with a flying crane for Tallulah, a luxurious cashmere scarf for Mr. Benchley, a Russian Cossack hat of Persian Lamb for Aleck, gloves for FPA, ties for Sherry, Marc, and Bunny Wilson, a deluxe box of Belgium chocolates to be sent off immediately with my note of thanks for Thanksgiving dinner to Edna, and, while she was busy in the hosiery department, a stunning little jet-beaded evening bag for Jane.

For Ross, a tortoise-shell-and-silver pocket comb, four pairs of men's stockings in primary colors embroidered with reindeers for the Marx Brothers, several exquisite, finely embroidered silk handkerchiefs for women friends to keep on hand (excuse the pun) for any lady I may have forgotten, and six boxes of Cuban cigars for any gent I may have overlooked. All in all, I'd done most of my Christmas shopping in one very productive afternoon.

Jane caught up with me as I was just settling the bill at Lord & Taylor's. She was a sight. Actually, I couldn't really see her at all, just the tam of her jaunty little red hat and the bow on her pumps, but I recognized the voice that addressed me from behind a stack of precariously balanced boxes. I removed the top two silver-foil-wrapped packages and looked into two very large brown eyes, the color of fine cognac.

"You've done no shopping?" she said in amazement. I thought that if I relieved her of the remainder of the load, she might sink to the floor, for her look of sheer exhaustion.

"*Au contraire*. I've had everything sent to the apartment, or I'd have needed a cart to see them home."

"That I should be so wise," she said, as I helped her carry her load out onto the street. It was after five o'clock, and the chances of getting a cab were growing slimmer by the minute, and as Woodrow Wilson was at home, the odds were really against us.

We decided to walk the seven blocks uptown to my apartment at the Gonk, and to rest with a drink or two before going on to dinner at Neysa's. As tonight was the regularly scheduled meeting of the Thanatopsis Literary and Inside Straight Club at Jane's and Ross's house, we wouldn't be missed. At least I wouldn't be, although Jane might. She'd had it up-to-here with the cigar smoke, the ashes on the carpet, the spilled liquor, the constant appeal for more of everything from the kitchen.

"I left a stack of salami-and-cheese sandwiches, pretzels, beer, and a gallon of gin"—Jane distilled the gin herself in her jerry-rigged bathtub still—"and told

Ross they were on their own," she said with frowning conviction. A worried look crossed her face, as if she dreaded the consequences of her absence. God only knew what would be the state of the house when she returned home. "I want the game moved back to their old digs at the Gonk."

She was referring to the room the club had kept for years for their Saturday-night games. "But Frank Case insulted Aleck," I said, "insisted that if there were to be poker games there, they'd have to promise not break any more windows or furniture, to keep their cigar butts off the carpet, and to not stiff the waiters."

"I've got to talk with Frank."

"No, you've got to talk with Aleck and Ross."

"Last week *somebody*, and I have yet to find out who, *somebody* knocked over my Great Aunt Lucille's soup tureen, right off the sideboard! No one claims guilt, and no one points a finger at the culprit."

"The boys stick together like stink on shit."

"But I'm afraid of letting Ross get too far from my watchful eye ever again. You know what happened last time."

Jane was referring to the game held last spring at the apartment of newspaper publisher Herbert Swope. When Ross fell into bed in the wee small hours of the morning, Jane found IOUs amounting to thirty thousand dollars spilling out of his coat pocket. "'There's nothing left for us to do but commit suicide!'" she'd said.

Money alone wasn't motivation enough for Jane to keep the game continuing at her home: "I've got to get the game *out* of my house."

"They've grown too comfortable, Jane, thanks to you."

"The Algonquin kitchens are far superior to mine," said the thoroughly modern woman who abhorred domestic husbandry.

"Perhaps, but the boys don't have to tip you two bits at the end of the night, either."

"Those cheap sons of—"

"They drop hundreds at every game and—"

"I'll show them, Dottie."

"—they get your place for free."

"Next week, no sandwiches!"

As we crossed the avenue at the corner, I was distracted from Jane's adamant speech by the sight of little Lincoln Douglas finishing up a shine on a pair of gentlemen's wingtips.

"Whattcha say?" asked Jane.

"That poor little boy, out in the cold all day," I said, indicating the kneeling child, whipping and snapping the flannel over the shoe. "That jacket he's wearing isn't much against this cold."

"What are you doing?" asked Jane when I told

her to stay put a minute.

A street vendor roasting chestnuts: The sweet, warm, smoky aroma drifted toward me like a come-hither finger beckoning me. I crossed the street and bought a paper bag filled with the hot, split brown nuts.

"Chestnuts, yum . . ." said Jane as I crossed back over.

Jane peeked over her boxes, as I walked past the Algonquin's entrance to where Lincoln had set up shop. He was packing things up for the night when I arrived.

"For you, Lincoln," I said, offering the child the bag.

His hesitation was painful to watch: the rich, mouthwatering, musky smell of the nuts seducing his senses; his upbringing and manners forbidding him to take the treat. His eyes flitted about as his mind and body warred.

"I bought these for you, young man. Don't you like chestnuts?" I said, more a directive than a question.

"Mrs. Parker, Ma'am," he said with a nervous stutter. He rose from his perch, but did not go for the bag. Sadly, I was reminded of the starving stray cat I once tried to feed a bit of meat, which wouldn't approach the food until it felt I was a safe distance away. This was no cat, though. Here was a proud, hardworking young man. The skinny youth's determination to fill his father's shoes (no pun intended) was admirable, and my concern came not from pity but from respect. And, of course, I pitied his situation, but was loath to ever let him believe I did. Everyone, especially children, must retain their sense of dignity. I've been accused of being a bleeding-heart. Maybe I am. My heart bleeds when I see the inequities existing around me. Lincoln's distrust was understandable, but it was the reason behind the distrust, the social history that created fear, that made me angry as well.

I smiled at the boy, but his eyes were cast down to the sidewalk. Did he see my gesture of giving merely as an impersonal conscience-driven act? Could he, so young, intellectualize a sentiment by my offering, or perhaps at least intuit it? Children are often acutely, painfully aware of the true inner motivations of adults.

"I bought these for you, but do you mind if I have one, they smell so good?"

"Please, Ma'am."

Jane arrived at my side. "Dottie—"

"Meet Lincoln Douglas, Jane. He's filling in for his father, Mr. Douglas. You know Washington, don't you? Lincoln, this is Jane Grant. Bring these chestnuts home to your father, young man."

It happened so fast that I thought I must have imagined it all, but as we turned to walk back toward the hotel, Lincoln having accepted the nuts for his father, I caught sight of a figure walking toward us. The man stopped, removed his peaked cap, and ran a hand over his head to smooth fair hair before entering an old Ford parked at the curb. The next thing I knew, Jane was pulling at my arm, asking what was the matter.

"Are you all right, Dottie? You look odd."

"I've had a ghostly visitation, I think."

"Where? I see no apparition."

"Just drove off in that beaten-up old Ford."

We hurried into the lobby where Douglas the doorman took the packages from our arms.

"Peter, was there a fellow asking for me a few minutes ago?"

"I'm sorry, Mrs. Parker, but I don't know if anyone inquired after you. I just now came on duty. Were you expecting a gentleman? Perhaps Harriet at the front desk—"

I interrupted the desk clerk, who was busily scribbling in the reservations book, the telephone receiver at her ear. "Blond fellow? Peaked cap? Right off the farm?"

"I'm sorry, Mrs. Parker, I didn't see any such person." Harriet rang for Jimmy the bellboy, and asked the young man if he'd seen such a character.

My heart began pounding loudly in my ears; I could barely hear Jimmy's answer, but his head shake was reply enough. I asked Harriet to order soda and ice sent up to my rooms. Peter handed Jane's packages to Jimmy, who followed us up on the elevator to my apartment.

Woodrow stood up from his bed on the sofa where he'd been napping, but was in no great hurry to greet us. I could tell by his spread-legged stance and buggy-eyed reticence that he was annoyed with me for having left him home all afternoon. After Jimmy placed the packages on the entry console table, I handed him Woodrow's leash and a half-dollar tip for his services.

We'd just thrown off our shoes when there was a knock at the door and a waiter entered with our drink supplies.

"Shall I make you a drinkie-poo, Dottie, darling?" asked Jane, pulling off her gloves. "You look spent."

"Straight up, would you, Jane?" I replied, throwing myself spread-eagle on the sofa.

Jane handed me the shot, which I threw back before returning an empty glass. "Thanks, I needed that."

"I can see that," said Jane, looking me over, and then, with her index finger lifting my chin to better look into my eyes, "Whoever's ghost you saw really frightened you, didn't it?"

"Oh, I'm fine now, you know," I said, shying

away from her deep scrutiny. "It's been a nasty couple of days, and it ended so suddenly when the priest murderer was killed. I suppose there's been no chance for the fact to sink in that there is no longer anyone to fear. The bad man is *dead*."

    I got up and walked over toward the window, parted the draperies to look out onto the street below. People bundled up against the cold, rushing along to their various destinations, traffic moving rather briskly, a delivery truck idling across the street, and somebody's magnificent new creamy-yellow Duesenberg—four doors, closed carriage, huge headlamps, hooded wheel wells, sleek running boards, sparkling chrome grills—pulling to the curb under the Algonquin's canopy.

    There was nothing at all out of the ordinary with the scene below; rather, the street was brightly lit, and newly hung holiday ornaments and colored lights displayed in storefronts along the street lent additional cheer to the evening. There was nothing sinister out there. All appeared benign, unthreatening. No, there was nothing evident, and yet there was *something* that lay concealed beneath the surface, lurking under the asphalt like a cancerous malignancy. I sensed it, even though I couldn't see it or give name to it. Whatever "it" was. Perhaps I was having a precognition of gloomy future events? There were gypsies somewhere in my line, after all, and my life, which to most readers of Frank Adams Pierce's column appears blessed with glamour and excitement, has really been a series of gloomy events with intermittent reprieves in the jovial, clever company of the Theatre elite.

It was foolish, this heavy feeling of doom, I knew. Jane's eyes bore into me, and I willed myself not to tremble. "Just my imagination gone off with me."

When we arrived at Neysa's studio, she was putting the finishing touches on a commissioned piece she'd spent the day working on for the cover of the *Saturday Evening Post*. We took pity on our friend, and suggested that instead of Neysa cooking dinner we walk down the block to the Dragon's Tail, a Chinese restaurant and front for a speakeasy. There we could have an inexpensive dinner of chop suey and enjoy a pot of potent "tea." By ten o'clock I'd pretty much washed away any residual feelings of dread that lingered. We made our way onto the street to walk Neysa back to her apartment house, and then went downtown by taxi to Jane's, where upon arrival we were greeted with gales of stale cigar smoke and loud, ribald voices.

I helped Jane carry in the catch of the day—her many purchases from the Fifth Avenue department stores, which we'd been shuffling around town all evening. We found sanctuary in her bedroom for a time, until we heard what sounded like the movement of furniture on the floor above, the location of Aleck's apartment. We left the room and joined the others, or rather, the meeting of the Thanatopsis Literary and Inside Straight Club, conducting the business of the week at Jane's dining room table.

The table was strewn with overflowing ashtrays, tumblers of booze, peanut shells, and the ravages of salami-and-cheese sandwiches. Jane stepped on something squishy, which upon further examination we determined to be the remains of a dill pickle for its greenish juices that squirted when heel met flesh.

"I dread going to the bathroom," she told me. "Who knows what I'll find. What's going on upstairs, Aleck?" she asked, removing her shoe and examining the debris on the carpet. "Sounds like creditors are repossessing your living room suite."

Jane was about to pick up a wet rag from the floor. "Who's missing a wet sock?" she asked, recoiling.

"You're disturbing me, woman!" Aleck balked. "Are you trying to point the fickle finger of fate at me? Can't you see I've got to—hit me with three, Ross," he said, discarding that number of cards.

"Three, two, one."

"Do you have to say it every time, 'three-two-one'?" bellowed Aleck. "We can take a visual count, for cry'n'outloud!"

"It's the way I do things, fat boy," said Ross, as he proceeded to deal out four cards at the request of George S. Kaufman, who sat expressionlessly, ignoring the squabble.

"Four, three, two, one . . ." said Ross, with slow

deliberation. "And two for Frank: two, one. And for me...." Ross laid his cards face down and made a series of peculiar faces. He twitched his mouth from side to side, flared his nostrils, knit his brows, and tried to look deadpan. The facial contortions amounted to the unpleasant expression one might see on a disgruntled vulture that lost its dinner to a street sweeper.

Finally, "*Hummmm*, I'll take one card," he said. But before doing so he took a horse chestnut from his vest pocket and with a circular motion rubbed it over the deck three times.

"Idiot," mumbled Aleck under his breath. "So, what have we got here?"

Bills were thrown onto the center of the table. The men studied their cards and then furtively studied each other as if to catch someone's bluff.

"Just a minute, Heywood!" said George S. to the rumpled, crumpled journalist. If anybody needed a new suit, it was Broun. "We agreed: Anyone looking at Connolly's face is cheating!"

"I'll raise twenty bucks," said FPA, throwing cash on the table and an inch-thick cigar ash onto his lap.

"I fold," said Broun, throwing down his cards, along with the remains of his salami-on-rye.

"Well, Connolly?" said Aleck. "We gonna sit here all night while you pray to St. Jude to fix your hand?"

"Yeah, all right, me, too, I'll fold," said Marc, his elbow knocking peanut shells onto the floor. Marc, a talented playwright, is an abysmal card player, therefore always encouraged to join the game.

"Too bad, boyo," said Aleck, "I could have used the extra cash."

"I'm in," said Ross, rising from his chair, crumbs scattering like dander from his clothes. In a ritual dance, he circled the back of his chair and resumed his seat.

"Can't you sit still? It won't change your hand, ding-dong."

Sherry tapped his cards for luck and kept his eyes down.

"Get this lad a drum," said FPA.

"The percussion section of the *George White Follies* ain't gonna change the bastard's luck," said Ross.

"Go fuck yourself," said Sherry.

"Would if I could," said Ross.

The men chuckled, and then Aleck took over:

"I'll see your twenty and raise you fifty," said Aleck, an eyebrow cocked up high above his spectacles.

"*Ah-ha!*" said Ross, "You're bluffing."

"I told you *not* to look at Aleck, either!" said George, relaxing back a little in his chair; but that shift in body position was no indication of whether

George held a good hand. He threw in fifty bucks. Ross followed suit.

The men turned to face Swope.

The *New York World* publisher was sitting in this evening, and the multimillionaire could put a wrench into things if he so chose. It was not uncommon for him to raise the stakes a thousand dollars just so that he could take a fifty-dollar pot. When he was bluffed into showing his hand, it was a fine night for the poor jerk who'd met his bet with a worthless IOU. And it was high stakes that could get Ross into big trouble. "I'll see your fifty," said Swope, beneficently.

Suddenly, Aleck noticed me leaning in the doorframe between the dining room and kitchen. A look of horror flashed over his face, the cigar stub fell from his lips and rolled onto the table. For a moment I thought he was having a heart attack, but then he addressed me with thundering accusation:

"Is the mutt here?"

"Mr. Benchley is at home and hearth."

A vein popped out despite the roll of fat on his neck. "The critter, the four-legged beastie, the Devil's advocate, the bug-eyed bastard, the—"

"Mr. Benchley would not appreciate being referred to in such terms, Aleck."

"*The DOG!*"

"Women have called him that, true, but you, Aleck?"

"Woodrow Wilson! Is he here with you?"

"Alas, the President of the United States is dead; 'My captain, my captain....'"

"Jane, is Woodrow here?"

"Only in spirit."

"Then somebody exorcise the bugger."

"If we don't pay the exorcist do we get repossessed?" said FPA.

"Shut up, Frank!"

It was getting out of hand. Aleck was throwing a fit over the possibility that I'd snuck in Woodrow Wilson. He could bash Ross and Marc about their superstitious foibles, but he had a few of his own: bad luck to have a dog in the room during a poker game.

"The pup is at home this evening. I'd not subject my Woodrow Wilson to your venom, you ol' snake!"

Woodrow'd been banned from the room before, and I didn't like to have his feelings hurt after I'd worked so hard to build up his self-esteem. "Now, if you don't behave I'll come over and tap your shoulder."

Aleck became contrite. "Sorry, my love." He turned back to the cards.

George S. won the hand. He has tremendous luck at cards without leaping from his chair or tapping things or rubbing his nuts on things.

Marc dealt the next hand, and I walked around

the table to stand behind Aleck. He removed two cards from his hand, which left him with an ace of spades, a ten of clubs, and an eight of spades. Marc dealt him the new cards face down.

Aleck gingerly lifted one card, and quickly set it down. Hesitatingly, he peeked under the other, and then brought his hand down with a loud slap. He dropped the three in his hand over the two on the table, and jumped up from his chair, nearly knocking me back into the sideboard.

"I'm out," he said in a choking whisper. He downed the dregs from his tumbler, and stumbling, turned toward me with an outstretched hand, indicating for me to refill his glass from the bottle on the sideboard. A troubling pallor had washed over his face; the trembling hand I steadied with my own as I refilled the glass gave me pause. Something was really wrong.

"Are you feeling all right, darling?" I asked, watching him throw back the drink. The others were busy with their game at first, until Aleck slammed down the glass and made for the door to the hall.

Jane, across the table and leaning over her husband, had watched Aleck, and rather than follow him out, as he was undoubtedly heading for the stairway and his apartment, came round to his chair and picked up his cards.

"I don't understand it," she said, as George swept up the pot. "Aleck had a great hand—two pairs.

Two aces and two eights."

"Swope, who had the chair next to Aleck's, pulled a face. "Dead Man's Hand," he observed, and then quickly leaned away from the cards Jane placed before him as if they emitted a foul odor.

A funereal silence fell over the table, before Heywood said, "And they're all black cards to boot!"

"Shit," I said, misunderstanding. "He could have won?"

"When Bill Hickok drew that hand he was shot in the head!" said Ross.

"Holy moly!" said Frank.

"That's just dandy," I said.

A shout sounded from the hallway, and from the urgency of the call, the men pushed away from their places and made for the stairs. Jane and I followed up to the second floor where we pushed through the hulks at the apartment's doorway and entered the apartment.

Looking through the living room and into the bedroom I watched Aleck, his arms supporting his weight as he gripped the doorframe of his closet. He turned at the sound of my appeal:

"Someone's stolen my opera cape!"

George S. Kaufman— Wins at poker without leaping, tapping, or rubbing nuts

Wild Bill Hickok— Was shot to death after drawing the "Dead Man's Hand"

Chapter Seven

Somebody's idea of a joke couldn't have happened at a worse time.

The Dead Man's Hand, comprised of black cards also signifying death, was a bad omen in itself. There were some coincidences that were just too sharp for card players to ignore. It was idiotic, for sure, but only a few hours ago I was shaking in my patent leathers from fear of some intangible malevolence in the air.

But there was little that Jane and I could do to rationalize Aleck's fear, once the men were ushered out of the room and we'd led Aleck into his big reading chair by the fireplace. The murderer was dead, we stressed; the theft of the cape was probably a silly prank by friends or, at worst, a mean-spirited payback from one of the many show-business people he may have insulted in his reviews. We played up the silly prank theory, but Aleck was having none of it.

After a frantic inspection of the apartment, in

which Aleck flitted about searching his desk, bureau drawers, filed papers, a strongbox that was unmoved from its hiding place, much to his relief—"My life is in there, turn your backs, ladies!"—nothing other than the cape, and, as he had also discovered, his top hat, were missing. The only indication that anyone had trespassed was a lone boot accidentally tossed aside by the burglar, thus preventing the closet door from closing tightly. We figured the robber entered through the unlocked front foyer door from the street, bypassing the card players safely in and out through the darkened hallway leading to the stairs.

"Thank God they didn't steal the gown I wore as Katherine in *Taming of the Shrew*."

Aleck, having founded the drama society at Hamilton College, had insisted on playing all the female leads!

Another half-hour of detailed inspection, where he discovered nothing else missing, but recovered several misplaced items—tennis racket, croquet wicket, and black feather boa—and Aleck took to his bed.

$100 REWARD! FOR THE RETURN OF RED SATIN–LINED OPERA CAPE AND TOP HAT TAKEN FROM THE RESIDENCE AT 412–414 WEST 46TH STREET. NO QUESTIONS ASKED. REPLY AT THIS PAPER BOX 409.

There was little else that occupied Aleck's mind over the next week. His mood reflected as much when at lunch. "I feel so violated."

I was relieved about this, however, in spite of his indignation, because he no longer held the misguided idea that there was some conspiracy to do him in; that a killer lurked in the shadows. It appeared we had finally convinced him the theft was nothing more than a prank.

One week before Christmas as we were gathering for our one o'clock luncheon, FPA arrived in a state of nervous agitation and carrying a sheaf of newspapers. As he sported a smile on his rubbery face, I awaited his remarks.

"'Bout time you got here," said Aleck, grabbing a newspaper from FPA.

"In the paper..."

"What's he talking about?" I asked.

"Copies of the *Chronicle,* from Dayton, Tennessee," said Frank. "I told you I'd use my contacts to find out about the murder."

"There's a crime wave going on down there," said Heywood.

"There's an article about Father John's murder," said Mr. Benchley, "which doesn't tell us more than we already know."

"And in a featured column entitled 'Around Town,' a week before the priest's murder, there's mention that Harlow Wayne Healy closed the doors of Healy's Hardware and Grain on Main Street, leaving a sign on the door stating, 'Gone Fishing,'" said Ross.

"All right, all right, but what does that get us?" I said.

"'Gone Fishing' in November?"

"Does your friend see some connection between this merchant going off and the death of Father John?"

"But there's this article, Dottie," said Frank. "Says here that back in November a Negro shantytown was burned to the ground one night, killing five people, three of whom were children. Because the incident made the national wire services, the sheriff of Fremont, where the crime occurred, was pressured to investigate and find the culprits responsible. He'd ignored many lynchings in the past, but now the governor and a congressman from the district called for a thorough investigation to appease the NAACP. An election was coming up; they weren't going to let this crime pass unpunished, as it spurred a cry of outrage from many progressive-minded supporters. This led to the Bureau of Investigation being called in, too."

"The Klan, then?"

"Appears so, but those bigots are so secretive, hiding under their nappies, that no one knows who's a member, and it's hard to point a finger at any one person. We're talking big businessmen, lawyers, doctors, politicians wearing the hoods."

"But that doesn't tell us anything about Father John."

Frank continued: "It seems that Father John might've seen one of the men take off his hood, because at the time of the fire, a little after midnight, the priest had been performing last rights on an old, dying Negro woman at her home, a shack in that shantytown, and he was the first to raise the alarm. He tried to rescue people, but to no avail."

"Frank, I don't get it."

"Harlow Healy suddenly closing up shop, the day after the fire," said Sherry.

"I asked my friend to check into the background of Healy and he found that his younger brother, Roger, best known as Rowdy for the obvious reason that his nickname implies, owned the store with Harlow. He also discovered big differences between the brothers.

"Harlow and Rowdy may have shared the same parents, but that's all they shared. They couldn't have been more different. You see, Harlow bought out Rowdy's interest in the business. The brothers didn't get along. And the connection to the darktown fire lies in Rowdy.

"After Rowdy left the business, Harlow put a hired man in his place as assistant manager. This did not sit well with Rowdy and many others in the community; people began bringing their business elsewhere. You see, Harlow gave the job to a Negro, a man who had worked at the store for many years, doing menial jobs, but was ambitious, hardworking, and smart. Burning down the Negro's house and several others along with it was a good way for Rowdy to screw with his older brother."

"And then both brothers disappear?" asked Mr. Benchley.

"So you're saying that Father John was running away across the country, no less, from an arsonist who was trying to kill him because he could turn him in?" I asked.

"Makes sense."

"It makes no sense to me. If this Rowdy person started the fire and had already escaped capture in Tennessee, why'd he want to kill the priest?"

"It seems to me that the priest was chasing Rowdy," offered Heywood.

"Why the hell would the priest be after him?" I asked.

"A reward for his capture?" said Aleck.

"Well," jumped in Mr. Benchley, "whoever was chasing whom matters not, anymore, unless it's strictly an intellectual pursuit in which you wish to indulge."

"What about the older brother?" I asked.

"Harlow? What about him?" asked Frank.

"Where's this Harlow, if he ain't gone fishin'?"

"Nobody knows."

"So perhaps Father John O'Hara was seeking

righteous retribution for the heinous crime because he felt a responsibility; his part in the crime having been as witness, unable to stop the criminal in the first place, unable to save the children," said Sherry.

"You wax eloquent, Sherry," I commented, "But it doesn't wax true."

"It's all over, thank goodness," said Aleck with enough finality in his tone to indicate the subject was closed once and for all. "Rowdy Healy killed the man who could identify him, and then he went after you, Dottie, because you'd seen his face, but his mission ended unsuccessfully, I might add, getting him killed in the process. Good riddance to bad rubbish!"

"You're darn tootin'," said FPA, adding his stamp of approval.

Case closed, time to get back to the party, was what they meant.

And although I had my doubts about Father John's heroism in seeking out the arsonist-murderer, my spirit was lifted, too, now that everything had been settled. All tied up with a pretty little ribbon and a bow.

Having been paid for several articles, a load of theatre reviews, and a short story, and with a collection of my poems close to publication, I was flush for a change. The holidays would be a bit brighter this year than last: Money *can* buy happiness—of a sort.

I spent my afternoons continuing my Christmas

shopping, took my sister Helen and niece and nephew to lunch at the Plaza, and, because I was very unsure about how I would look in it, consulted with Tallulah at Bendel's on whether to buy a cashmere coat with monkey trim at collar, cuffs, and hem. I saved a ton of cash when Lula pointed out that because of my diminutive stature the profusion of long black fur gave me the look of the Capuccine variety, begging the question, "Where's Giuseppe, the organ grinder?"

"Well, that's decided," I said, throwing off the coat. "The last thing I need is a monkey on my back."

And then I saw it: A marvelous Persian lamb, light-gray wrap-over coat, buttons at the hip, rolled shawl mink collar, called out to me. A snazzy slouching hat of the same fur with charcoal-gray velvet banding completed the look.

I was sporting my new ensemble when I arrived late at lunch a few days before Christmas, and had just settled into my chair between Aleck and Mr. Benchley when our waiter, Luigi, came to inform me that I had an urgent telephone call. Woodrow and I walked to the desk and I picked up the receiver.

"Mrs. Parker?" whispered an agitated voice. "This is Michael Murphy."

It took me a few seconds to put name to face.

"Father Murphy of St. Agatha's—"

"Yes, of course, Father Murphy. What can I do

for you?" I said.

"I've been trying to reach Mr. Benchley all morning. He gave me his card."

"Would you like to speak with him? He's here, in the dining room—"

"Mrs. Parker, is it possible—I can't talk about it over the phone, but it's—"

"Yes?"

"It's urgent that I speak to someone about John's murder."

"Have you telephoned the police?"

There was a hesitation, and a loud intake of breath on the other end of the line.

"Father?"

"What if I'm wrong?"

"About what?"

"I don't know what I should do."

His distress was palpable. The only thing to do was to wait, silently, in hope that he'd continue. He did. "Please . . . I wonder if you or Mr. Benchley might come. There is something I'd like you to see. I'd like an opinion about it, and there are things about him—"

He stopped in midsentence.

"What things about him, Father?"

There was no response, although I repeatedly called his name.

And then: "Can you come to the rectory?"

"Yes," I replied, mentally checking my appointment calendar. "I believe so." I couldn't answer for Mr. Benchley's afternoon commitments, but I'd walk over with Woodrow Wilson immediately after luncheon. The relief in his voice was evident before I rang off. Could it be really *that* urgent, that it couldn't wait an hour or so?

But on rethinking, it might be very important in solving the mystery of *why* Father John was killed, even if catching the murderer was no longer an issue. And there was something about his voice that prompted me to reconsider waiting until after luncheon to go to the rectory. Perhaps I sensed fear rather than distress.

I returned to the table, stood behind Mr. Benchley's chair, and told him about the telephone call. He immediately put down his knife and fork, swallowed down his drink, and stood from the table.

"Are you going to eat that?" I asked, pointing to the remainder of the T-Bone on his plate.

"Help yourself," he said, after I quickly wrapped the meat in a linen napkin and stole a steaming popover from the basket Luigi was placing on the table.

No one came to the door when we rang the bell at the rectory, and after a couple of minutes, and repeated knocks, Mr. Benchley tried the doorknob.

There was a gloomy air to the hallway, as we called out, announcing our presence.

"Nobody home."

"I don't understand it. Maybe he didn't figure we'd get here so soon."

"Then he's taken a walk, or he's in the church. Yes, that's it, he's in church."

Turning to leave for St. Agatha's, a thought came to me.

"Let's wait in the library for his return."

"I suspect you're remembering a half-full bottle of fine Irish whiskey," said Mr. Benchley, a silly grin on his face.

"Actually not," I said in defense of ulterior motives. "Woodrow Wilson is hungry, and I want to give him the steak bone. But since you mentioned it, I could do with a beverage to wash down the popover."

"*Ohhh*, Mrs. Parker," he gurgled a chuckle.

"*Ohhh*, yourself, Mr. Benchley!" And I opened the pocket doors in search of refreshment.

I went directly to the window seat, took off my coat, and then removed the napkin from my purse and presented the bone to Woodrow. Mr. Benchley went to the cabinet where stood the bottle of hooch.

"*Ohhh*, Mrs. Parker," he said, smacking his lips.

"*Ohhh*, Mr. Benchley," I replied, as I moved aside the sweeping bullion-fringed drapery to view the front stoop and the street beyond.

"*Ohhh*, Mrs. Parker!" he said again.

"Are you going to '*Ohhh*, Mrs. Parker' me all day? Pour me a drink for cry'n'outloud," I said, biting into the popover. "I've had no lunch, no morning coffee, no nothing to—why are you standing there like the fool you are, holding the bottle and staring at the floor?"

"*Ohhh*, Mrs. Parker!"

"What *is* it with you?"

Leaving my comfortable perch I stepped over Woodrow, who was doing quite a number on the bone on the Persian carpet, and made a beeline to Mr. Benchley. He was standing there frozen. "If there's no ice in the bucket, fine, I'll take it straight up."

"There's no ice in the bucket, Mrs. Parker, because that proverbial bucket has been kicked."

"What are you babbling about, you nincompoop, the bucket's right there!" I said, pointing at the silver vessel on the cabinet. I popped the remainder of the bread into my mouth, took a tumbler from the tray, and then turned to retrieve the bottle that he held clutched against his chest.

And that's when I saw him.

I swallowed hard, and the bread went down like a rock.

Father Michael Murphy lay prone behind the wingchair at the fireplace.

"*Ohhh*, Mr. Benchley."

"My sentiment exactly."

"I see what you mean," I said, forgetting the glass in my hand and taking a nervous swig from the bottle. "Are you sure he's dead?"

"He's not catatonic!"

I peered around the chair that blocked much of the priest's body to meet the opened-eyed stare of Father Michael.

"*Ohhh*, Mr. Benchley," I whined, and Woodrow looked up from his dinner to concur with his own call of the wild.

"Let's not start that again, Mrs. Parker."

"Oh, the poor soul!" I could have cried then and there, but for the possibility that the murderer was still in the house. "What should we do?" I whispered.

"I don't know," he said, taking the bottle from my hand. He took a swig from it and handed the bottle back to me. I stood dumbfounded; my Mr. Benchley *always* knew what to do, and *never* would have taken his liquor from anything but a clean, iced glass. He worried me.

But, then, suddenly, like a hot poker shot up his—well, you know—he bolted around the chair and stooped to examine the dead priest.

Following his lead, I tripped on a candlestick that lay on the floor nearby. A bloody candlestick, I should say. I was about to pick it up to move it aside, when Mr. Benchley violently grabbed my wrist.

"Don't do it!" he shouted, and I instantly understood. For I was about to do the one silly thing I had found so annoying in the books by popular mystery writer Ariadne Oliver! Her innocent characters were always picking up the murder weapon—guns, bloodied knives, pokers, frying pans, candlesticks—leaving prints to incriminate themselves. The poor saps were always at the wrong place at the wrong time, never had alibis, were the last to see the deceased alive, and invariably had a pair of muddy Wellingtons crammed into the back of their wardrobes. Now I realized that I was behaving like a character in an inane mystery story!

"I suppose we must call the police."

"I suppose we must," I whispered.

"Why are we whispering?"

"The murderer might still be—"

"*Ahhh*, yes; in the room."

"In the house."

"I see your point."

"But, where is the housekeeper?"

"Mrs. Daniels, wasn't it?"

"Perhaps she's out doing her Christmas shopping or something."

"Or she might be lying dead somewhere in the house!"

"*Ohhh*, Mr. Benchley!"

"Enough! We've already played that game!"

"You started it, and I can't think of anything else to say."

"We better search the house, see if she's here."

"Search the—are you out of your mind?"

"It's been suggested—"

"But, what if the killer is still in the house?"

"Why are you so sure he'd risk discovery? Why would he be lurking about when he could be long gone by now?"

"The killer's always lurking about in Ariadne Oliver mysteries!"

"Yes, that's so, but we're not *in* an Ariadne Oliver mystery, are we? We're in a Dorothy Parker Mystery, my dear."

"That's true," I said, seeing his reasoning. "But, shouldn't we take a weapon or something before we go around dark corners and peek into closets?"

"Do you see anything around here that could be used to protect us, Woodrow Wilson notwithstanding?"

I scanned the room: A vase with chrysanthemums, the candelabrum, a picture frame, a paperweight, and a newspaper that might be useful in swatting a fly was all that was at hand. And then:

"This bottle might pack a wallop!" I announced.

"In more ways than one, I can see that."

He took the bottle from the table, poured the remainder of its liquid into a tall glass, gulped a mouthful down—"for reinforcement," and then we made our silent advance into the hallway, Woodrow at our heels, his toenails clicking like castanets on the marble floor. I picked him up.

The silence of the house was unnerving, so much so that when the doorbell clamored, I was so spooked I screamed out. Woodrow leaped from my arms, took up the cue and started yapping, running circles round me and Mr. Benchley, and then made an attack at the door.

As the knob turned and the door creaked open we watched with bated breath. Sunlight ushered in Alexander Woollcott.

"I thought I'd find you here!" he said accusingly, and then, looking us over, noting the bottle, gripped by its neck in Mr. Benchley's hand and held high above his head, "You're not going to strike me with that thing, are you?" He turned to me. "I heard you scream, Dottie. Bob didn't strike you, did he?"

"Don't be an idiot," said Mr. Benchley. "Of course I didn't strike her!"

"I demand to know what's going on here!"

"Come all the way in and shut the door, for Chrissake!"

"I see you've finished off the bottle, all right."

"How'd you know we were here?"

"I asked at the desk who'd called Dottie that she'd leave without a word!"

"Snoop."

"Yes, that's true, but after all that's happened this past week, I was a little worried about you."

I was about to say, "Aleck, that murderer is dead," as I had been repeating to Aleck whenever he would fall into a funk over the burglary of his cape and hat, but now I was not sure that I believed all of us were safe from harm.

"What's going on here? Where's Father Michael, and why are you skulking about in the dark wielding an empty bottle?"

"We were about to search the premises."

"The 'premises'?" chuckled Aleck, removing his hat and loosening his red scarf. "You sound like the police investigating a crime!"

"We are not the police, but we are investigating a crime."

Aleck turned to look at me for clarification.

"Why are we whispering?"

"We were looking to see if the other murderer is still about."

"Benchley, what other murderer? What fresh hell is this?"

"Be quiet, and stop stealing my lines, Aleck," I said.

'Well, Bob, want to explain what's going on here?"

"Father Michael in the library, with a candlestick—"

"This would make a good board game," I said.

"—and the housekeeper, Mrs. Daniels, is nowhere about."

Aleck stood there coyly smiling, anticipating the punchline. When it didn't come, he looked from one to the other of us and said, "And . . . ?"

"And?" I asked,

"Aleck," Mr. Benchley reiterated, "Father Michael in the library, the murder weapon a candlestick, and—"

"Yes, yes," he nodded impatiently, "but I don't get it."

"What's not to get?" Mr. Benchley was losing his patience.

"The joke, the game."

"No game, Aleck," said Mr. Benchley. "Father Michael's lying dead in the library, the murder weapon is—"

"You serious?"

"*Aaarrrggghhh!*"

"*Ohhhh*, Mr. Benchley!" said Aleck.

"Not again!"

With all the noise we'd been making with knocks, screams, and whispers, whoever might have been hiding had surely escaped out a window by now and was long gone.

Aleck and I lined up behind Mr. Benchley, I sandwiched between the men, Woodrow taking up the rear, as we gingerly ascended the stairs, freezing at each creak of step, until we finally stood huddled on the top landing.

We were about to proceed along the hall toward the doors of the first bedroom when the front door flew open to reveal Mrs. Daniels carrying in a flood of sunlight, her door keys, and her grocery bags, and a startled expression upon seeing our shadowy figures atop the flight of stairs. She screamed bloody murder at the sight of us.

We returned to the first floor, Woodrow in the lead, and after retrieving the fallen packages, helped the housekeeper to sit on the velvet sofa in the hall. We explained our presence, our unpleasant discovery, and our relief that she was unharmed.

There was much wailing and chest beating, and when there was an opening to speak above the racket, I asked if I could call someone for her. Getting no reply, I led her into the kitchen, where I sat her down at the table. She grabbed me around the waist and cried wetly into my new lamb coat. But I didn't mind, really, as I patted her surprisingly soft gray hair; and she smelled comfortingly like the housekeeper I remember from my childhood, a combination of soap and bleach.

I reached over to grab a towel from the sink rack to wipe her eyes, and then, as I've heard tell that the cure for all the maladies in the British Empire is a "cuppa," I put on a kettle and searched for the tea. I tossed Woodrow a biscuit from a tin, took a seat across from the housekeeper, and waited for the water to boil and the men to return from their inspection of the house.

"At what time did you leave the house, Mrs. Daniels?"

"Eleven o'clock, to go see my sister in St. Claire's Hospital. She had her gall bladder removed."

"And was the Father alone when you left?"

"Yes, he'd just returned home from visiting Mr. Charles, the church deacon, who's been down with fever."

"Has anyone else come here to see him today, anyone visiting, anyone come to the door today at all?"

She shook her head, and said, "Just me and Father Timothy. He's gone, now."

"Timothy Morgan? Didn't he leave weeks ago?"

"He stayed on."

"I thought he'd just come to claim Father John's body and was heading home."

"No, Father Timothy sent his poor dead godfather's body back to Tennessee, but he stayed on these weeks, and I think he would have stayed through Christmas, if Father Michael hadn't told him a little white lie."

"When did he do that?"

"Yesterday, it was. I don't listen to private conversations, but they was in the hall, and Father Michael was saying that guests would be coming tonight to stay for the holidays. 'Course there was nobody coming, and I never heard the Father ever speak a lie before. But, good riddance."

"You didn't like Father Timothy?"

"I know them Jesuits is different sorts of priests, but he wouldn't even assist Father Michael in the mass when our good deacon, Mr. Charles, came down with the influenza."

"And how was Father Michael this morning? In good spirits?"

"Worried about our Mr. Charles, you know; the

old man's near ninety. And he didn't read his paper, even; said mass at seven, hardly touched his breakfast, and he loved my eggs and kippers."

"And . . . ?"

"Oh, and then he went to see Mr. Charles, and when he came home took the mail from the hall and went into the library like he did every morning I can remember, to read and answer his letters and make his calls. I heard him talking on the telephone when I left the house."

"So he said and did nothing else unusual?"

She shook her head.

I measured out the Twinings from a tin, poured the boiling water into the teapot, and brought it to the table. As I fetched cream from the icebox and cups from the cabinet, Mrs. Daniels's sobs rose in a series of crescendos.

"Mrs. Reynolds across the street," she finally choked out.

"She was here?"

"No."

"Shall I go fetch her?"

"No, I don't want her here."

"Then what about her?"

"Maybe she saw something. She's always snooping out her window," she said with contempt. And then, accusatorily, "Had her eye on the Father, she did."

"You mean she was in love with him?"

"Fallen hard like the angel Lucifer, the devil! Always spying through her window. I saw her with her glasses one day."

"Opera glasses?"

"Yeah, the little ones, like. Always coming here with cakes and muffins, after she'd see I stepped out the door. She was trying to tempt him into a life of sin!"

"Well, they say the way to a man's heart is through—oh, never mind that. I get the picture. She had a crush on Father Michael."

"No, Father Timothy!"

"I see what you're saying. You think maybe she saw whoever killed Father Michael come into the house."

"The brazen hussy!"

She fell into a crying jag after a sip of her tea.

I left to reenter the library to fetch something more medicinal to calm the hysterical woman. Trying not to look in the direction of the corpse, I went for the bottle of sherry in the cabinet before spotting an unopened bottle of Kentucky bourbon, which would not now, or in the future, be missed by the man on the floor. I grabbed the bourbon and shot back into the kitchen to spike Mrs. Daniels's tea.

The spiked tea went down quickly, followed by another fortified cup, and then Mrs. Daniels took a sip of plain tea, too, and was more agreeable to taking a lie-down until the police arrived.

We would have to interview the brazen hussy across the street, it appeared, but shouldn't we just leave it for the police? I was contemplating when best to call in the authorities when Mr. Benchley and Aleck entered the scullery, giving voice to my thoughts.

"No one's about," announced Mr. Benchley.

"Where's the woman?" asked Aleck.

"Mrs. Daniels knows nothing much," I said, and then told them about the conversation between Fathers Michael and Timothy, who'd obviously overstayed his welcome and was politely sent on his way with a little white lie. "Father Michael had no visitors before she left at eleven. He was in the library answering his mail and making telephone calls when she left. But there is the woman across the street who Mrs. Daniels says keeps a watchful eye on the house. Mrs. Daniels believes she had designs on Father Tim."

"Then we should interview the woman, don'chathink?" said Mr. Benchley.

"Let's do it then."

"I'll call Cousin Joe down at the precinct, let him know we have another dead body," said Aleck.

"Oh, Aleck, I don't want to spend another afternoon sitting around on hard oak chairs, staring at gas-chamber-green walls and criminals' mug shots while trying to convince the knuckleheads that I didn't kill anybody!"

"I can attest that you didn't, my dear."

"Thank you, Mr. Benchley, that's very big of you."

"Don't mention it."

"I won't—ever again. Fred, dear, don't you think, perhaps, that Father John's murderer is not dead after all? I mean, are there two killers? I rather doubt it."

"It's an epidemic, is what it is," said Aleck.

"That man who shot at you, what's his name, Rowdy something, got killed in traffic, we know he stabbed Father John. But with Father Michael now murdered it means there's more than just one killer around. Someone else is out there killing people, and until we three know why, we're in danger, too," said Mr. Benchley.

Something nagged at me.

"Father Michael not only wanted to tell us something about Father John's murder," I continued back on track, "he also wanted to show us something, before calling in the police."

Mr. Benchley suggested that we look around the library for that 'something' Father Michael wanted so urgently to show us, something to do with the murder of his friend, Father John. Whatever he may have stumbled across, I doubted that we would find anything, if only because the killer probably wouldn't have killed the priest without getting any incriminating evidence from him first.

Mr. Benchley put on his gloves, and standing in the doorway I watched as he quickly opened drawers and closet doors and file cabinets.

"*Hot-diggitty-dog!*" he exclaimed, pulling out a file labeled "John O'Hara" from the unlocked cabinet. He pulled out a handful of personal letters. "Return address, Father John's church in Tennessee. These we read tonight, might be something in these."

My eyes to the floor and away from the corpse, I registered something out of place. Either the floor was uneven and the priest had wedged a piece of cardboard under a leg of his desk, or something had missed the wastebasket and had not been retrieved by the scrupulously neat Mrs. Daniels. While Aleck stood at the desk, placing the telephone call to his Cousin Joe, I got down on hands and knees and pushed between Aleck's legs to further inspect my discovery.

Aleck squealed, "I won't even let my tailor do that!—Oh, not you, Joe, although I wouldn't let you do it either. I was talking to—Oh, all right, we won't touch anything.... No, I'm calling from the telephone in the library. Yes, a few feet from the body. Gloves? No, I'm not wearing any—oh! fingerprints? Well, I'm wiping mine off with my kerchief as we speak, and now the desk and—Why are you yelling at me? I'm sorry, would you repeat that? Dottie, dearest, stop crawling around, you're making me nervous . . . . What, Joe? *Damn!* Hold the line! I just knocked over the inkwell! Bob, would you hand me something for the spill . . . . Yes, Bob Benchley's here, too. He found the body. Yes, all right, Dottie, you found him, too—What? Oh, Bob's just looking through some files. No! But he has his gloves on. All right, we won't touch anything. All right, I'll tell them. Joe? Joe? Operator?"

Click-click-click . . .

Aleck looked down at my upturned face, and as he helped me up from the floor he said, "I suppose he'll send someone; we were disconnected. Whattcha got there?"

"An envelope, didn't quite make the wastebasket."

Mr. Benchley crossed the room to peer down at the envelope addressed to Father Michael with the return address, Father Timothy Morgan, Grosse Pointe, Michigan.

"It's postmarked December 22, 1925."

"Odd."

"Nothing inside," I said. "Have you searched the desk drawers, Mr. Benchley?"

We made a cursory search, but came up with no letter, just a large number of Christmas greetings from folks wishing Father Michael a Merry Christmas.

The trashcan was empty, thanks to Mrs. Daniels, and looking on all surfaces around the big room, we found nothing that might have been contained in the envelope. That meant that the letter was opened *after* Mrs. Daniels had tidied up the room in the morning, *after* Mrs. Daniels had left to visit her sister in the hospital. *Possibly just before Father Murphy's telephone call to me at the Gonk.* Was whatever was contained in the envelope the something he wanted to show us? Could it be that the something in the envelope was important enough for someone to kill for?

I stepped over Father Michael (who'd become so much a part of the landscape of the room that I no longer felt queasy) and with a poker pushed aside the blackened bits of wood and ash. Heat rose from the remains, indicating a fire had only recently burned itself out.

"So we have a couple of old letters from Father John dating back, the last postmarked September, and an empty envelope of a letter received this morning from Father John's godson, Father Timothy. Odd."

"Why odd?" asked Aleck.

"Because according to Mrs. Daniels, Father Tim's been staying here all these weeks. He only went back home to Michigan at dawn this morning."

"Maybe the letter was lost and was just delivered."

"Perhaps . . ." I said, putting the envelope in my coat pocket. I clipped on Woodrow's leash, and then

Mr. Benchley and I left Aleck to wait for the police as we crossed the street in search of the Brazen Hussy.

We rang the bell of the second-floor-front apartment in the brownstone numbered 242. This was undoubtedly the residence of the Brazen Hussy, as when we descended from the front steps of the rectory we saw the curtain move and the glint of sunlight reflected on glass.

"Whaddayawant?" came the sweet musical strains of a voice not unlike the guttural blast of a muted trombone.

Speaking into the box: "I'm Mr. Benchley, Madame, and I'm with Mrs. Parker, here, and we'd like to speak with you, if that's all right."

"Don't want any."

"Doesn't she sound pleasant?"

"We're not selling anything, Mrs. Reynolds. We came from St. Agatha's across the street."

The only reply was the click of the door lock release, so we entered into the hallway. A flight of stairs led us up to the second-floor landing. We knocked on the door facing the front of the house, which stood ajar, the aroma of roasting beef wafting out into the hallway, and we were bidden to enter.

The woman described by Mrs. Daniels was a very pretty redhead, and no more than thirty years of age. She was sitting in a chair beside the window, and it took me a moment to see that the chair had wheels and was of the sort used by invalids. And then another woman who perfectly matched the gruff voice through the callbox entered from the kitchen.

The room was well appointed; the furniture stylish. The same could be said of the redhead. Once our introductions were made—her name was Hermione Reynolds, and the gruff-voiced hired woman was Miss Winny Winkle—we told of our mission. Miss Reynolds said that she often sat by the window to watch the street. She'd recognized us from before, entering and leaving the rectory several times. It was all she had to do until her broken leg, a compound fracture, healed and the cast could be removed three weeks from now. She knew Father Michael as she'd attended services at St. Agatha's most Sundays before her accident. She'd seen the youngish priest, Father Timothy, whom Father Michael sent often to administer communion to her until she was on her feet again and could attend mass, leave early this morning carrying a suitcase, and saw Mrs. Daniels leave the house around eleven. She saw no one else, other than the mailman, approach the house. She asked why we were inquiring, and we told her of our grim discovery, at which point she turned to the window, clutched a fist to her chest, and bowed her head. She didn't turn back to look at us as we made our goodbyes, making me wonder how deeply upset she must have been. Just as we opened the door, we heard her say, "Poor old soul," as she continued her frozen gaze down on the street.

We were on our way back across the street to

meet Aleck at the rectory just as two police cars, sirens blasting, pulled up to the curb, and blue uniforms emerged from each. Unfortunately, a couple of carloads of reporters had tagged along, the men having been hanging around the police station waiting for a call to come in to alert them to a juicy lead for the late editions. We'd have to enter the rectory through the church entrance to ward off their attention.

"Here we go again," I said to Mr. Benchley, and later, to the detective interviewing us: "Detective, we've *got* to stop meeting like this!"

There was something bigger going on for a second murder to have been committed. If Father John could have led the Feds or the police to the capture and conviction of the missing Healy brothers from Tennessee, because he had *known* for certain of the brothers' involvement in the darktown fire, why the circuitous journey to New York via Michigan? Why not just tell the authorities in Tennessee? Certainly Father John had to be stopped from going to the police. The question, posed by the insightful Heywood Broun, kept nagging at me: *Was Father John in pursuit of the culprits or had they been chasing him?* I don't know why the positioning mattered, but it might have something to do with his death.

And now there was another killer out there. What did Father Michael discover, or have innocent knowledge of, that could have made somebody want to kill him, too? If only Mr. Benchley had been at the

Royalton to receive his urgent calls, or if we could have arrived at the rectory sooner, perhaps we might have prevented his death! I knew that there was nothing we could have done any differently; we left our luncheon only minutes after I spoke with the priest on the telephone. And yet, I knew it would haunt me, and I'm sure Mr. Benchley as well, that we were not able to get to him in time.

Aleck, Mr. Benchley, and I decided that if we were still in any danger our best line of defense was to go about our business as usual, keeping away from the police station and our faces out of the newspapers, so that our involvement—our connection to both murders—would appear to be nothing more than incidental to the killer. The murderer might not quite understand that murdering one of us would bring the entire city down on him. Our fame here in New York and across the nation had made us celebrated figures, and if one of us was killed by his hand, a dragnet would move at full steam to track him down. Huge rewards would be posted—Swope alone would put up a hundred thousand dollars, especially if he could secure an exclusive story for his paper. Killing any one of us was suicide.

Once the alarm was out reporters converged like rats emerging from the sewers on trash day. These men, the young ones and the old, wore the uniform of the hardboiled newsman—ties askew, suits rumpled, shoes scuffed and in need of repair or the trash bin, oil-stained hats affixed to shaggy heads—and all looked equally haggard. They had gathered in a tight bunch at the rectory's front door. After having chased cars from police stations around the city, where they'd spend long hours waiting by telephones for something to happen (hopefully, a big heist or a big bust, but above all a lead story that they could call in to their newspapers' city desks), they were thirsty for details.

The detective on the case saw the value of a plan we'd concocted to divert attention from ourselves and downplay our discovery of the dead priest. Especially when we suggested that the press might spin a story that would send the citizens of the city into a panic. Certainly, every man of the cloth would be a potential victim. And then there were the "crazies," the crackpots who'd take a shot at us just for the chance to be in the limelight!

So after the police made a statement to the effect that there had been a tragic "accident," Mr. Benchley went outside to address the eager newsmen with a hastily written statement:

"Woollcott, Benchley, and Parker stumbled onto the body of Father Michael Murphy when they arrived at the rectory of St. Agatha's earlier this afternoon. The celebrities had gone to the rectory to discuss with Father Michael the final details of a musical show they had been planning for the benefit of the homeless orphans of the city, to be performed next spring. Mr. Benchley is quoted by this reporter as saying, 'We enjoyed working with Father Murphy. It is sad that he fell and hit his head on a candlestick. But, we will prevail; the show will go on for the children of the city!'"

We had to hope that at least some people would buy that story. And of course, *now*, because Mr. Benchley cannot tell a lie, we'd have to do a show for the benefit of the city's orphans. At least one good thing will come from this tragedy.

Within a few hours presses were printing variations of the story that the priest died accidentally, and we three were set free and sitting in my apartment, reading and rereading Father John's letters.

Aside from a few paragraphs in which Father O'Hara described his impressions of the Scopes Trial, the life of a parish priest in a small Tennessee town was far less than exciting, concerned with services, sacraments, births and deaths, and helping the sick and the poor. These day-to-day references could not have been of much interest to anyone who wasn't in the "God Business": that Mrs. Woodward's appendectomy went terribly wrong, killing her and leaving six children under the age of eleven motherless, and the death of an infant from scarlet fever, were the most dramatic and compelling events to be noted. Many reports of monies earned through various events, such as bake sales and white elephant sales, and the theft of a year's supply of votive candles were tedious and led us no closer to finding the reason leading to the priest's murder. Sometimes I think such letter-writers fill pages with such mundane stuff in an effort to validate their correspondence when there is really nothing worth reporting. But as I read on I realized that there was nothing mundane at all about his life. Rather, here was a man conflicted, a conflicted soul in a world of conflict; a preacher of love and charity in a region rife with ignorance, bigotry, greed, and contempt. I heard a tone that reflected not only the tedium of his daily ministrations, but the frustration at his helplessness in effecting improved living conditions in the poverty-plagued pockets of the rural districts. Although feeling ineffectual and realizing the thanklessness of his dedicated efforts, he soldiered on. I sensed that a profound loneliness had burdened him as he tried to shoulder the grief of others, while finding none on which to lay down his own troubles. Was he depressed? Or was it simple weariness and a need for a change of scene that sent him off on a trip around the country in search of the human connection offered through the company of his godson and old friend?

Me and a distraught Mrs. Murphy

Bury the lead!

Chapter Eight

I'd often found this time of year heart-wrenchingly depressing—the forced, almost excessive cheerfulness. There were lights everywhere, trees everywhere, bells, bows, tinsel, and holly everywhere, plenty of booze everywhere, handsome men everywhere, and music everywhere. You'd think that would make a girl happy. But I was traveling alone through the strings of parties, lights, and glitter. I'd no man, no husband to come home to. No children. And that's what Christmas was all about. The celebration of the birth of a Child, and deep within me there was a yearning for a child of my own.

Every day I'd see skinny little Lincoln Douglas buffing away at gleaming shoes, his little hands bare in the cold damp, his back arched against the wintry wind.

When I'd stop to get a shine, his hooded eyes stayed downcast; and once, when I arose from the folding chair and handed him two-bits, he forgot himself and I caught his eye. His shyness was palpable as he quickly nodded his thanks and bowed his head to stare down at the sidewalk.

I wanted to cry.

I wanted to shake him, to make him look at me and see that he should not be frightened. I only wished to be of help in any way I could. He needed a decent coat, but I knew he would not accept my charity. Lincoln Douglas had been well taught to be afraid of well-meaning white people.

An idea popped into my head. Lincoln would get a warm coat.

I don't know what made this season bearable, except for the fact that Aleck and Mr. Benchley were unusually attentive. Even Edna did not grate on my nerves when she'd appear at luncheon several times a week, now that her *Showboat* was finished. I sought distractions, if only to quell the underlying sense of menace haunting me since Father Michael's murder.

Jane and I lunched and Tallulah, who also was alone, was always game for an afternoon cocktail or a steak at our favorite speakeasy, Tony Soma's. I suppose they remembered the events of last season when Eddie and I parted ways and a failed affair with a newspaper reporter sent me on the skids to land in the hospital by way of my foolish attempt at ending my life. I'd forgotten that an affair is just that, a single event with a start and end time. Silly me. I didn't think anybody'd really care if I popped off. I thought they just wanted me around to provide the entertainment, as I'm always good for a fast and clever retort to brighten any conversation. My wit has made me famous; my wit has brought me into the sphere of the geniuses of my generation, but I don't know that I belong in such a world. I have to work so hard to be witty. Yet, it's all I know.

My acid tongue has cost me friends, too, because sometimes I don't know when to keep my mouth shut. I almost believe it when I say I don't care what people think. I don't know that I'm so very droll, so very sophisticated. It's hard to be amusing, to keep up the pretense of being anything very special.

Most of the Round Tablers are alone in this city. It's a tough place to make a success. Most have no family close by. And the understanding we all possess is that you're only as good as your last show, or book, or joke. Too soon you can become yesterday's news, and we all want to forget yesterday in hopes of a better tomorrow. So we live for the moment: fast and furious.

But I do have friends, I learned, and this season they made sure I was not lonely. And as Christmas approached I joined into the spirit of the holidays.

Mr. Benchley arrived at my rooms on Christmas Eve morning carrying a large box covered in red foil and brandishing a huge green satin bow. Woodrow Wilson barked furiously at the foreign object blocking Mr. Benchley's face, and stopped only when he had placed it down on the edge of my desk.

He bade me turn away and cover my eyes.

"The ones in back of my head?"

"Don't be ridiculous, Mrs. Parker," he said as he pulled off the ribbon and lifted the lid. I admit that I began whining a bit, from impatient excitement, and Woodrow responded to my angst with several whimpers of his own, as we heard Mr. Benchley scuffling around.

"You and the President ought to start a singing act. Vaudeville is dying, and you two can quickly put it out of its misery."

I'd no time for a comeback for the sound of strange and intermittent screeches that alternated with bars of music and voices. As I turned, Mr. Benchley stood back with a look of satisfaction as the Coon-Sanders Nighthawks Orchestra piped out "Yes, Sir, That's My Baby."

A radio!

"It's grand!" was all I could say, admiring the cathedral-shaped box. I gave Fred a hug and Woodrow pulled at his cuff.

Mr. Benchley leaned over to pat my pup and then reached into his pocket from where he withdrew a steak bone wrapped in white paper. "You don't think I'd arrive without your treat?" Woodrow made a fast exit to the bedroom with his treasure.

As it was Christmas Eve, Mr. Benchley would

take the train home in an hour to spend the holidays with Gertrude and the children. He was concerned about me and Aleck alone in the city, inviting us to his home for the holiday. But Aleck and I preferred to remain in town. Truth is, Gertrude and I have never really warmed to each other. Aleck has a standing invitation for Christmas Eve dinner with Edna. I'll spend the eve with Jane and Ross, and on Christmas Day I'll join Aleck for what always proves to be a sumptuous dinner at George and Bea Kaufman's. It was decided that we would begin our inquiries once again into the deaths of the priests immediately following Christmas Day.

It had been a smallish group at luncheon these past weeks. George S., Irving, and Harpo and his Brothers were busy with their show, *The Cocoanuts;* George Gershwin had an opening on the thirtieth for *Song of the Flame,* and Ira was busy with lyric writing, too, for next season's show. Alfred Lunt and Lynn Fontanne were out of town for tryouts, and Ross had a deadline for his failing magazine, *The New Yorker*.

I suspect the tourists were disappointed when popping their heads into the Rose Room hoping to see a Marx Brother or two, or a glamorous Lunt or two. What they got was Aleck, Mr. Benchley, and me along with a scattering of newspapermen they might recognize by their bylines, if not their pictures.

One day at lunch, I voiced my concern about little Lincoln Douglas.

It was just Aleck, Mr. Benchley, Heywood Broun, Mark Connelly, Robert Sherwood, Bunny Wilson, and Edna at the table.

"It seems his father, Washington, was beaten up by some thugs," said Heywood. "They put out his lights for a couple of days, broke his arm and a couple of ribs, too."

I voiced my dismay.

"He'll live."

"But, why? What'd he do to deserve—"

"He let too many people know his plans," said Broun.

Heywood Broun is a respected journalist, sportswriter, and theatre critic, even if you'd never guess it to look at the frumpy old thing. The Harlem community, especially the Negro intelligentsia, admire and respect him. He lectures at Columbia University, and has brought to public attention the talents of many Negro artists. Last year he showed me a poem by a young student, entitled "The Weary Blues," published in a colored journal called *The Crisis*. The kid nailed it, all right: the struggle of his race, the plodding on, in just a few phrases in jazz refrain. It was he, Langston Hughes, whom we'd met last Thanksgiving night outside the Cotton Club.

"Washington was saving up his nickels so that he could rent space at the Shoeshine Palace on Sixth Avenue. He needed twenty-five dollars for the first month and another ten dollars to buy the leather chair from the guy who was giving up his spot. Washington was going to go down to the shine parlor with the money, but the night before he planned to pay up, he stopped at a joint on Lenox Avenue to collect the last couple bucks he needed from this bootlegger he'd done a truck run for. He was feeling good; things were looking up; he'd be making good money at the Palace.

"He had a couple of shots and went out smiling, according to the barkeep. Once out the door he was jumped, dragged to the alley, beaten, and rolled. Spent a week in the hospital. Lincoln's the oldest of the three children. Wife works nights at a laundry."

We came up with a plan.

Christmas spent with Aleck, Jane, and Ross warmed the frigid days. Snow fell on Christmas Eve, and by morning several inches lay over the cityscape like a fresh start on canvas.

As soon as Mr. Benchley returned to Manhattan and resumed his usual activities, I found my place again. My spirits rose, as they usually do when he's around. Silly how I depend on him. But he adds lightness, brightness, to my days.

The night before New Year's Eve we set out onto the icy streets for the opening night of the Marx

Brothers' show at the Lyric Theater: Aleck, Mr. Benchley, Bunny Wilson, Marc Connolly, Sherry, Edna, Heywood Broun, FPA, and I. All but Edna and Marc would write reviews, but we all sat in the critics' circle like a string of footlights beaming up at our friends, hoping the show was as good as we expected. I *do* like writing good reviews, believe me, because I truly want to see good theatre, even though I'm best known for performing rather clean and efficient autopsies and insuring the rapid demise of hopeless cases. The Brothers are such wonderful entertainers, and with Irving's music and George Kaufman's book I don't know that anything can go wrong. I don't suffer fools easily, but these fools I welcome.

After an early dinner at the Gonk we piled into two cars that Aleck had ordered for our ride to the Lyric Theater, timing our arrival to best advantage. Curtain was at 8:45 P.M.

The street traffic was heavy, and it was slow going as we made our way across the avenues, scooting around trolleys at the congested intersections at Times Square, where Seventh Avenue and Broadway crossed like a big X marking the grid. Pedestrians moving at a brisk pace slowed to a snail's crawl as people emerged from the subway station at Times Square and 42nd Street. Running north and south on both the East and West Side train lines was the Shuttle that connected both sides of town from Grand Central Terminal on the east to Times Square Station on the west. This link to both sides of Manhattan made the Theatre

District an important crossroads, a meeting place for all to gather for special events, at times of crisis, and for mass celebrations. And the sheer glamour of that crossroads could not be denied, as was evident in the spectacular array of brilliantly lit signage that hung from the surrounding buildings, dangling above the avenues, no longer with just the old-time white lights that gave the district its name, *The Great White Way,* but now with the new, brilliantly colored lights, advertising everything from stomach tonics to cigarettes in a rainbow of color.

The excitement stirred up by everyone rushing to an evening of wonder and adventure that is live theatre became evident with the noise of the traffic reaching a crescendo as drivers impatiently engaged their horns one after the other as they stood idling in line. The honking lasted for long intervals until fading to silence as wheels rolled on once again. The cavern formed by the tall buildings echoed the start of another jam-up a few blocks away, the sound reminiscent of cicadas chirping from tree to tree on a hot summer day in the country.

We arrived at 8:40 to alight on a red-carpeted sidewalk, lined by hundreds of onlookers. Dazzlingly decked-out first-nighters hung about under the marquee, surely on display with hopes of being noticed and admired. They lingered outside the open brass doors chatting-it-up or having a smoke before entering the lobby. The haughty arrogance of the elite struck me at times as comical, but if you saw it from my perspective, the swells were oddities on display for a crowd, strutting and fluffing their feathers, and serving as a kind of sideshow for the shop clerks and housewives who'd gathered along the sidewalk hoping to catch glimpses of the rich and famous.

We were met by the rest of our party inside the lobby, and we trooped into the orchestra section, smiling to so-and-so and so-and-so, waving to this one and that one, stopping to shake the hand or kiss the cheek. And because we had arrived with only minutes to spare before the curtain rose, most of the audience was already seated as we tramped down the center aisle toward our seats, so our party was duly noted and fawned over like royalty. Makes me laugh, Mr. Benchley giggle, and Aleck, gloat.

And we did not disappoint: Edna wore a lovely gown of fawn-colored crushed velvet under a luxurious dark-brown sable evening coat. A headband studded with champagne-colored crystals adorned her dark bob. She looked lovely holding onto Aleck's arm as he, sans stolen cape, but wearing a dramatic black greatcoat with a cape-like collar over his tails and a new top hat perched on his head, waltzed grandly from the lobby, nodding graciously at people on both sides of the aisle.

Mr. Benchley, always impeccable, in top hat and tails, a sprig of holly on his lapel, took my arm as we brought up the rear. I did not have such a glorious coat as Edna's, but I knew I looked quite fetching in my red satin gown, fabric gathered in the rear to form a train and with a deep V neckline. I wore a string of gold pearls dropping to below my waist and matching drop earrings. Over the gown I wore a brocade coat of red and golden thread, cuffed, collared, and hemmed with fringes of gold-dipped feathers. A single feather to match the coat's trim adorned my new shingle-cut hairdo and completed the effect.

I do clean up nicely.

George S. Kaufman nervously made his way from the orchestra pit, where he'd been in conference with the director and Irving Berlin, to join his wife Bea at their seats in the last row of the orchestra section. Sam Harris, the show's producer, followed behind, but made for the lobby.

"There's Artie over there," said Aleck, as we entered our row.

"Who?" asked Edna, sloughing-off the magnificent fur.

"My friend Artie—Arthur Garfield Hays, the attorney."

As Mr. Benchley relieved me of my evening coat, I looked over the several rows to see a very handsome man of forty-something years nod in our direction before leaning in to speak into the ear of a rather worn-out-looking character of hang-dog expression seated next to him.

"That's Darrow, Clarence Darrow, the attorney,

sitting next to him," said FPA, moving forward to sit between me and Edna.

Aleck turned suddenly and took my elbow. "Artie's married," he said, meeting my eyes over his spectacles. Was it a dare, or had he seen the glint in my eyes?

The second bell rang and within a few seconds the houselights dimmed. We settled in our seats as the curtain was lit in brilliant blood-red glory and the conductor lifted his baton to signal the orchestra's attention.

The frantic overture began with highlights of the coming musical numbers, and settled into a romp as the curtain parted to reveal a set depicting a hotel in Florida.

We laughed for an hour and a half straight, watching the boys' antics, and after an intermission break for spirited libation—a little hooch from a flask to doctor the ginger ale—we returned for another hour of side-splitting laughter. The audience would recover from one gale of laughter only so they could hear the next laugh-provoking line; the chortling and chuckling would replace the guffaws in an effort at self-control, only to be led by the boys into another wave of full-out screams. At one point I turned to observe the sophisticated ladies and gents in the row behind us, the glow from the stage lights filtering out enough for me to see the red-faced contortions of bellowing fellows and the mascara-marred cheeks of the now-graceless goddesses. Funny was funny, low humor or high, and through laughter we shared a common humanity.

Aleck was beside himself, so high one might have thought he'd sniffed cocaine. The Brothers were his discovery, you see, and although they were no more than a half-dozen years his junior, he embraced them, especially Adolph (Harpo), with fatherly affection. More than anything, he wanted them to succeed. As for George S., well, he'd started his career as Aleck's assistant at the newspaper, and Aleck had watched him progress into a top-notch playwright. As for Irving? They'd been friends for years. Who didn't love him? The man could do no wrong. Nothing made Aleck happier than to watch his friends succeed. Especially if he had played a role in their success.

By the time the curtain fell at the close of Act Two and the curtain calls went on and on with whistles and cheers and thunderous applause, and huge bouquets of flowers delivered into the arms of the cast, the Brothers continuing their antics during a standing ovation from the audience, we were all in high spirits.

And tonight, rather than rush out of the theatre before the houselights came on to compose and phone in his review, Aleck led the delegation of Round Tablers around the orchestra pit, up through the proscenium, and out through the wings.

We moved slowly out of our row; people were chatting, in no hurry to leave the theatre, it appeared, as if hoping against hope that the curtain would rise for a third act of Marx Brothers' lunacy. As we entered the aisle, Arthur Garfield Hays, and his companion, Clarence Darrow, greeted us. Aleck and Hays shook hands, and with a hand at his elbow, Aleck moved his friend in the direction of the stage, where we paused for introductions to be made. I noted that the dour-faced Darrow looked rejuvenated by the evening's fare. The sallow complexion I'd observed earlier was ruddy, now, and his gray hair had a renewed luster. I'd seen news photos of the man taken during the two great trials of this past year, and the impression I'd gleaned from them was that of a folksy, slump-shouldered, frumpy old buzzard with thumbs permanently affixed to suspenders. So I was surprised to notice that he had such a capacity for joy; there was a bit of a kick in his step, and when he smiled, the residual effect of three hours of fun lifted his hound-dog eyes to crinkle attractively at the corners.

And Hays, well, *there* was an attractive man, if ever I saw one. Not a pretty boy, mind you, but a man of substance, brilliance, character, and dedication to righting injustices. More than any aphrodisiac, those qualities could make me swoon. But it wasn't for nothin' that he was fair of face, too. And when Hays took my hand and looked straight into my eyes and addressed me with a deep, mellow baritone, "A pleasure, Mrs. Parker, a real pleasure," I was hooked. *Damn*, I thought, *why do I always fall for the married ones?*

Mr. Benchley needled my spine. "Careful, Mrs.

Parker, your lust is showing."

 Mr. Darrow smiled down at me in greeting from his great height, so I'd no chance to elbow Mr. Benchley in the ribs as deserved. Mr. Darrow offered me his arm and we moved onward, following Aleck, Edna, and Hays backstage. FPA, Sherry, Marc, and Heywood tagged behind while Mr. Benchley brought up the disapproving, tongue-*tsk*ing rear.

 We wove our way through a spider web of ropes and cables that flew the backdrops of sets, as dozens of stagehands and technicians, on cues from the stage manager, raced about on various tasks. Chorus girls and boys still in costume and greasepaint dispersed to their dressing rooms. Sam Harris, Irving, and George and Bea Kaufman were beaming as they cheerfully thanked and back-patted members of the cast; it was rare to see George S. so animated as he appeared this night: talking, laughing, joking. He may be a quick-witted scoundrel at times, but he was basically a shy man.

 Aleck kissed Bea, and slapped the men on their backs with congratulatory sentiment. He introduced Hays and Darrow and then continued on the path toward the dressing rooms. Mr. Benchley was duly admired by many chorus members and several techies with whom he'd worked when starring in Irving Berlin's *Music Box Revue of 1924*. And FPA, too, was quite a man-about-town, and there was scarcely a chorine who wouldn't sell her mother into slavery for a mention in his column. Frank and Mr. Benchley lagged behind as we climbed the steel stairway to the Brothers' dressing room.

The wonderful smell of greasepaint, sweat, and the musty charge of electric stage lights blended in perfect proportion, a perfume that once sniffed could seduce any young thing into devoting one's life to the Theatre. Once snared in the atmosphere of this vapor and then exposed to the exhilarating rain of applause, one becomes addicted. It's a good thing I have no talent for singing, dancing, or acting, or I'd be among the fallen.

Aleck knocked on the dressing-room door.

"Who's there?" came the reply from within.

Oh, it was going to be a knock-knock joke.

"Aleck"

"Aleck who?"

"Aleck to come in."

The door was thrown open, revealing Chico, face white with cold cream and a cloth in his hand bearing evidence of flesh-colored face paint. He stood there in his underwear.

"Aleck to come in—to some money, too," he replied.

Groucho turned from the mirror to face us as he tore off his fake moustache: "Let's see your money. There's a charge, you know, for the second show."

Aleck entered the dressing room cramped with bouquets and standing arrangements. Someone had sent a wreath made entirely of prickly pear stalks. Cleverly, the boys had posted dozens of congratulatory telegrams on its thorns.

"I haven't a cent on me," said Aleck. "Perhaps I might arrange a little loan from one of my friends."

"All right, then, that'll be fifty thousand francs," said Groucho.

"I've a dollar," said Hays.

"I'd say you were worth more than that!"

"Sold!" said Chico, rushing over to grab the buck Hays removed from his pocket. But Harpo beat him to it, offered the hat from his head, with his wig caught in the crown. Hays dropped the dollar into the hat.

Groucho came over with his usual bent-duck walk, his arms behind his back to peer up into Aleck's face.

"So you've no cash of your own, you freeloader!"

So this was the second show, I thought, and Aleck was going to let them play it out.

These boys are as zany offstage as they are onstage. They didn't give a crap that men of dignity had come to honor them with a visit. Marie of Romania could bestow the honor of knighthoods, and Harpo would grab her sword and fence about like a demented Douglas Fairbanks.

"I've not a centime," replied Aleck.

"You must have some loose change somewhere," insisted Groucho, as he started unbuttoning the impeccable white satin vest of Aleck's evening clothes.

Harpo pulled out Aleck's pants pockets.

Chico undid his tie.

Zeppo took Aleck's greatcoat, folded it neatly, and presented it to Darrow to hold. He handed Aleck's walking stick to Hayes.

Harpo indicated he wanted Sherry to hold out his hands. Harpo attempted to slap the offered palms several times, and of course, Sherry pulled away in time to avoid contact. I was next enlisted into their lunacy. I held out my palms and instead of slapping them, Harpo reached into Aleck's top hat, from which he took, and then placed, a set of jacks into my cupped hands.

Heywood was next ordered to display both palms, and he complied with a giggle. Again from the hat Harpo removed a small sack. He opened the drawstring, took out a handful of marbles, pretended to swallow them and then, seeing the top hat was empty, he put it on his own head, and slapped Heywood's palms before he could retract them.

Harpo laughed and spun around the room.

By this time Groucho had removed Aleck's tailcoat and vest, and was busy removing the studs from his shirt.

"Wait a minute!" interrupted Chico, unbuttoning Aleck's trousers. He reached a hand down in through the waistband and pantomimed the removal of a handful of items.

Aleck's trousers fell to the floor. He didn't blink an eye as he stood regally before us in white silk underwear. He was enjoying being a part of the act.

"Let me see those," insisted Groucho, and Harpo and Zeppo leaned in to watch as Chico slowly unclenched his fist to reveal the treasure within his palm: two tiny rhinestones for all to see.

"The family jewels!" the Brothers shouted in unison.

Aleck laughed, "My, they're bigger than I thought."

George S. popped his head in the door, and upon glimpsing a nearly naked Woollcott, he moaned, rolled his eyes, and quickly departed.

Groucho turned to Mr. Benchley, who'd just walked in to join us, and said:

"I'll bet there's a jackpot in those pants!"

Catching on quickly, Mr. Benchley said, nodding, in all seriousness, "So I'm told, so I'm told."

Groucho moved in toward Edna, and then circled her, his eyebrows raised repeatedly as he nosed in on her ample, bejeweled bosom.

"I see you've brought the Woolworth Building

with you, Aleck!" he said, reaching out a hand, which Edna promptly slapped.

"I was just admiring your fifty-first floor," he said, backing off. "Your radio antenna ain't so bad, either..."

As Aleck began to re-dress, he made the introductions all around. The Brothers nodded and bowed and went about their business of dressing into evening clothes. We bade them farewell, promising to see them soon after Aleck called in his review, and we made for the stage door and the alley leading to the street.

Hays thanked Aleck for getting him the first-night tickets, and Mr. Darrow expressed his gratitude for being included in such an enjoyable, if unlikely, experience. Declining the invitation to join us for a late supper and the cast party, the attorneys strolled with us toward the curb where Hays's car was already waiting to take him and Darrow home. Street and pedestrian traffic had dispersed by now, and fetching cabs should not be difficult.

Hays waited for his liveried chauffeur to step out of the driver's compartment to open the door for him and his friend, but after a moment passed without the man's appearance, Hays opened the door himself, and was about to bid Darrow enter when he turned to us and asked: "Are you sure I can't drop any of you somewhere?"

I couldn't help myself. Here were two very...

compelling men. At least one was compelling me, and I didn't want to lose the opportunity of spending a few minutes alone in his company, even with Mr. Darrow as chaperone. I spoke up before my companions could put on my brakes:

"I'd be grateful for a lift to the Algonquin," I said, moving swiftly now past Mr. Darrow and into the car.

"Mrs. Parker," interjected Mr. Benchley, "you've dropped your glove."

I wasn't about to fall for such a ploy; I supposed he thought he could just pop into the seat next to me so that he could monitor my behavior, the stinker!

But he had retrieved my glove, for I saw that I held only one in my hand.

I expected Mr. Benchley to bounce into the seat beside me, but he did not. Rather, to my surprise, everyone appeared to turn away from the car as their attention was drawn to a disturbance a few feet along the sidewalk.

There were shouts as Hays was rushed by a young man, coatless, his shirt soiled and disheveled, a trickle of blood running down from his brow.

"Walter!" said Hays, at the sight of the distressed fellow. "I don't understand," he said, looking into the car and at the capped profile of the driver sitting behind the wheel. "Who's driving? Why aren't—Oh, my Lord, you've been hurt."

But I was to hear no answers, for suddenly the door slammed shut, the car bucked, throwing me rudely back against the seat, and the next thing I knew we were speeding away from the curb.

"Wait, driver!" I shouted lamely, trying to aright myself so as not to land my rump on the floor. "You've forgotten—"

I grabbed the seat in front of me and saw not only the driver but another figure in the seat beside him.

Before I could object, a blanket was thrown over my head. I felt a scuffle, and then a bulky presence leaning in next to me.

I fought as best I could to find my way out from under the suffocating hold of the blanket and the stronghold of the arms that held it in place. My headband slipped and I found myself with a nose full of feathers, adding to my panic of claustrophobia from the musty woolen shroud. I couldn't scream, I couldn't escape; my arms were pinned, and when I heard a laugh, I felt the cold, damp gooseflesh of terror rise in me. I struggled to exhaustion, but it did no good. I reasoned, finally, as the car rumbled over the cobblestones, that if I did not desist in my struggle, whoever had me in his clutches might not be reluctant to knock me out with his fist. It was doubtful I could escape the power that held me hostage, for I was wearing out from lack of air and brute resistance. If I were to have any chance of escape, I'd better adjust my thinking. I stopped moving and slumped into a feigned faint. It proved to be the right play, for even through the heavy cloth I could discern two voices.

"I think she's dead," said the voice closest to me, the man gripping me. He shook me a couple of times, and I felt my neck snapping in whiplash. I wanted to scream, but squelched the impulse. "I think she's dead!"

So there were two men who'd kidnapped me: the Driver and the Gripper.

The Driver said: "She's not dead, you dummy, only fainted, probably."

"She's suffocated!" said the Gripper.

"Get hold of yourself!" yelled the Driver.

The pressure loosened around my head, although the cover remained. I desperately wanted to take a deep breath, but instinctively knew it was better to play dead. Could the men hear my heartbeat? It reverberated loudly in my ears.

The car whipped around and I was thrown from side to side, and would have fallen hard to the floor if the Gripper hadn't had me firmly in his clutches.

The tires skipped—we'd crossed over streetcar tracks—and then the *rump-rump-rump* of a subway train passing overhead on the el. The car swung around a corner. For a time we were whizzing down a thoroughfare; we were traveling down an avenue; lots of stops on cross streets, and now it was smooth like macadam. Most of the avenues had been paved over the old cobblestone.

We came to a jolting stop, and if it hadn't been for the Gripper my head would have hit the windshield.

Horns sounded in multiplicity; a fire engine's siren whirred faintly in the distance, and soon the brisk *clang-clang-clang* of the fire truck's bell announced its impending approach; dogs barked. Shouts and police whistles filtered through my black prison.

The Driver blasted his horn with angry fury, cursing a blue streak while maneuvering the wheel from side to side as if to clear some obstacle. The fire siren was getting louder and louder, signaling the truck was coming closer and closer. The alarm was ear-splitting, the Driver's cursing more and more vivid. I smelled the bitter odor of fire smoke, and knew we were in the vicinity of some great conflagration.

Now the whining of the siren had doubled and the clanging bells rang out zealously announcing the joint arrival. I sensed we were in the middle of it all, perhaps dead in the path of the trucks, for all of a sudden a truck horn bellowed like a ship's foghorn upon us, and I could hear the incensed shout of a policeman ordering drivers to pull aside.

But the Driver was not about to obey.

The car lurched forward. A sharp turn followed by a spine-jolting bump and the irate shouts of the policeman told me we were riding the sidewalk.

Leaving in our wake startled voices and hair-raising screams, we thumped and rumbled along, hitting objects in our path, with the screech and scrape of metal as we barreled down the sidewalk.

A street-corner alarm sounded, and a new onslaught of police whistles followed, and soon came the whine of police car sirens from several directions.

I was thrown ruthlessly to my side, and on landing managed to find the door handle. The Gripper couldn't see my hand resting on the handle, as the blanket obscured it. I was about to risk it, jumping out of the car, for I felt a reduction in speed.

But before I could make my move, a new sound: It was as if the car's engine was suddenly in the cab with us, and the sound of the wheels clunking along cobblestones reverberated intensely. A thud: We'd hit something metallic. A cat screeched indignantly.

We were in an alley! The closeness of the buildings' walls enclosed us, and I anticipated that if I tried to get out of the car, now, I'd hit a wall and probably roll under the vehicle's tires: a sorry end.

I knew that should the alley not lead to a side street, but dead-end at a wall, it would be the end of the ride and perhaps the end of my life! For how could I hope to find a means of escape from my captors when blocked on three sides? Where would I run?

But as soon as it began, the echo disappeared, and I knew we were out on the street again.

"Stupid, stupid, stupid!" said the Driver as we raced over cobblestones.

"But I did what you said. It's not my fault she got in the car!"

"Shut-up!" yelled out the Driver. "We've got to get rid of her."

They meant me.

The car suddenly stopped.

The Driver said, "If she wakes up and makes a sound, break the bitch's neck."

Eyes had been squeezed shut against the dark, against my fate, but now I opened them.

A door opened and slammed, and a new presence was in the car, in the front seat; I smelled his cologne.

"Where's the other one?"

"There was a mix-up," said the Driver. "We have a woman."

"How the hell . . . ?"

The blanket was tugged and lifted.

Playing dead was harder than I thought, but I forced my body to remain limp, my face toward the back seat. I was sure I wasn't going to fool anyone; my heartbeat thumped so loudly in my ears I was sure it could be heard a block away. Would they kill me in the car? Would my body be discovered floating in the East River alongside some knocked-off bootlegger's?

I hadn't a chance of escape—not in the shoes I was wearing.

"She's not dead," said the New Man. "She's just passed out."

Oh, shit!

I was rolled over, and felt panic rising like a painful tingle coursing up from deep within my belly.

Dear God—if you exist—dear God, if you can hear me, and of course, as you are all powerful, omnipresent, you can hear my thoughts—dear God!

"It's that bitch, Parker," said the New Man. "Now you've done it!"

A slap, followed by a cry of surprise. The Driver was on the receiving end.

"It was supposed to be two birds with one stone; and you bring me a goddamn mouse!"

"I'm sorry, Sir, but she just got in and—"

Another slap put a period on the Driver's objection.

"Did she see your faces? Can she identify you?"

"No, we threw the blanket over her head, soon as she got in the car."

"Dump her over there by the trash, and you idiots get the hell out of here. I don't want to hear you're still in this city tomorrow morning."

"What are you going to do?" asked the Gripper,

out of arms' reach of the New Man.

"What do you think I'm going to do, you lame-brain flunky! Now it's going to be more dangerous to take them out! More of our people at risk and months of planning down the drain. Throw her in the garbage, dump the car, wipe off your fingerprints, for chrissake, and get out of town."

The car door opened and slammed.

They hastily wrapped me in the blanket, and then I was carried over the shoulders of the Gripper. A shoe fell off, and my purse fell from my arm when I let my arms dangle. I braced myself mentally for a landing on hard ground and metal cans, but when I finally hit the ground it was with less impact than I had anticipated. I remained motionless until I heard the car gears engage and the whine of reverse gear. Screeching tires on the cobblestone faded into the hum of regular traffic before I threw off my shroud and opened my eyes.

I rose slowly to my feet to assess the damage to my person. I was bruised, for sure, although I couldn't see the evidence under my disheveled clothing; fingers caught in the tangles of my hair, a bird's nest complete with mangled feather left behind.

I hobbled through the alley in search of my missing shoe, a bare light bulb over a doorway lighting my way, and found it kicked close to the wall of the building, my purse, a few feet away.

Afraid to enter through the alley door and into

the building for fear of confronting the New Man, I quickly walked toward the street, hoping for the sight of lots of people, but was disappointed. My city that never sleeps was caught snoozing on the job!

To my left was Fifth Avenue, the northwest corner. I stood on the side street, and instantly knew the lay of the land. Mady's Speakeasy was a few doors away, and that meant a telephone, and rescue, and safety from the fiends of the night.

But before I ventured into Mady's I turned back once again toward Fifth Avenue. The alley I had been dumped in—the door by which an overhead lamp had lighted my way—led to a place I'd forgotten about; a place noted and ignored because of all the crazy events that had been occurring to me and my friends. And here it stood before me: the clue, its connection to the two murders, another attempted, and tonight's kidnapping.

The University Club loomed big, like a neon sign calling my attention.

Oh, crap, I thought. This is bigger than anything I could have imagined. I made the leap to understanding that brought me back to the little priest from Tennessee, and now I couldn't just let it lie. But I couldn't go to the police and tell them of my kidnapping. A police dragnet out to capture my kidnappers might serve merely to send the assassins underground and into hiding until the heat was off. It wouldn't serve in snagging the entire ring of conspirators. These people weren't out to kill *me*; they didn't bother when they'd had their chance just a couple of minutes ago.

The threat to the lives of Clarence Darrow and Arthur Garfield Hays would remain until the leading players in this scheme were caught, and I suspected that there were lots more people involved than the three men who took me on the little ride across town. They were the small fish; we had to snag the big fish, and I suspected that the New Man, if not the big mackerel, would lead us to a bigger catch of the day.

These murders and the ones planned for execution were motivated by hatred and prejudice: a personal, deep-seated effrontery in the minds of the transgressors. This was happening in New York City, one of the most liberal places in the country. Who was to know who else was involved? Maybe it wasn't just the Ku Klux Klan of the South, but a Klan right here in my city!

I walked to the corner of Fifth Avenue to flag a taxi to drive me down the dozen blocks home. A car screeched to a stop and Mr. Benchley leaped out. He ushered me into the backseat, where sat Aleck and FPA.

Once escorted safely back to my apartment and wrapped cozily in my wooly robe, a couple scotches warming me up, I relayed the details of my abduction; then the men told me about the chase that ensued.

It had become evident that the intended kidnapping victims had been Darrow and Hays, from the words overheard by Hays's chauffeur when he had been tumbled out of the limousine by the culprits. My friends secured a taxi to pursue the limousine, leaving Edna in the charge of the attorneys. When I asked if the police had been called in, they were unsure, but a call placed to Hays at his house told them he had not called them as yet, believing my life might be in danger if ransom was what the kidnappers were after; the loss of the automobile was of no importance to him. Whether Hays was aware that my abduction was the result of a botched plan to snare himself and Darrow, he didn't say, and I acted dumb, playing down the episode: I was fine, I said, just fine. And look for the limo near the docks, I said.

I turned to my friends and told them everything I had deduced after my little adventure, and that it was time to investigate and stop the murderers from going any further.

"You, Mrs. Parker, will do nothing."

"That's right, Dottie, dear, we can't be chasing you all over the city. My old heart just can't take it," said Aleck.

"Shit!"

"We'll take care of things, all right, Dot," said Frank, smoothing his comb-over and puffing on his cigar, a self-assured smile stretching his bat-like features.

I wanted to crown all of them with a frying pan—if I'd had one handy.

"Never-you-mind, Mrs. Parker," said Benchley. "Tomorrow I'll check things out at the University Club myself—ask around, get the general lay of the land, so to speak."

"I'll so-to-speak myself, if you don't mind!"

"Now, Dottie, darling, don't be cross," said the fat man. "You can't get into the Club. You're a woman."

"But they'll let you in, Aleck?" I said, testily, recalling Aleck's drama club photos from Hamilton College.

"It's a gentlemen's club, and even if you were a guy, you didn't finish high school let alone graduate from a university," said the smug puffer.

"I finished top of my class at Harvard, was editor of the *Lampoon*, and can mingle with boys from lesser schools," said the idiot Bob Benchley. "*And* I know all the words to "The Whiffenpoof Song," even if it *is* a Yale abomination—the published words, too, not only the dirty lyrics: *We are poor little lambs that have lost our way, baaa baaa—*"

"Oh, *baaaa*, yourself!" I said.

"It's little things like that—knowing all six verses—that'll get *me* in."

"Is that so?" I said, not really expecting an answer.

"That's right," said Benchley, and Hear-No-Evil and See-No-Evil nodded in agreement. "It's too dangerous, Mrs. Parker. Men swimming naked in the pool and such things. You know what they say," said Big Brute Bob.

"Oh? What *do* they say, whoever 'they' are?"

"A woman's place is in the kitchen."

I snatched the tumbler of scotch from his hand and finished it off. "If that's your philosophy, it's no wonder you can't get a woman in the bedroom." They thought they were so smart, but as I was just a little cluck, and had no frying pan, I'd find a way to cut them down to size!

It was time they learned their lessons.

"Goodnight, you big bruisers," I said sweetly, and pulled closed the curtain to my bedroom alcove.

The next morning I telephoned Jane: "'A woman's place is in the kitchen,'" was all I had to say to the woman who detested domestic husbandry.

Next, I put a call in to Edna: "'A woman's place is in the kitchen,'" was all I needed to say for her to slam down the receiver and rush down to my rooms.

Inspiration struck! I telephoned Groucho Marx, who, always ready for outrageous adventures, more than happily agreed to my plan, and by noon Jane, Edna, and I were greeted at the stage door of the Lyric Theater.

The Brothers

University Club~Groucho need not apply for membership

Chapter Nine

One had to pity the Brothers' dresser for the work involved in setting their dressing room straight. If the condition of the room this morning was any indication of his labor, the Marx Brothers should kiss the fellow's feet. Knowing them, they probably would, just to embarrass the man.

The dressing tables were sparkling, the smudges of greasepaint and clouds of powder washed away off the surfaces of mirrors, chairs, floor; screens uncluttered of last night's tossed costumes, the floral arrangements whisked off to various hospitals, the congratulatory telegrams posted neatly on corkboard, wardrobes sponged, pressed, and hanging in order of wear, hats on hat forms, shoes polished and ready, personal props at the ready to be retrieved, the pancake makeup, liners, rouges, clown white, and makeup brushes washed and lined up on each table. The mirror lights brought cheer to an otherwise dreary room walled with brick and topped with ceiling pipes.

"This is going to be a challenge," said Groucho with nervous relish.

He ordered us to remove our hats and coats and then lined us up like troops. He told us to stand straight, shoulders back, chest out, and nodded up to Edna. She rolled her eyes, and he backed off. Scrutinizing each of us, he duck-walked a zigzag between and around us, pinched Jane in the ass, and at her cry of surprise, clapped his hands for our attention.

"All right!" he shouted, and then he assigned each of us to one of the three costume racks. "Chico!" he pointed to Jane. "Harpo!" he pointed to me! And to Edna, "Zeppo!"

"And I'll be Groucho!" said Groucho.

For the next twenty or so minutes we dressed accordingly. I donned Harpo's fright-wig, the strawberry-blond curls giving me pause—perhaps I'd bleach my hair one day. Jane's hair was shorter than Chico's, but his pointed, dark-green felt cap gave the right impression. A subtle touch of greasepaint, fake eyebrows trimmed to size, face putty to thicken my nose, and we possessed the appearance of the Brothers' far-distant relatives.

Edna was told to brilliantine her short bob and comb it straight back.

"What about my makeup?" she asked, her face clear of cosmetics.

"You don't need any," said Groucho. "Just put

on Zeppo's double-breasted suit, and you'll look more like him than he does."

At the face she pulled he added, "If it makes you feel any better, throw on that fedora. There! Now you look more like a man than Zeppo!"

From the words she spat out telling Groucho precisely into which orifice he should stick the fedora, I was surprised that she didn't just walk out of the theatre, leaving us to fend for ourselves.

"She needs a moustache, Groucho," I said, "or she'll be mistaken for George Sand or some other cross-dressing woman."

"I'm the only one wears a moustache around here!" he said, as if it were some great badge of honor. "But, all right, if you insist," he said, trimming one from his enormous supply into a pencil-thin lip-liner. A bit of spirit gum to glue the piece in place, then the fedora, and she was set.

The plaid pants, the vests, the neckties, the jackets were too big for me and Jane and had to be pinned in places. Suspenders helped keep the pants up, but Edna wore the suit quite well (after we ladies banded her breasts, that is).

"Groucho, you don't look like yourself," I said, when we checked our appearance in the mirrors.

"Almost forgot," he said, and started adding the heavy brows and iconic moustache that was his trademark. He frizzled his hair to stick up and out at the sides, after parting it in the middle. The addition of the glassless spectacles, oversized cutaways, off-kilter bowtie, and a cigar completed the look of sheer lunacy.

"Ready, boys?" he asked as we continued to adjust our clothing.

"We'll never get past the gatekeeper," I said.

"The Marx Brothers are welcomed anywhere," and in an aside, "and if we're not welcomed, we go anyway, and if that doesn't work, we go anywhere else."

"There's no arguing with that kind of logic, I'd say!"

"There's no arguing from you, *period!* You say nothing at all. Remember: You are Harpo onstage and mute."

Edna chuckled, "This will be a day to remember, the shutting of the meanest mouth in town."

"You!" said Groucho to Edna. "Do nothing but nod when spoken to. Keep your hat down over your eyes."

"What about me?" asked Jane, the little Chico. "Any pointers?"

"Don't keep looking at your fingernails, keep your hands in your pockets, jiggle your keys, thumb your suspenders, spread your legs when you stand and uncross them when you sit, but most important of all, try not to look like a fairy. It'll get in the papers and ruin a good man's reputation. Best yet, stay out of sight, and when you can't do that, wedge yourself between Harpo and Zeppo and maybe no one will notice you." He handed me Harpo's bicycle horn. "Here, Dottie, if you must speak, beep!"

We were off and running now, like fools rushing in where angels fear to tread. And when our taxi pulled up at the main entrance of the University Club, I felt the flutter of fear in my belly. They weren't butterflies, no! More as if very wise angels were thumping and batting their wings in wild warning through my innards.

With Groucho in the lead I tried to remember the tips he'd given us to help make our disguises believable: (1) Harpo and Chico were always in motion. (2) We were not to *prance* around like Chaplin, but to *scoot* around like spinning dreidels, skipping occasionally to regain balance. (3) Edna as Zeppo was to do nothing but stand beside Groucho and appear as manly as possible.

Jane and I scooted to the door of Stanford White's Italian Renaissance palazzo-style mansion on the northwest corner of 54th Street at Fifth Avenue, our trousers threatening to fall or to trip us up in our oversized shoes that were stuffed with newspaper. Passersby slowed to stare at the motley crew, and at one point, a woman and child stopped dead in their tracks, blocking my path. I beeped my horn in the woman's face, and she moved on quickly, clearing the way.

The uniformed doorman looked at Groucho with trepidation as our intrepid leader sidled up to the fellow and looked him up and down. Straightening his epaulettes and playing with the bullion fringe, Groucho then saluted as he passed through the entrance. He didn't get very far before the befringed captain of the guards caught the tail of Groucho's cutaway.

"If you like my suit so much, there's this guy on Tenth Avenue can get you one from a guy on Seventh Avenue, who knows this tailor on Third . . . ." He flicked his cigar and turned to enter the door.

"Sorry, Sir, but this is a members-only club."

"And how do you know I'm not a member of this club?"

"Ah, well, I don't—"

"Do you have any reason to believe I am *not* a member of this highfalutin' institution?"

"Well—"

"I didn't think so!" said Groucho as he opened the door himself and held it for his "Brothers" to enter. He saluted: "Give my regards to General Pershing. Tell him I'll meet him at the Russian Front at eight P.M. That's the restaurant next to Carnegie Hall on Fifty-seventh."

Groucho broke through and rushed forward into the magnificent, green-marble-columned reception lobby. The place reeked of money, from the great expanse of marble under our oversized shoes to the impressively gilded vaulted ceilings soaring several stories over my curly blond wig.

By now we'd attracted some attention.

A smattering of a dozen or so young men appeared from various corners to watch the amusement. And within moments a stiff-collared man of forty-something, trim and elegant in a dark gray vested wool suit, on whose lapel was pinned a Phi Beta Kappa key, approached us with the attitude of a southern belle protecting her virtue. He sported a neat, if substantial, black moustache and had wavy dark hair softened with streaks of gray at the temple. When he opened his mouth to speak the space between his front teeth lent a whistling sound to his speech: Here was the gatekeeper.

"May I help you gentlemen?" he asked with a curling lip and a slight hesitation on the word "gentlemen."

"P-r-r-r-ofessor Beaur-r-r-regard Shrimpleton Schlepper-er-er," said Groucho, rolling every *r* while shaking the man's hand violently. "That's quite enough, my man, you'll throw out my back before you get the chance to throw out the rest of me. Now!"

He wasn't going to give the man a chance to speak; before the fellow could recoup, Groucho charged ahead: "My sons and I are seeking membership in your vastly overrated inner sanctimonious. We Schlepper-er-ers are graduates from the most contentious and pretentious halls of academe, holding degrees in Parasitical Psychology, Adenoidal Anatomy, and Convoluted Geometry."

"Sir—"

"Doctor! Call me *Doctor* Schlepper-er-er! That's a *schlepp* with three *errrrrs* after it. I hold a PhD in High Colonic Physics, as well as a master's degree in Scientific Absurdity *and* an MOC!"

"MOC?"

"Master of Ceremonies!"

By now we'd attracted quite a crowd of young men who knew exactly who we were, or thought they did: the Four Marx Brothers. And by the sound of the laughter, we were a hit!

I beeped my horn.

"What is it my boy?" asked Groucho.

I beeped again.

Groucho nodded, and turned to the gentleman for directions to the men's room. Once directed, I nodded in response, uncrossed my quivering legs, and with a beep of thanks, snuck off in the direction of the lavatory. But rather than follow on from the directions, I walked to the open door to my right.

I peeked in, and knew I was at the entrance to the famous reading room that faced Fifth Avenue.

I'd often walked past its street-level windows facing the Avenue. If one looked up, one could see between the parted draperies wingchairs in which sat rather stodgy-looking old fellows, doing whatever stodgy old fellows do in private clubs. I had wondered about such places, envied, even, the idea of their masculine camaraderie. But, hadn't I'd found my own little place among men in my seat at the Round Table? I suspect that together we do most of the things that go on in such formal clubs: We eat, drink, play games, talk politics, tell dirty jokes, and promote each others' careers. We, too, have a closed, exclusive club. Our requirements are rigid: smart, sassy, savvy, members only. Be boring and you are out on your ass, banished from the table. Of course, we are Hottentots compared to these *pillars of society*. As long as he had a university degree and six letters of recommendation for membership from other members, a gentleman could play in the library, dine in the dining room, swim in the pool, and keep rooms in residence at the University Club. Oh, you didn't have to be rich, necessarily, to qualify, but it didn't hurt.

As I looked around admiringly at the masculine opulence, at the graceful swags of hundreds of yards of spun-gold fabric lining those draperies and glistening in the cheery winter sunshine, my curiosity of many years was sated. I knew, now, what lay within the glorious rooms that I had merely glimpsed from the street, and it was spectacular.

And on the wall, Gilbert Stuart's George Washington stared down at me, his lips a tight, straight line of disapproval set over wooden teeth.

I knew I wasn't inconspicuous, not in what I was wearing, but if I could place myself in hiding I might be able to see or hear something that could lead to the capture of the New Man, whoever he was. All I had to go on was a voice. He sounded a lot like Scott Fitzgerald: cultured, slightly affected, belying traces of America's Heartland. But his was a warmer-sounding, deep, resonant voice, not boyish or buoyant in tone like Scott's, and to hear him speak, you'd never guess the real character of the man was imbued with the hatred of racial prejudice. Prejudice transcends ignorance, I suppose; I've never understood it, really. I've always seen people in terms of their talents, their wit, their accomplishments, the quality of their characters. This hatred is based in fear, though people like these would be loath to admit it, even to themselves. Their hatred is self-justified, I think; much of it is not born of simple ignorance, and then cultivated and bred. You don't always see it flagrantly displayed here as you do in the South, with lynchings and cruel segregation. It is like a banked fire: silent, smoldering beneath the ashes, but hot and ready to burst into destructive flames when stirred up. Am I naïve to think that after sixty years people would have seen the injustice of slavery? That the Klan would have been laughed out of town? But, of course, the South didn't *willingly* give up slavery, did they? It had to be wrenched out of their grip. And there are always little people who feel better about themselves and their condition when they can feel superior to others and have something or someone to hate and look down upon.

There was nowhere for me to hide. The palms in the corners wouldn't shield me; the various chairs scattered about the richly paneled and carpeted room wouldn't do, either. I caught an alarmed eye behind the pince-nez of an elderly fellow who'd looked up from his newspaper. He did a double-take, his glasses fell to his lap, and then he shook his head, poor thing, disbelieving what he was seeing as if his eyes were deceiving him.

The old man made a little choking sound, which caught the attention of an attendant, another guardian of the gate ready to serve the members and ready to call in troops of bouncers to throw out the riff-raff.

The only thing I could do was walk in boldly. Perhaps the attention I could draw in this hushed place might prove useful in my search. So I came in blasting. My bicycle horn, that is.

Startled, frowning faces looked up from their books, and there was a string of *hurrumps* thrown my way and a couple of clutched chests, and within seconds I was corralled on either side, at each elbow, by two attendants who lifted me straight up off my feet and carried me vertically out of the room, my big shoes dangling. I was carried in this way into the front lobby and toward the entry door, having to pass the commotion of youthful members ignoring the pro-testations of the more elderly staff and membership, as Groucho distributed complimentary tickets to the evening's performance of *The Cocoanuts*.

"Put Harpo down right here," directed Groucho when he saw me floating between the men. "I see you've found a new means of transportation."

They stopped in their tracks, looked over at the Gatekeeper, who nodded, and lowered me to my feet. I squeezed the horn.

Everybody below the age of thirty laughed and then cheered. I took a bow and beeped three or four more times until Groucho said, "Stop the yakking, Son." And to the crowd that had gathered: "Once he gets started, you can't shut him up."

And through the laughter and excitement at meeting the Four Marx Brothers came a familiar voice.

Before me stood the indomitable Mr. Benchley!

He adjusted my crushed-down top hat, pressing down *hard*, sending my curly wig to meet my glued-on bushy brows. "You're attractive as a blond, dear, but you must do something about those eyebrows."

I beeped at him, straightened my wig, and pulled up my pants.

And then, appearing at his side was a familiar face. The handsome fellow we'd encountered at the opening-night party for Noel Coward's new play, *Hay Fever*—the man, Pinny Somethingorother, who'd offered his car to take a distraught Aleck home . . . the beautiful town car . . the creamy-yellow *Duesenberg!*

He was about to speak, but when he looked at me he must have seen the light dawn in my face through my ridiculous disguise, for in the instant that our eyes locked I remembered the Midwestern, cultured, if slightly affected tones of his voice, similar to Scott Fitzgerald's—the same inflections, the flat vowels—and I knew that he and the New Man were one and the same. And through the makeup, wig, bushy eyebrows, and all he must have seen the recognition in my face, for he turned on his heel, found an opening in the throng of men, and bolted through.

"You see," babbled on Mr. Benchley, unaware of my discovery, "you scare off lots of rich, eligible bachelors with those brows, not to mention the nose hair, Mrs. Park—Hey! Where're you going?"

I beeped my horn repeatedly as I gave chase after the assassin while tugging up my trousers. He was headed for the entry doors, but just as he was about to make it to freedom, blue coats, brass buttons, and visor caps, the uniforms of New York's Finest, were piling out of a paddy wagon and running past the doorman for the lobby.

The crown of Pinny's light-auburn hair shifted, and I followed him toward the rear of the building. Elevator doors closed before I could catch up to him.

There had to be stairs, I thought, and turned to see the sheets of wide, white marble and white wrought-iron railings.

I tripped and fell to the floor, and Mr. Benchley was at my side helping me up to my feet. I kicked off my shoes—they were only slowing me down—and retied the sash that served as a belt to hold up the trousers. I told Mr. Benchley of my discovery, and then took off up the stairs, beeping my horn all the way, hoping the policemen would follow me up. Whistles rang out, and there were shouts to "follow that man!" A score of clicking heels, like castanets, sounded on the marble steps behind me.

Logic told me that Pinny knew quite well the layout of the club. He could be anywhere. If he had a room at the club, he might have retreated there. There was no way I'd be able to find him if he'd sheltered himself behind one of the scores of doors on the residential floor. With no idea on which floor he'd gotten off the elevator, when I reached the landing I looked at the elevator's floor indicator, which had stopped at the number four.

Onward I trudged up the steps, my trousers proving troublesome. At one point they fell to the floor, and the only thing I could do to carry on was to step out of them. The shirt I wore came to my knees, and anyway, I didn't care much about modesty at a time like this.

I reached the fourth floor and had to make a decision. The elevator was on its way up to the seventh floor. Straight ahead was the library, and I figured there'd be lots of places for him to hide if he had in fact gotten off on this floor.

I entered and hid between the door and the wall as the herd of charging policemen and curious members thundered up the stairs to the floor above.

Once out of their reach, I turned to see the wonder of gilded columns supporting a series of arches that ran the expanse of the remarkable library, the H. Siddons Mowbray ceiling murals, painted in rich, warm, deep blues, greens, and fiery reds. I raced through the room, peeking around the corners created by each arch, and saw no one but a few gents reading at tables.

If he were on the lam, he wouldn't hide where he'd be trapped. A thorough search would eventually reveal him.

So back to the elevator I ran, so exhausted from the chase that I decided, as I probably had lost the trail, to ride up in ease to the seventh floor, where the elevator indicator had marked the stop. The doors opened and the attendant paid me no mind, merely asking which floor I wanted.

I was winded from the chase, but managed to puff out, "Redhead, tall fellow; on which floor did you let him out?"

"Floor seven, Madame."

I was no longer fooling everyone with my disguise. "Seven, then."

The doors opened at the landing facing the

dining room, where scores of men were seated for luncheon.

He could be under a table; linens draped to the floor might work temporarily until a waiter or busboy or the foot of a diner betrayed his presence.

I stood poised at the door, ignoring the maître d's fierce glare, then pushed past him to stand in the middle of the room. Conversations halted, eyes burned through my costume, several men laughed and a couple applauded, as I scanned the unoccupied tables for any movement of the linens. I could go left or right through the room, but I had little time to make a decision, so I confronted the maître d' and asked if the redheaded man had entered the dining room? His eyes betrayed him. They flitted to the left, and, before he could grab me—the crazy, pantless person who might harm a club member—I was off.

The police were entering the dining room from the hall as I was forging my way through waiters and busboys, repeatedly excusing myself, then knocking into a waiter, upsetting a tureen he carried and sending it crashing to the floor. The maître d', with his captain at my heels, slid across the aisle on a sea of split-pea soup, like the Babe stealing second base.

The kitchen was a perfect avenue of escape, I realized, as I pushed through a swinging door—the wrong door as it appeared, for I collided with another waiter. We stood chest-to-chest, staring at each other for a long moment, a tray loaded with shucked oysters caught between us. The slimy crustaceans slithered down between our bodies, one nasty critter finding its way in through my shirt collar to remain there, wiggling in the waistband of my bloomers.

It appeared that I was moving in the right direction, for ahead in the distance of the huge kitchen there had been another mishap, cleanup being attended to by mop and bucket. Chefs were screaming obscenities in bilingual rants, hats were flying, pans were banging, and I ducked in time to avoid a firm left hook aimed at a dishwasher by a *sous-chef*.

I beeped my horn and everybody froze for a second, saw me, then ignored me to resume their fights.

Around the maze of counters and butcherblocks, I took a slide through squashed squash and landed on my knees. Pinny was in the distance, and I had to stop him.

Dozens of plucked chickens lay on trays at hand's reach, and I grabbed a bird and flung it like a quarterback toward the forty-yard line, but hit a rack of crystal glasses that toppled and shattered in a melodic shower.

Continuing my progress, or should I say, my trail of destruction, my jacket caught on the edge of the stove. In attempting to free myself, my elbow knocked over a vat of mashed potatoes on which I slipped, falling face-forward onto my belly. I was sliding down the aisle toward a wall. My arms flung forward to break the crash into a baker's rack. It did stop my slide, but my hands grasped several freshly baked apple pies in the process. While I was rising from the floor the wire shelf under my grasp gave way, tumbling onto other shelves. I licked the tasty samples from my hands and the syrupy bicycle horn and pulled myself up to a standing position, only to be confronted with a hysterical pastry chef beating his chest like an angry gorilla.

There was too much commotion for me to get to the pantry, where I was sure he was hiding. I crawled over a marble, flour-powdered pastry table, and somehow avoided being clobbered by that ubiquitous murdering frying pan, now employed and aimed at my derrière by the pastry chef, as if ready to swat a troublesome fly. I made it to the floor before it made contact with my behind. But his swing was not aborted in time, for the pan hit a fifty-pound bag of flour instead. The room exploded into a blinding cloud of snow.

I entered through the door of the vast and extensively shelved pantry where canned goods, boxed fresh produce, hanging cured meats, and basins of iced shellfish enough to feed a city were stored. The ice lockers took up an entire wall.

Could it be so simple? Could he possibly have found refuge here? Perhaps behind a tall cardboard box, or the onion sacks in that corner?

A rectangle of sunlight led me to an open door

where a fire escape descended to the alley.

He's gone, I thought, *out into the streets, lost to us as he hides among millions of people.*

As I stared out at the cobblestone alley, the same alley where I had been literally dumped out with the trash, Mr. Benchley arrived to look over my shoulder.

"Gee, you look swell," he said, appraising the damage: my egg-batter-dipped, apple-seasoned, dredged-through-flour self. "Looks like you're ready for the fryer!" he said, slapping Harpo's top hat, which he'd retrieved somewhere along the way, back atop my head.

"Are you making love to me, Mr. Benchley?" I said, snorting out the powder that clogged my nose. "Well, now's not the time. There's a murderer to catch."

A police officer came running down the alley from the side street, and soon the pantry was a sea of bluecoats entering from the kitchen, strong-arming my other "Marx Brothers" and trailed by dozens of young club members who had followed the fun.

There were few of us who hadn't been smacked by flying entrées, splashing soups, and slimy seafood. Mr. Benchley stood before me with a leaf of escarole replacing his coat handkerchief and a smudge of flour on his cheek. In spite of the fact that the assassin had gotten away, there was the residual exhilaration from the chase, and messy as it was, there had been a sophomoric joy in the craziness that I doubted had ever existed in this staid environment before.

The police cleared the room of all but me, Groucho, Jane, Edna, Mr. Benchley, and the resident manager. Two police officers remained by the order of a Big Kahuna captain who was sporting lots of edible decorations on his uniform. We were told to sit on the wooden crates, and then that officer in charge, Captain Mahoney, questioned us.

Mr. Benchley took the lead, starting with my kidnapping of the night before, meant to abduct Clarence Darrow and Arthur Garfield Hays, and the dumping of my body in the trash bin. Mr. Benchley had arrived at the club in order to investigate.

"Investigate what?" asked the Captain, overwhelmed by the futile chase and the incongruous cast of characters sitting before him.

"Well, you see, it's a long story."

Captain Mahoney wiped traces of tomato soup from his face, pulled up a fruit crate, and sat down with a sigh. "I'm listening."

"You know about the murders of the two priests, the first, Father John, falling into the arms of Mr. Woollcott on Thanksgiving morning, and the second, Father Michael Murphy of St. Agatha's, bludgeoned the other day?"

"What does that have to do with you ransacking the University Club? A lot of very important people are members here, and I've got to arrest somebody or the Chief will—"

I jumped in: "Well, you see, the murders are related."

"To what?"

"The conspiracy to assassinate Darrow and Hays," I said.

"The reason Mrs. Parker flooded the kitchen with vegetable consommé and sent the carcasses of several plucked and oven-ready chickens into oblivion, was to stop the presumed assassin."

"What were you doing here?" I asked Mr. Benchley, accusatorily.

"I said I'd follow up the clue of the stationery from the club we found in Father John's trash. I had the photo of the priest and I showed it to several men, who recognized him. The manager remembered that a priest was looking for a man by the name of Healy. And then I ran into the fellow whom we'd met at Noel's party, Pinny Somethingorother, and he invited me to his room for a drink and a—"

"And a knife in the gut! He probably planned on killing you there. He had to suspect you knew he was involved!"

"But, I had no idea! How did *you* know he was involved?"

"His voice. The man my abductors reported to last night told his flunkies to dump me out there. I pretended to be passed out so I couldn't see his face. He sounded like F. Scott; you know, hoity-toity. I connected the voice to the man the minute I saw him with you. And he knew that I knew."

"That's enough! I'm asking the questions here!" barked the Captain. "Let me get this straight: You're telling me that two priests were killed by this Pinny guy, and he also wants to kill the two lawyers?"

Groucho couldn't resist: "You know what they call two dead lawyers, don't you?"

"What!"

"A good start!"

"Quiet!"

"You know what they call two dead priests?"

"What did I just say?"

"All right, all right! He's no fun," Groucho said to no one in particular.

I said, "Yes, Pinny is involved in a conspiracy and in the killing of the two priests. First Father John was killed, probably because Father John knew of the plan to assassinate the lawyers, and then Father Michael got killed, because the priest eventually found out *why* Father John was murdered. The Wild-Haired Man, Father John's killer, stepped out in front of a car, you see. We think there's a widespread plot planned by the KKK. Pinny may just be a middleman, if not the assassin himself."

"When did you come to that conclusion?" asked Mr. Benchley.

"Last night. When he scolded my abductors for the botched-up kidnapping, he said something about there being 'more of our people at risk.' So there must be others involved."

"I'm asking the questions!" said Captain Mahoney.

"What was the question?"

"*Aaarrrggghhh!*"

The captain pulled himself together: "All right, now! Why does the Ku Klux Klan want to kill these lawyers in the first place?"

"*Ahhh!*" said Groucho, "now we get to the *Krux* of the Ku Klux Klan! Say *that* fast five times."

Mr. Benchley said, "Darrow has agreed to defend one Henry Sweet, the father of Dr. Ossian Sweet, a Negro physician. Dr. Sweet had the audacity to purchase a home in a white suburb of Detroit earlier this year. When his home was stoned by gangs, his father, Henry, got his shotgun and shot into the mob, killing a man. This comes on the heels of last summer's Scopes Trial—"

"The 'Monkey Trial'?"

"The very one," said Mr. Benchley.

"That was a lot of monkey business, if you ask me," said Groucho.

"Well I'm not asking you!" hissed the Captain.

Mr. Benchley continued: "Lots of good Christians viewed Darrow's defense strategy of picking apart William Jennings Bryan's testimony, and his challenge against the rationale of the seven-day Genesis of the Bible in light of Darwin's theory of evolution, as reprehensible; the death of Bryan soon after the trial's end exacerbated that angry sentiment. And now Darrow, the emissary of the Devil himself, is to defend a Negro who shot a white man."

"Well," said Edna to Jane, who had been sitting quietly on a sack of potatoes next to her, "at least now we know why we've been running around like lunatics!"

"You need a reason?" asked Groucho.

"How did the police get here so fast?" I asked the Captain.

"I called them," said the manager. "Brute force was needed to extricate you theatricals from the premises."

"What? You got a club full of wimps? You had to call the police to do your dirty work?" I asked the pompous ass. I'd have liked to further tighten his already-tightened necktie, but his expensive suit covered in God-knows-what was vengeance enough for his snobbery.

"You were running amuck, causing scenes," said the little shitter.

"And you've been harboring a murderer!" said I. "The important thing now is: What can we do to catch these terrible men before they kill again?"

"Nothing. You do *nothing*. You leave it to us, the police and the FBI. All right, I'm taking you all down to the station," said the Captain. He turned to the manager: "Do you want to press charges on these people?"

"As Mr. Benchley is a member of our club, and considering the circumstances—"

"And the fact that you've got two tickets for this evening's performance of *The Cocoanuts* I've already bribed you with...," said Groucho.

"—we can forget the incident."

"Very well," said the Captain. "Let's get these folks downtown to the station."

Jane and Edna fought off the grips of the officers with their cries of objections. "How dare you manhandle me!" yelled Jane.

"Do you know who I am?" demanded Edna.

"You're Chico and Zeppo, or somebody in between," growled one big brute.

Mr. Benchley moved to my side, in an effort to escort me more gently to the door.

"On what charge do you arrest me?" said Edna.

"Yeah, on what charge do you arrest her?" asked

an indignant Groucho.

"Impersonating a Marx Brother," answered the Captain, sarcastically, "and in a minute, I'll add resisting arrest to the charges."

"But I *am* a Marx Brother," insisted Groucho.

"Yeah, *sure* you are. And I am Marie of Romania," said the other policeman.

"Hey," I said, "That's *my* line you're quoting, you big oaf!"

"Look at that moustache," he said to Groucho. "I bet I could pull it right off, it's so phony."

"You mean like this?" Groucho pulled off his moustache.

"My point, exactly!"

"Yours is a phony if ever I saw one," said Groucho.

"Oh, yeah?"

"I bet I could pull it right off," said Groucho, giving a wickedly strong tug at the policeman's pushbroom whiskers.

There was an unattractive grunt of pain from the officer, who released his hold on Groucho long enough for our friend to make a break back through the kitchen. The crash of pots and pans was signal he was causing some upset beyond the swinging doors.

"Forget about him," ordered the Captain. "It's these people we want, anyway. They're part of a murder investigation."

The door to the alley was opened, and we were about to file out into the alley where the paddy wagon awaited our transport, when I stopped short. The door to the alley had been open when I arrived in the pantry, signifying Pinny had found his means of escape. But, why hadn't he been picked up or even seen by the police who'd already covered the exits? I didn't know why, but I had the strongest urge to remain in the pantry. Maybe it had been a ruse, that opened door. But, where could he have hidden?

I whispered to Mr. Benchley. He nodded.

When the others had gone out through the alley doorway, I pulled down on the lever of the meat locker. The door opened to reveal a butcher-knife-wielding Pinny, who came running out at me, the blade aimed at my chest.

Mr. Benchley's mighty tennis backhand proved useful as the frying pan he gripped made contact in an upward swing. Pinny crumpled to the floor.

Boys of the club

Jane, Edna, and I posing with Groucho ("and I am Marie of Romania")

Marie of Romania

Chapter Ten

If it hadn't been for Aleck's cousin, Joe Woollcott ("from the normal side of the family, *not* the sissy side," Joe always stressed), we'd probably have spent the night in jail. Worse still, our faces would have been plastered all over the evening papers. Fortunately, when we filed into the stationhouse the reporters who usually hung around waiting for tips were either still outside the University Club waiting to be told why the police had been called, or at another newsworthy event, a bank robbery at one of the larger banking institutions downtown. Of course, there were enough witnesses at the club to say that the Marx Brothers had arrived seeking membership, and had given out free tickets to their new Broadway show. And wouldn't you know, Groucho himself, having escaped from the police, gave an interview on the pink Milford granite steps of the clubhouse, alongside the manager, who smiled and offered Groucho and the Brothers honorary membership. Pumping the man's arm in a handshake, he replied, "Please accept my resignation. I don't want to belong to any club that would accept people like me as a member." Smiling for the cameras: "But it's been a lot of laughs, and let's not do it again."

After a couple of hours of giving and signing official statements, we were allowed to leave. Edna, exhilarated and rather pleased that I had included her in my little adventure, had a car sent over to pick us all up and to deposit us wherever we needed to go. We were a rag-tag crew getting into the limo, and the consolation was that nobody other than Joe, Captain Mahoney, and a couple of officers knew our real identities.

After Woodrow Wilson had licked the remnants of whatever food had crusted on my neck, and I'd located and disposed of down the toilet the stinking oyster lodged in my underpants, I lowered myself into a hot bath. I could feel the exertions of the afternoon stiffening my body. Everything was beginning to ache; I had bruises in places I couldn't see from my assault on the club's kitchen. What I wanted was a warm bed and several glasses of imported cognac to ease me into sleep, but I was ravenously hungry, too, as I'd tasted nothing all day but bits of apple pie that found their own way into my mouth.

I was stepping out of the tub, with the intention of calling room service for some dinner, when there was a knock at my door.

Aleck and FPA stood there decked out in evening clothes.

"I thought for a change of pace we'd have a bit of supper at the Waldorf before the show," said Aleck, entering and pulling out from his coat a bottle of genuine French cognac. FPA followed him in, offering a box of fine French chocolates.

"You've read my mind," I said, "about the cognac. Is it the real stuff or rotgut with motor oil added for color?"

"It's the real thing, my dear!"

"Bless you."

Oh crap, I thought; tonight was the opening of George Gershwin's new show, *Song of the Flame*. As Aleck poured all around, and I broke into the box of chocolates, I began to tell the men of the events of the day, of which they had already been briefed by both Mr. Benchley and Cousin Joe. They chuckled and Aleck was exceptionally jolly at the knowledge that all the assassins were dead or locked away.

"Joe told me that the man they caught wasn't saying a word."

"You mean, the man *I* caught, don't you?"

"Yes, ma petite enfant, the man *you* caught."

"He's not who he claims to be," I said. "The real Pinchus Seymour Pinkelton, or Pinny as he called himself, is someone the police have yet to identify. The real-deal drove off in his Duesenberg several weeks ago for his lodge in Michigan's Upper Peninsula. He hasn't been seen since. Aleck, Frank, I don't want to go to the opening tonight. I'm spent, and can review the show next week."

"You and Benchley and Edna, too, are lazy creatures indeed."

"Mr. Benchley's not going with you?"

"All right, get some rest. Tomorrow's New Year's Eve and we have that charity affair."

After the men left, I called room service for a steak and the usual accompanying side dishes. Jimmy the bellboy arrived to take Woodrow Wilson on his evening constitutional. I'd just settled down with a second cognac when Mr. Benchley arrived. He hadn't eaten yet, so I called room service to double the dinner order.

The food revived my spirits and the cognac relaxed my worn-out muscles. Mr. Benchley and I sat around listening to the Paul Whiteman Orchestra playing *All Alone,* and their new hit, *The Charleston,* on the radio broadcast.

We were chatting playfully about our friends when Marion Anderson's new recording, *Nobody Knows the Trouble I've Seen*, began to play. Our mood mellowed as we listened.

Mr. Benchley asked if he had left his cigarette lighter in the apartment sometime during the past few days. I looked through my purse before remembering that I indeed had the lighter; I'd lit my cigarette with it but failed to return it, as moments later we found the dead body of Father Michael Murphy.

"I think it's in my coat pocket," I said, heading for the closet to check the pockets of my new Persian lamb coat. "I've got it; squirreled away for the winter," I said, pulling out the lighter along with a handkerchief and a crumpled piece of paper. It was the envelope addressed to Father Michael from Father Timothy Morgan of Grosse Pointe. The correspondence, or whatever the envelope had held, was missing.

I walked back in from the bedroom and tossed the lighter to my friend.

"I'd forgotten about this, Fred," I said, looking at the postmark and then handing him the envelope. "Father Timothy left New York a few days after this letter was sent from Grosse Pointe."

"What does it mean, do you think?"

"There's only one way to find out what was in the envelope. We've got to call Timothy Morgan and ask him," said Mr. Benchley.

I called down to the desk and asked the operator to get me on the line with St. Thomas of Aquinas Seminary College outside Grosse Pointe, Michigan. It would take some time, she told me, as all the lines were busy, but she would ring up as soon as she connected.

An hour later, still with no luck reaching Michigan, Mr. Benchley and I broke out a new deck of cards for a game or ten of rummy, while Ben Bernie crooned *Sweet Georgia Brown.*

By eleven o'clock, Mr. Benchley was asleep on the sofa, Woodrow Wilson tucked under his arm, the two snoring and whistling in rhythm with Bessie Smith's rendition of W.C. Handy's *Careless Love Blues.*

I was about to turn off the radio and go to bed when the telephone rang. It was the hotel operator calling to say all the circuits were busy and she had still not reached the party I'd requested. "Try again in the morning," I told her.

"Nodded off . . .," said Mr. Benchley.

"No kidding."

Woodrow Wilson leaped off his chest and came to sit before me with a smile of anticipation on his face.

"No, we are not going out, little man. It's time for bed." I looked over at my friend, who'd risen off the sofa, handed him his hat, kissed him on the cheek, shut the door behind him, and went to bed.

New Year's Eve morning 1925 dawned clear and crisp, I am told. I rarely see that time of day unless I am returning from a very late evening.

Woodrow Wilson woke me at ten o'clock, anxious for some action. The poor little critter had been housebound these past few days, with me gallivanting around town discovering dead bodies, chasing assassins, spending my spare time at the police station, and generally running amuck and making a fool of myself in oversized trousers.

"All right, all right," I whined, dragging myself out of bed. And I literally was dragging, as it felt like every bone and joint in my body would snap into fragments if I moved too quickly. I caught my profile in my wardrobe mirror, and was awed by the color and size of the bruise on my left buttock. Another lovely blue circle, reminiscent of, and about the size of, Lake George, had spread across my upper-left thigh. At least the right side of me was unmarred, I thought, as I went about my morning toilet. I quickly drew on hose and threw on an old woolen dress and my coat, slipped into a pair of soft old shoes, put on a cloche and a little lipstick, and grabbed Woodrow Wilson's leash.

He led me into the elevator, then out into the lobby, where I ordered coffee and sweet rolls to be sent up to my rooms.

As I walked toward the doors, I glanced over to my left, to the small room that once was an old office, but now, according to the small, tasteful sign above its entrance, was the new Washington's Shoe Parlor. Peeking in, I glimpsed Washington Douglas, his arm recently freed of its cast, shining the shoes of one of his first patrons.

Thanks to Frank Case, Washington now was an equal partner in the hotel's new business. For a nominal monthly fee, he had use of the space, and all of the hotel's business. Every night, shoes were left outside the rooms by residents for shining.

Thanks to Aleck, FPA, and Mr. Benchley, Washington had three brand-new leather chairs with footrests in the shop. Edna, Jane, and the rest of the gang chipped in and sent a special delivery from Santa of toys, clothing, candy, and a goose with all the fixings to the Douglas's apartment a couple of days before Christmas. Heywood and FPA began their own little advertising campaign for the shoeshine shop with regular mentions in their columns of who met whom, who said this funny thing or that, while getting a shine. Little Lincoln and his siblings would return to school after the holidays sporting new winter coats, leggings, boots, gloves, scarves, and caps. Today, he was helping his father set up supplies on the shelves.

I was happy.

Joseph, the Gonk's daytime doorman, patted Woodrow, and then addressed me:

"Mrs. Parker," he began, "my mother thanks you for the handkerchiefs you sent her at Christmas." It is always smart to have a few extra presents on hand at the holidays.

"How is she feeling, Joseph? Any better?"

"Oh, much, thank you. The doctor says she'll be fine and up and around in a couple of weeks." She'd had her appendix removed.

"That's good to hear, Joseph," I said, and was about to follow Woodrow's lead when a car drove up, and Joseph opened the passenger door. "Oh, and Mrs. Parker?" he added after the passenger got out and he'd closed the door after him, "I was wondering . . ."

I waited as he opened the entry door to the lobby, expecting a request for hard-to-get tickets to a show for him and his fiancée, Sarah. Instead, when he arrived at my side, he asked, "Remember you and Mr. Benchley and Mr. Woollcott, too, wanted me to be on the lookout for 'any unsavory characters,' as Mr. Woollcott put it—any strange-looking man hanging around?"

"I remember, Joseph, and eliminating Messieurs Ross and Broun from our luncheon club, have you noticed anyone unusual?"

"Well, there's been this car," he said, and smiled as he spoke with admiration, "this beauty of a motor, a touring car it is, a buttery, cream-colored one, with shiny, wire-spoked wheels and grand headlamps and chrome you can see your face in—sixty-five hundred dollars of pure—"

He ended his reverie abruptly and came back to earth. "A Duesenberg, you know?"

"You should be an automobile salesman, Joseph."

"Do you think so?"

"Yes, I think I saw that car out front, once," I said, recalling the one parked in front of the Gonk a few weeks ago when I had looked out onto the street from my window. Of course, I'd seen lots of pretty Doozies around town. Swope has a gorgeous green one. So do the Fitzgeralds, but theirs is red. And now that I recall, that scoundrel Pinny has a white—no!—a buttery-cream-colored Duesenberg!

"Strange thing is, the car always pulls up a few feet from the canopy, and just sits there for five or ten minutes. Nobody gets out and nobody gets in. The other day, I went over to speak to the chauffeur, but the car pulled away from the curb as soon as I approached, and this morning—"

"You saw the car *today?*"

"An hour ago. It drove past a couple of times—three times."

"Call the police, Joseph," I said, dragging my unrelieved pup back into the lobby. I handed the leash and two-bits to Jimmy, asked him to walk Woodrow, and followed Joseph to the desk, where he informed Frank Case, the hotel manager, of my request to telephone the police.

Frank Case called the station, asking Joe Woollcott to send a plainclothes detective around through the Algonquin's delivery entrance at Mrs. Parker's request. Ten minutes later, the detective sat down across from me at a table in the Oak Room, right off the lobby. I sipped coffee as I told the detective about the Duesenberg, its connection with the man arrested yesterday who was suspected of murder, and the planned assassination of Darrow and Hays. The car, I suggested, is probably the same automobile belonging to a missing man from Michigan, Pinchus Seymour Pinkleton, whose identity the assassin had assumed.

The detective told me it would be best if I remained at the hotel, and if I had to go out, to be accompanied by friends. I didn't like the idea of being a prisoner in my own home.

"Well, Mrs. Parker, if the auto was here this morning, it means whoever is driving it is looking for someone here. Or waiting for a chance to do something. I'll have a few plainclothes officers sent over to watch the building."

Woodrow returned, a kick to his step, and we went back up to my rooms, where I telephoned Mr. Benchley at his apartment and told him about the automobile. He'd stop up to escort me down to luncheon in an hour, and, "by the way, did you get a call through to Father Timothy in Michigan?"

I told him I would ask the operator to try the call again, after which, to keep my mind off unsettling thoughts, I spent the next hour knocking off a review for *The Bookman*.

The telephone call went through when we were just about to disband the luncheon, during which

Groucho embellished wildly on the crimes of the day before, and I corrected with the truth. Mr. Benchley followed me to the telephone to listen in.

It quickly became clear that Father Timothy Morgan would not be able to come to the telephone, let alone receive a message from us, because he had been found dead five days ago, the victim of an accident, a deadly accident.

"He was found dead in his car, crashed down a ravine," said Father Matthew Pasco, who had taken our call.

"*Oh, my God!* When did this happen?"

"As I said, last week. Were you a friend of Timothy's?"

"We met him when he came to New York."

"He was distraught over the news of his godfather's death. When he read about it last week, he was inconsolable."

"Last week?"

"Yes, there was a letter of condolences from Father John's bishop informing Timothy of his death."

"Are you saying he just found out about Father John's murder, a couple of days before he crashed his car?"

"That's correct. Murder, was it, did you say?"

"But, when Father Timothy came to New York to—"

"New York, did you say? As I told Father Michael at St. Agatha's in New York, when he telephoned the other day, I believe Timothy's distress may have contributed to his accident because he took the news rather hard."

I fell silent while trying to tie the threads together, prompting him into polite smalltalk:

"Were you very close to Timothy when—"

"We met only a few weeks ago."

There was hesitation on the other end, and a couple of aborted phrases.

"Father Pasco, I met Timothy Morgan a little over a month ago in New York City, during his stay at St. Agatha's with Father Michael Murphy."

"Well, that is impossible, my dear. Father Tim has been *here*, and has not made any trips to New York. Now I don't know what this is all about, and it is a very sad time for us, here—"

"I am so sorry, Father, but please bear with me for another minute. Was Father Timothy visited by his godfather last month?"

"He was."

"And could you please tell me if you sensed anything unusual about the visit?"

"I don't know what's going on here. I don't know why you're asking these things. Unless you have some kind of official standing—"

"I understand, Father Pasco. You will be receiving a call from the New York City Police Department very shortly."

I turned to a puzzled Mr. Benchley when I rang off: "Father Timothy is dead, but he's not the man we knew as Father Tim. The real Timothy Morgan hadn't left Grosse Pointe, and certainly hasn't been in New York recently."

FPA had lingered in the lobby to chat with an old friend after leaving the dining room. I asked him up to my room for a drink and a talk with me and Mr. Benchley. When we were settled in, Mr. Benchley took the floor.

"Here's what we have, Frank," said Mr. Benchley, starting from the beginning: "Father John is killed. Dottie sees the Wild-Haired Man fleeing the scene. Soon afterwards, Dottie is shot at and I chase the Wild-Haired Man, but before I can grab him, he gets hit by a car."

"Wait," said Frank, "let me write this down." He fetched a pencil and a notebook from his pocket.

"All right, then," said Mr. Benchley, "we can surmise that Father John knew something, and we can assume he could identify the Klansmen who set the darktown fire. But I don't think that witnessing that fire and knowing who set it was the real reason for his flight from Tennessee."

I cut in: "You mean he found out that the Klan had bigger fish to fry?"

"Yes, I do believe so, even if you did carelessly choose a rather distasteful analogy, considering."

"Oh, dear!" I said, contritely. I hate clichés, and that one just fell out of my mouth. "I didn't mean—"

Mr. Benchley laughed, "No, of course you didn't, my dear girl. Now, we don't know if he told everything to his godson, the real Father Tim, but I believe he knew about the assassination plot to kill Darrow. And that's why the intrigue—"

"Yes," I said, "There had to be something really big going down for someone to bother with impersonating Father John's godson for nearly a month."

"The fact that Father John came to New York, went to the University Club, where the assassin was staying, is too much of a coincidence for him not to have known an assassination plot was in the works," said Frank.

"Precisely. And that is the motive for murder number one. Now, yesterday morning a letter arrives for Father Michael from Father John's godson, Timothy, postmarked Grosse Pointe *the day before Tim crashes his car*. Father Mike has just returned home from visiting a sick deacon at the hospital and finds the letter among the mail. It makes no sense to him, as the man he believes to be Father Timothy has been living with him for a month."

"But it's only speculation as to what he learned when he opened the envelope and read the letter from the real Father Tim," I said.

"It must have been confusing and then became disturbing, after he telephoned Father Pasco in Grosse Pointe, so he called Mrs. Parker, and you know the rest of the story. I doubt we'll ever know everything that was written in that letter," said Mr. Benchley. "But, the imposter Timothy had already left for the train back to Michigan—or so everybody was supposed to think. The imposter knew the real Father Tim had been killed, and he had to get out of there—or make it appear he had left town. He probably suspected that Father Michael knew something funny was going on. Perhaps he tripped himself up in simple conversation with the older priest. Whatever transpired, he had to get rid of Father Michael to protect himself and keep the plan on track."

"Murder number two," said Frank.

"Father Michael's call to the Michigan Seminary College confirmed that he had harbored a criminal this past month."

"Then I am kidnapped, foiling the first plan to nab and kill the lawyers. I connect the voices of two seemingly different men, and discover a co-conspirator, the fake Pinchus Seymour Pinkleton," I said.

"The real Timothy Morgan must have been about to give it all away, after he heard about the murder of his godfather," said Frank. "That's why they wacked him; made it look like an accident. Murder number three."

"There are lots of people involved in this," I said. "Somebody gave the order to take out the real Father Tim. I'll bet our imposter is still in town, still part of the plan to kill the lawyers."

"I believe you are right, Mrs. Parker."

I shivered.

Could it be the fake Timothy Morgan is driving around in a sleek new Duesenberg? I wondered.

Frank piped in: "I don't know what's going on except there's a priest-killer and a lawyer-killer, too. And then there're arsonists on the run. I thought it was one of them arsonists stabbed the old priest on Thanksgiving?"

"The fire alone was probably not the reason for killing Father John, but I suspect the players in both the arson and the attempted kidnapping are the same," said Mr. Benchley.

"Now, what is it that you need me to do?" asked Frank, chewing on the end of his cigar.

"How fast can you get wire photos from the Scopes Trial, Frank? Courtroom photos. We've got to try to identify people who are involved in this conspiracy."

"Oh, I see; you suspect the killers are home-grown Tennesseans, is that it? Maybe went to the trial?"

"You said you and Aleck had a friend down there who wrote for the Dayton paper? Maybe he can help identify these Klan assassins. Maybe they were hanging around the courthouse during the trial."

"I'll put a call in, pronto. Anything else?"

"Yeah, what about any missing persons from the area? They might be involved, or perhaps the missing are additional victims; you never know."

"Well, there were those brothers—the darktown fires?"

"Yes, well, one of them is dead; I was there, Frank. But, yes, ask your reporter friend if there are photos of the other brother, Harlow. I gather he was an important figure in the town of Dayton?"

"I recall it was a town outside of Dayton. Fremont."

"Well, they both might have come to New York as part of the plan," I said.

There was a knock at the door.

Mr. Benchley opened it to receive a long florist's box from our bellboy. He tipped the youngster a dime.

"Well, Mrs. Parker, it's not your birthday, is it? What did you do to deserve this?"

"Oh, shut up your nasty little mind and give me that box."

I placed it on the coffee table and removed the ribbon and lifted the lid to reveal a dozen branches of creamy-white camellias. The heady fragrance and fresh beauty of the flowers took my breath away.

Mr. Benchley moved for the card, but I slapped his hand before he could steal it away.

"It's obvious that a gentleman sent them, a man of some class and distinction," he said, all-knowing. "Or some swell asked his mama what would impress . . ."

The card was the sender's personal stationery. I removed the note from the envelope and turned away from my nosey friend.

> *This offering is hardly thanks enough for the great service you have performed for me and my friend, Mr. Darrow.*
>
> *We would be most pleased to have you and your guests join our party at the Cotton Club tonight for the midnight festivities and show.*
>
> *Forever in your debt,*
> *Arthur Garfield Hays*

"Who're they from, my little darlin'?" asked Frank.

"Let me take a guess," said Mr. Benchley. "The flowers were sent from Lily Walters Florist on Park Avenue, the notepaper, quality stock from—"

"Art Hays," I said to end the teasing speculation. "Gee, he's grand! The flowers are to thank me for helping to snag the assassin, and to invite me to the Cotton Club tonight."

"I suppose I'll find a corsage when I return home," said Mr. Benchley.

"Be a good boy and put these in some water."

"You already have a prior commitment for tonight, my dear Mrs. Parker."

"We have the New Year's Eve party at the Friars Club, yes, but I can pop off after an hour to join Messrs. Hays and Darrow uptown."

"You little witch!" said Mr. Benchley with a chuckle. "It says here, 'guests,' you and 'your guests'!"

"All right, of course you can come, if you promise to behave yourself."

"As long as you promise, Mrs. Parker, to behave *your*self."

"I am the model of grace and discretion."

Frank let out a sharp, startling cackle, and then, repentant, "Sorry, but the way you said it . . ."

"And, yes, Frank, you will join the party, too."

"I expect Aleck is attending the festivities?"

"No doubt. And we should invite Edna, as Aleck is escorting her to the Friars Club."

"We'd better hire a wagon to take us up."

"Jane and Ross?"

"Other plans."

"You and Gertrude will come up for a drink before we leave, Mr. Benchley?"

"She's not coming to the party after all, I'm afraid. The children have the chicken pox."

"Oh, I'm so sorry to hear that." I said. "Perhaps you need to get back—"

"I've never had the pox, so I mustn't return while the boys are contagious."

I wanted to send my friends off on their way so that I could prepare for the evening's festivities. I hadn't a thing to wear!

"So, Frank, would you get on that right away?"

"Oh, you mean the photos and stuff? All right, Bob, I'm off to do your bidding. See you later."

"I'm leaving, too," echoed Mr. Benchley. "I'll pick you up at eight o'clock, then?"

"Fred," I said, stopping him at the door, "do you think Hays and Darrow are well-enough protected?"

"I doubt they would have invited you to join them tonight if they weren't. Aleck said Hays hired Pinkerton guards. I'd not worry about it. As of yesterday, the assassins' plans to attempt anything in New York had to have been aborted."

"I suppose you are right," I agreed. "With the real Father Timothy killed, the imposter somewhere out there, and we don't as yet know the true identity of the man we captured yesterday, these hateful people are bound to need time to regroup. They'll try it again, somewhere else, in some other city, I fear, and I'd just like to see them all caught and put away before that can happen."

"See you tonight, my dear," said Mr. Benchley, patting my head and turning to leave.

"Oh, and Fred," I said, breaking off a camellia blossom from a stem, and slipping it into his lapel buttonhole, "thanks for the frying pan back-swing, yesterday."

"A pleasure, my dear, don't mention it."

I turned toward my bedroom closet. What on earth should I wear tonight?

Arthur Garfield Hays, married

Chapter Eleven

The camel-colored crushed velvet? No, I decided, I'd wear the plum satin dress with the handkerchief hemline. But then I thought that the black crepe Chanel with my floral embroidered tunic looked chic. Suffering the agony of women everywhere while wrestling with which attire seemed most appropriate for an occasion, or the most provocative, I finally settled on the beaded bodice, beige silk Molyneux with satin trim and draped, plunging neckline. There were comfortable shoes to match, nude-colored satin two-inch heels with T straps — I wanted to dance tonight, in spite of my aching muscles.

I'd finished arranging my hair, placing the toque Jane had given me for Christmas on my head. The finely constructed headwear with its detailed jeweled touches was stunning. I was sorry Jane was not joining us tonight to see me wear her marvelous gift.

I removed two of the five strings of clear crystal beads from around my neck, as I believe in the fashion philosophy that less is more, and added only one bracelet to my left wrist. *Done*, I thought. But the truth is, I'm never done; I keep on second-guessing myself, and I continued to fuss about while waiting for Mr. Benchley and FPA to arrive for a cocktail before we walked the few blocks up to the Friars Club on 48th Street.

I fussed over which wrap to wear, the chocolate-brown velvet cloak with turquoise lining or the silver foxtail–trimmed cape? I threw on my cream-colored satin evening wrap coat and was surprised that it was a perfect complement to my dress. It wasn't the warmest of choices, but we were only a few blocks away from the club, and later I'd not be outside longer than it took to nab a cab for the Cotton Club.

Mr. Benchley arrived a few minutes past nine o'clock, saying FPA would meet us at the party. He was happily tipsy, I'd say. Oh, he was never one to get really soused. He'd just become more jubilant when he'd had a few under his belt, more droll, the timbre of his baritone more lilting, giggles escaping more freely, as his conversation would spill out with a smile and a chuckle, effervescent, like champagne pouring out from the bottle. Tonight was for merriment, as the whole city would be out and about celebrating.

There would be parties everywhere, at every hotel, in private homes, even on the street. In less than three hours, thousands of people would welcome in the New Year, gathering at Times Square to watch as the big ball was lowered from the old New York Times Building at One Times Square, the very center of the X that marked the crossing of Broadway and Seventh Avenue. Streamers and confetti would fly out windows, as would any thought of the Volstead Act as champagne corks popped all around town.

Of course, such merriment could prove depressing; seeing the old year out might cause introspection—*What the hell did I do? What have I accomplished? The clock is ticking, one more year gone down the drain.*

But there is always the hope of a new year ahead: another chance, another shot of gin, another party, another man might come along and chase your blues away. *Put down that razorblade.*

Mr. Benchley uncorked the bottle of imported bubbly he had procured from his trusty bootlegger, a reliable source for "the sauce." While he poured, he said, "Did you know the police found Hays's Limo abandoned by the docks? And right next to it was a Duesenberg matching the description you gave to the police? A freighter sailed this morning for Panama, from that very pier. They're checking the passenger roster and searching the ship for stowaways."

"If they left on that ship they must be idiots to think they could get very far; and I don't think they're stupid. But you think we're all safe, now? That the threat to Hays and Darrow is over?"

"Well, it seems that three of the gang are out of the picture. And with the Pinkerton guards and the extra police on the lawyers, it'd be suicide to attempt an attack. Anyway, Darrow is leaving in the morning, heading back home to Chicago, with guards at his side."

We drank to each others' health and to a prosperous and wet New Year. Woodrow finished off the ounce of champagne I had poured into his dish, after sneezing from the bubbles, and Mr. Benchley presented him with a delectable portion of rare roast beef, sent up from the kitchen as a special treat.

The Friars Club's membership is composed of the theatrical and literary figures of our city, a fraternity of sorts not unlike our Round Table but grander in number. It, too, began its history with the casual gathering of press agents who met regularly to dine. And not unlike my vicious circle, their numbers were increased by actors and vaudevillians. Women may not apply for membership, but are wined and dined by the "brotherhood." That will have to change someday.

Aleck and Edna, and the Gershwin brothers, George and Ira, Irving Berlin, and FPA arrived soon after we walked through the clubhouse doors. We took the table that Aleck had arranged for us, and soon the champagne was flowing.

The entertainment promised to be lots of fun, with Fred and Adele Astaire, Jimmy Durante, Will Rogers, and newcomer Bob Hope hamming it up. My trying month of murder and mayhem faded away in the warm, festive atmosphere.

Frank, pulling out a small manila envelope from his jacket, handed it to me across the table. "Wire photos from the Scopes Trial."

"Thanks, Frank." I was about to slip the package behind me, where the chair back met my own, for safekeeping. I really didn't want to look at them tonight. *But*, I thought, we *had* asked Frank to get them, and there *had* been some urgency to the request. Of course, that was before the limo and the Duesenberg were located, and the knowledge that the steamer probably carried the assassins away.

"Aren't we going to look at those now?" asked Mr. Benchley. He proceeded to unwind the string from its closure. There were three photos, one taken in the courtroom and two of the crowds outside it.

"Here is a wire photo of the Healy brothers, posing in front of their store," said Frank. "Harley is on the left; Rowdy, the younger and the 'real piece of work' I told you about? He's on the right."

"This can't be so," I said, staring at the smiling face of the Wild-Hair Man, who Frank insisted was *Harley*. And standing reluctantly next to him with a frown was the man I recognized as Father Timothy, a.k.a. Rowdy Healy! "I don't understand . . . but I think we've been after the wrong fellow all along!"

In the courtroom photo stood Darrow and Bryan, the courthouse packed with press and observers, mostly men, as the jury took their oath. One street photo was of Darrow, looking directly into the camera, and his team of lawyers in the forefront with townspeople crowding around. The other photo showed the lawyers with the defendant climbing the steps to the courthouse, townspeople, again, in the background.

I was looking for the faces of the men involved in the murders, trying to determine if others were involved by analyzing their poses in relationship to other figures in the crowd. I saw nothing, and pushed the photos toward Mr. Benchley, just as Lionel Barrymore and his brother Johnny stopped by our table to say "hello." There was a lot of chatting and joking around, chairs pulled up to join the already-crowded table. The orchestra was tootling out a heavy-handed brassy beat for the dancing couples. Then Humphrey Bogart, a talented young actor who debuted on Broadway this year, asked me to dance. It was quite brave of him to ask me, really. I am looked upon as a bit *formidable*—if one *can* be just a bit formidable.

I had on my dancing shoes, so we hit the floor doing the Charleston, a new dance craze, to the popular song, *Yes, Sir, That's My Baby*. After Humpy—he didn't mind the nickname or the implication—returned me to the table, Mr. Benchley touched my arm.

"Dottie," he said. (I knew that what he was about to say held some importance, because he addressed me by my first name.) "Notice anything unusual about the courtroom photo?"

"I see lots of suspenders."

"Exactly!"

"What's new?"

"There are only a couple of women in the courtroom. See, the two hats here, one over there?"

"All right," I said, wanting to know what he was getting at but wanting more to leave my worries behind me and trip the light fantastic for the rest of the evening with handsome young men.

"No, don't look at the dance floor, look at the picture, specifically at the woman on the left, second row."

"What about her? Am I supposed to know who that is?"

"Pay attention—stop tapping your toe and look at the picture again."

"Spoilsport!" But I did as told. The photo was pretty good, as far as wire photos go; not too many dark lines obscuring the paper. "Oh, crap! It's *she*."

"I'd bet my wife on it!"

"Keep your little hausfrau out of this, Benchley!"

"The man to her right, isn't that . . . ?" I said, stopping short, waiting for Mr. Benchley's opinion.

"You're *darn tootin'* it is! Hello, Timothy Morgan, *Father* Timothy Morgan—a.k.a. Rowdy Healy!"

"We've got to call the police, Fred! That's the woman across the street from St. Agatha's rectory, Hermione Reynolds was her name, wasn't it?"

"Yes, and if she hasn't left town she could be the one person the police could break for the identities of the whole murdering gang!" said my friend, and off he went in search of a telephone.

Mr. Benchley's departure attracted Aleck's attention from a jovial conversation with Edna. "What's with the boy genius?" he asked.

"Aleck, we have to leave the party. What time are we to meet the lawyers at the Cotton Club?"

"After eleven-thirty, I suppose; the lecture should be over by eleven."

"What are you—"

Sobriety struck me between the eyes.

"*What lecture?*"

"Darrow's giving a lecture in the Great Hall at Cooper Union tonight. Should be over by eleven, and then they'll drive up to Harlem."

"Cooper Union!" It all made sense. "*Oh, shit*, of course he is!"

As soon as Aleck said the word *lecture*, I realized I had stupidly ignored a giant clue.

"In the steps of Abraham Lincoln," boasted Aleck.

"Oh, shit, I hope not!" I said; then off to the cloakroom to fetch our coats.

Mr. Benchley was on the phone, giving the address of Hermione Reynolds to the police. I stood beside him, waiting, looking at one of the street photos.

And that's when I saw it, clear as day.

The eyes, grayish-white in the black-and-white press photo, a straw hat obscuring the hair, but it was definitely him—the Wild-Haired Man—the murderer of Father John O'Hara, the man who'd tried to plug me, the man struck down dead on the streets of the city!

I grabbed Mr. Benchley's arm, and he covered the transmitter with a hand as I shared with him my discovery.

"Get men down to Cooper Union, right away," he said to the night-desk sergeant at Joe Woollcott's precinct house. "Darrow's there and there may be an attempt on his life tonight!"

I asked the hat-check girl to give the photos to Frank with instructions to get them over to Joe Woollcott at the police station, and we flew out onto the street. Without a word to each other, we headed downtown for the college.

It was ten o'clock, and it would take divine intervention to snag a taxi on a night like this. We were a couple of blocks off Times Square, where already there had gathered fifty thousand people waiting for the stroke of midnight to ring in the New Year. Just out the door, we were engulfed in the party atmosphere of loud, rambunctious revelers, moving in large gangs toward Seventh Avenue and the Square.

It appeared that the younger set were out tonight taking to the streets in their finery. Everyone was laughing, playful, intoxicatingly wild, encouraged by imbibing forbidden nectar and wearing devil-may-care cloaks of youthful prosperity; victory cries risen from the horrors of death and ashes in the trenches: *Carpe diem!* Seize the moment! Tomorrow we will all be dead!

We plowed our way against the onslaught of pedestrians, toward Fifth Avenue. Perhaps by some remote chance we might secure a taxi heading downtown.

Just as we reached Fifth, a cab pulled up to the curb, discharging a rowdy bunch of kids. But, as luck would have it, a burly fellow in a pointed party hat pushed in front of us and grabbed the door handle.

The gods must have smiled down on us, for while I was wishing Woodrow Wilson was with us to do his little taxi cab shuffle, Mr. Benchley had taken action.

"Sorry, old sport," he said, grasping the elastic strap on the man's paper party hat and giving it a good snap, "police emergency! We're commandeering this cab."

"Why, I never—!" said the man, cupping his chin from the sting of the assault, as Mr. Benchley put me into the cab. He grabbed Mr. Benchley's shoulder and spun him around. Fred must have seen the right hook coming, for he ducked and the fellow's hand made contact with the steel of the automobile.

"Sorry, old sport, Harvard Boxing Club's lesson number one—duck!" apologized Mr. Benchley, as he joined me in the cab and closed the door, leaving the fellow to nurse his injury as we drove away from the curb.

Below 34th Street the traffic was lighter and we were making good time. *Good time for what?* I asked myself. Could Darrow already be dead? If so, the attorney's death was our fault for not reading the clues. Why had I dismissed the importance of the Cooper Union lecture schedule we'd found in the trash from Father John's room at the rectory? Why hadn't I thought about it after finding the assassin's connection to the University Club—the stationery, a clue found along with the lecture schedule? I never bothered to look closely enough to see that Clarence Darrow was to speak tonight. At the time, though, any connection between the murder of the priest and an assassination conspiracy hadn't presented itself. If it had, Mr. Darrow's life would not be at stake now. But that was no consolation for our mistake. The only hope for Mr. Benchley and me to redeem ourselves for the oversight was to arrive in time to stop the assassin, and we were the only two people who had a chance of identifying him. In an audience of hundreds, only we could point out the inconspicuous man waiting for his opportunity to shoot Darrow.

Mr. Benchley handed the cabbie a buck as we

pulled up before the lecture hall at Cooper Union College. The streets here were relatively quiet for such a festive night, other than the rumble of the el train on the tracks overhead screeching to a stop at Union Square. We entered the lobby of the hall to be met by a gentleman at the door.

As Mr. Benchley explained why we were there and asked if the police had arrived, I walked through into the hall.

Mr. Darrow, dressed in a dark suit and bowtie, stood on the stage giving his talk. There were occasional waves of muted laughter, so my presence did not distract. I circled the back aisle, scanning the heads, but it was a futile task, as the seating was a curved arena with a dozen columns obstructing my view of faces. The lights aimed upon Darrow on the small stage served only to back-light and make silhouettes of the heads in the audience.

I stood in place for a moment, trying to decide what best to do. Was it really logical for the assassin to place himself in the middle of the audience, where he would be immediately apprehended when he'd done the nasty deed? Assuming he didn't want to die a martyr, wouldn't he choose a spot that gave him an avenue of escape? Perhaps in the gallery, to take to the roof and down to the street, or backstage, where he would be shielded from the audience's wrath completely.

I looked and saw that the hall didn't have a balcony. He had to be in the audience—or backstage.

Mr. Benchley and I were the only people who knew what the assassin looked like, but what if the shooter were someone other than the man who had impersonated Father Timothy? That would make finding the killer in this crowd impossible.

The police had arrived, I could see, for when Mr. Benchley walked into the hall from the lobby he was accompanied by two uniformed officers.

"Where are the Pinkerton men?" I asked Mr. Benchley.

"One in the audience and one outside, according to the manager. The police have the building surrounded and several officers are on the roof," he told me, while squinting his eyes in search of the killer in the audience.

"What time is it, Fred?"

"It's nearly eleven."

"I'll bet he's waiting for Darrow to finish so that he can take a shot during the applause, and make his break in the confusion at the exits."

"That's probably right, but I don't see our Father Timothy anywhere yet. You stay put; don't do anything," he whispered. "I'm going around to backstage from the outside entrance."

I knew the assassin's weapon of choice would be a gun. It would be a terrible sort of poetic justice in a demented mind to kill the modern-day champion of

Negro equality in the very room where more than sixty years ago Abraham Lincoln, emancipator, addressed the audience in his bid for the presidency. Would the hatred and violence never stop?

There was more laughter from the audience, and I looked toward the stage and Darrow's grim face, as he ambled slowly to a position downstage, allowing the laughter to grow. There was the power of a pregnant pause and the control of a great speaker in his deliberate delivery.

I froze when I glimpsed a slight movement at the edge of one of the three dark curtain panels filling the arches that backed the high platform on which Darrow was standing. Then something appeared at the break in the curtain, and within a split second I knew it was the muzzle of a gun.

I hurried down along one side of the shadowy wall of the circular hall. Ahead and next to the stage was a door at audience level leading backstage. Quickly, I disappeared into the wings, pretty certain that from where the assassin stood he hadn't seen me approach.

I expected a great expanse of space, but this was a lecture hall, not a legitimate theatre. A narrow hallway with arches echoing those on the proscenium gave little distance or protection from the gunman. I also expected a great number of policemen backstage, but there was no one, and I wondered why there was not even a stage manager. That's when I saw the man tied up and gagged, sitting in the corner.

I had no way to make contact with the men in the lobby, and little time to spend untying the poor fellow in the corner. Darrow was about to finish up his talk in a few minutes, I could sense it, as the chuckles from the audience were growing stronger now, and I was certain he intended to end on a high note.

How was I to stop the shooter?

I looked around me. A length of wood was lying on the floor, and I knew I could use it as a flat club if I had to strike out to defend myself. Perhaps I could get around and club the assassin from behind—that is, if he didn't hear or see me approach and shoot me first!

Was I insane? What was I doing here? Why couldn't I have left this to the police? Why didn't I listen to Fred and just stay put? I picked up the wood and was contemplating my next move, when suddenly Darrow ran down the stage steps and into the audience. There was pandemonium in the crowd as Pinkerton men pulled him to the floor and the policemen filed in, pointing weapons toward the stage.

Holy crap! I thought, *I'm going to get shot by either friend or foe, but definitely by somebody toting a gun!*

I made for the street stage door, aware that there would be policemen ready to greet the assassin on his way out. But, oddly, I came out onto a lobby, not outdoors. The hall was a fan-shaped structure within a square-shaped building.

Five guns were pointed at my face.

Mr. Benchley glared at me.

When they determined that I was just a simple idiot who got caught at the wrong place at the wrong time, they put their guns down on the ground, which I thought odd at first, but I sighed with relief, eager to clear the door so that the squad could enter and take the assassin.

But they didn't move, and I didn't understand why they didn't just push me aside and storm in. But, as I looked over my shoulder, understanding dawned. "Father Tim" stood pointing a gun at my head, and I decided that was a good enough reason for the cops to lay down their firearms.

I was to be his ticket out of the place, the hostage, and I began to see how foolish I had been to choose this way out. I'd walked right into his hands, and now, after using me as his shield, he'd kill me for sure. He led me to a door leading out into the night. "I'll have no trouble shooting you in the head if you try anything."

I was so scared I couldn't swallow, let alone answer his threat. He had to keep me alive for a while, anyway, and maybe I'd get rescued before he finished me off.

Chaos ruled outside the entrance to the hall, and he brought us directly into the fray, one hand at my back, the other holding the gun at my waist, as we blended into the mix of men and women scattering away along the sidewalk. We walked north across the square at Astor Place, and then down through the subway kiosk stairs with scores of others who went on through the turnstiles toward the northbound platform of the subway el. We had no sooner arrived than an oncoming train prompted people to quicken their paces through the turnstiles to board it before it left the station. The cars came to a prolonged and screeching halt, loud enough to tear one's heart out. But before we could get through the turnstiles, I was pushed to my knees.

And suddenly, I was free! He had released me with a push as he leapt over a turnstile.

Of course it was insane to follow the man who'd just held a gun at my head, but I never said I was sane. If the doors had closed on the car he'd just entered, and I didn't follow, he would get away and probably try to kill Darrow and others again.

As a fellow put his fare into the turnstile's slot, I pushed him aside to go through. I could hear him cursing at my back as I slipped into the car, pushed in by the throng of passengers. Before the doors closed I glimpsed the bluecoats led by Mr. Benchley arriving at the gates.

Fred took the turnstile in a single, graceful bound, and hit the doors just as they began to close. As he was wedged between them, the engineer was forced to open the doors once again. Mr. Benchley was in.

Bluecoats, frustrated at failing to stop the train, blurred and disappeared as the subway train jolted forward and moved out of the station.

"How did you find me?" I asked as we wormed our way through a party of swells. I wound up in a dead-end wall that turned out to be a big-bosomed matron blocking my progress.

"Your white satin coat is distinct, in a sea of black, my dear, shines like a beacon in the night."

"I think he's in the car up ahead."

"And why are you following him?"

"I don't know. Death wish? Pills are easier, I'd say."

"You mustn't die, Mrs. Parker. Whatever would we do without you?"

"We'll get out next stop: 14th Street."

The train pulled into the station and we exited. When the doors opened there was a scurry of passengers and we were carried on the wave leaving the car.

I spotted him then, getting off the train, too, one car ahead of us, and just as I caught sight of him he caught sight of me and doubled back in. I hate to be challenged or double-crossed, and there was a score to settle with the man. I grabbed Mr. Benchley's hand and pulled him back in as the doors closed on us.

It was the same thing at 23rd Street, the shuffle

out and then back into the car, but at 28th, as we started our exit, we saw bluecoats swarming the platform and we knew he would not risk getting off. Mr. Benchley caught the eye of one officer, and he signaled the killer was on the train, but the doors closed before anything could be done to alert the engineer to stop. At 33rd, the subway train did not stop, and I figured it was by order of the police. We were coming into Grand Central Station at 42nd Street, and I expected a veritable wall of blue to greet us on arrival.

But, my fear was that he had a gun and might try to take another hostage, possibly shoot his way out, killing innocent people out for a night of celebration.

The train pulled into the station slowly and screeched to a prolonged, earsplitting stop. There were no officers on the platform that I could see, and I wondered *why—how could this be?*

We waited as people piled out of our car, and positioned ourselves just outside the door while others entered.

"*He's off!*" I yelled at my friend. "He's off the train. See him?"

In a wave of derby bowlers, apple caps, and fedoras, his blond head bobbed along distinctly.

"I don't."

"He's right there, no hat, the only one without a hat. See now?"

We moved toward the hatless figure and stayed a good distance behind, following him up the iron stairway, wondering whether he was headed for the street or intended to blend into the crowd weaving about in the huge Grand Central Terminal. If he did that, he could run down any of a dozen track ramps and board and hide in almost any sleeper car of a train scheduled to leave at midnight, and be lost to us.

Up ahead was a line of policemen standing like a barrier. As soon as he saw them, he positioned himself next to a young couple, talking to them as if they were acquainted and sticking close to them as they turned toward the long, white-tiled corridor leading to the Shuttle, the short, one-stop train connection to Times Square.

Usually at this hour, only a few people might be walking along this corridor to the Shuttle, but it was New Year's Eve and the crowd was rushing to get to Times Square in time to witness the countdown to midnight and the dropping of the ball from the Times building.

The subway train was already in the station and the platform was unusually crowded. Up ahead we could see the hatless head of our quarry getting into the first of the three subway cars.

What were we going to do, I asked Mr. Benchley as the train pulled out of the station and into the tunnel. Yes, we had had opportunity to yell out to the officers standing watch at the terminal entrance, but that might have started a gunfight, with lots of people killed or wounded. But, what were we doing now? Chasing him to where? Truth was, we didn't know *what* we were doing; we had no plan. We were just chasing the Devil, and if we weren't careful, we'd get to Hell before he did!

All of a sudden, I was knocked into a big, burly man who caught me in places he shouldn't have laid his hands; Mr. Benchley was down on the floor in missionary position over a sprightly matron, through whose eyeglasses flashed a surprised, though not discontented, look. The train had come to a rude and violent stop. People had their hats knocked off at best, or sprained and bruised body parts at worst, and quickly I surmised that the emergency brake inside one of the cars had been pulled to stop the train. The interior lights went out and we were cloaked in darkness.

God knows what was going on in the dark; there were gasps of shock, cries of pain, a few obscenities, gurgles of laughter, and a good amount of shuffling among the tangle of bodies. I heard a scream, and then Mr. Benchley's voice: "I beg your pardon, Madame. Dottie? Where—Oh, there you are!" Auxiliary lights came on, shedding a dim pall over the scene. He took my hand.

We were stopped in the tunnel between stations. Probably just under Bryant Park.

"He's going to get out by forcing open the doors," said Mr. Benchley.

He was going to use the dark cover of the tunnel to make his escape.

Then, the hum of the motor as all the doors opened; the lights flickered and became brighter. The conductor was walking through the cars looking for the culprit responsible for pulling the brake cord. Mr. Benchley tried to tell the man what was going on, but he didn't seem to understand, accusing *us* of having pulled the cord, only stopping his accusations when several people vouched that we were telling the truth.

"He's out in the tunnel," I said.

Mr. Benchley was silent for a long moment. Then he spoke, a frown revealing strong consideration. "You know, I don't think so. There's no place to go but back to Grand Central or on to Times Square. No; he's on the train. I think it was a trick to make us think he jumped out."

"So, he's heading for the Square where he can blend into the crowd."

The train shook and coughed to a start, and within half a minute we pulled into Times Square Station at 42nd Street.

Mr. Benchley was right; he had remained on the train, and we were first out of the car. Now our man would have to get to the stairway and up to the first level toward the street before we did; the stairs were closer to us than to him. He would have to cross our path to get to the stairs, and Mr. Benchley bolted through to stop his progress. *Oh, crap, Fred's going to get shot*, I thought, as I let loose a bloodcurdling scream.

People stopped in their tracks to turn and look at the screaming demon standing in the middle of the platform, but it was enough of a distraction to slow the assassin's progress, allowing Mr. Benchley to pull at his coattails as the man hit the stairs running. The tug was enough to throw him off balance and bring him down hard, his back hitting the hard edge of a steel step. He toppled over to sprawl face down and flat out on the platform. The gun he'd been holding had flown from his hand to spin like a top an arm's-reach away.

Mr. Benchley threw himself over him, a knee placed strategically in the small of his back. As he leaned over to secure the weapon, the lessening of his weight on the assassin's back gave the killer opportunity to throw Mr. Benchley off and over to the ground, where he lay supine for a long moment, winded. As the men rose to their feet, the gun once again was pitched aside in their scuffle. It landed at my feet. I picked it up. It weighed so much more than I thought it would, this deadly, molded piece of metal cradled in my shaking fingers. "Father Tim" saw that I had his only hope of defense and lunged toward me. So frightened was I that he'd use it on me once he had wrestled it from my hand, that I pitched the gun over the heads of onlookers in the direction of the subway tracks. I heard it hit the tile wall and fall down into the recessed well. For a second time, Mr. Benchley grabbed at the culprit from behind and swung him around. It was not the best move to repeat; the men stood face to face, and this time the wily rat administered a swift and accurate kick to the groin. With Mr. Benchley doubled over in pain, the assassin took full advantage of the opportunity to escape. He sprinted up the stairs, his path cleared as no one in their right mind wanted to grapple with a madman.

I followed and let out another scream that could land a person in an asylum. It was the right thing to do, however, for I had actually forged my own path. Frightened, people got out of my way, and when I reached the landing I was met by half-a-dozen cops charging down from the two stairways leading from the street.

They looked at me, and they knew who I was, and that the assassin was close to their grasp.

But where, exactly, was he? Suddenly I'd no idea where he'd disappeared.

Mr. Benchley made it painfully up the stairs, and we were surrounded by a crowd of passengers and police officers. One woman pointed to the street, saying, "He went that way." A young couple pointed to an archway in the distance, and we decided the man couldn't have gone up the stairway at the same time the cops were descending from the street. The only other path of escape was through the door beyond the arched opening, just off the downtown platform of the Broadway Line, around the corner from where we stood. And that door led directly into Hubert's Museum.

Mr. Benchley and I, followed by at least six uniformed men, bolted through the Museum's entrance. Only a half-dozen years ago this was the subway entrance to one of the most spectacular lobster palaces in New York, Murray's Roman Gardens. Its doors closed after the war, when drink became illegal. People must have been more thirsty than hungry, for they turned to the speakeasies for quenching.

Hubert's Museum was a freak-show exhibit, and a very successful one at that. Mr. Benchley and I had intended to take a drunken tour through the place someday—it was the kind of lunacy that one needed to be tight to enjoy—but it appeared that that "someday" had arrived dry. The night had been freakish enough already—I could do without any more freaks. But as we entered the dark, gloomily lit entry and raced toward the ticket booth and turnstile, we encountered the first of many.

A woman in the ticket booth was pointing at the curtain just beyond the entry turnstile and ranting her displeasure. As Mr. Benchley lifted me over, before leaping over it himself, followed by the cops, she continued raving over the dime admission we'd failed to pay.

The long corridor we entered was lined on both sides by four-foot-high velvet curtains topping waist-high platforms, on which, when the curtains parted, were displayed the various advertised oddities. There were only a handful of people viewing the exhibits in the dimly lit room, as it was nearing midnight and the greater attraction tonight was the countdown to the ball dropping outside in the square.

We ran past the display of shrunken heads, two-headed snakes, and the three Filipino midgets on their little stage, one of whom asked why we were in a hurry, and "why the cops?" Mr. Benchley asked if a hatless man had run past, and they nodded and pointed the direction.

Martha, the Armless Wonder, one of the advertised headliners, couldn't point when we stopped at her vignette, but with a toss of her head in the same direction she wished us luck.

The Carlson Sisters, "Twin Fat Girls," finished each others' sentences:

"A hatless man?" He went—"

"—that way, toward the—"

"—flea circus!"

Once arrived at Professor Heckler's Flea Circus, where sixty trained *Pulex irritans* were performing gymnastic leaps and summersaults, playing football, carrying flags, and jumping ropes, we were ignored. If we hadn't been pressed by a more urgent purpose, we might have been so transfixed by the talent and skill displayed before us that we'd have forgotten we weren't at all tight.

We exited the museum the way we'd arrived, and the screaming ticket seller was soon soothed into silence when Mr. Benchley pushed a dollar bill through the hole in her glass booth.

"He's gone," she said, "the man you were chasing."

We piled out through the door and onto the subway platform where we were in time to watch the scuffle between our prey and one of the police officers.

Mr. Benchley grabbed my arm and placed me behind him, shielding me from danger.

A shot fired, thunderously, for the echo reverberated within the tunnel, and I struggled to get free to better see what was happening. A policeman down, shot in the foot, the assassin on the run with the cop's service revolver.

It's dangerous to shoot off a gun in such a confined space with hundreds of people going to and fro like ducks in a shooting gallery. People were scurrying for the stairs up to the street, their screams of fear mingled with the screams of celebration a few feet above us out in Times Square.

Our man was searching for escape, and with every turn he had to retreat and try another path. And in the confusion of the crowded subway, passengers made mad dashes for cover. Mr. Benchley held fast my hand, dragging me along.

"I saw that door open," he said, while assisting a young woman fallen down in the rush before him. "The old loading platform of the building."

I knew what he meant: When the *New York Times* built its offices marking the cross-point on the X that was Times Square back at the turn of the century, the company had created a loading dock area to more quickly transport newspapers by means of special trains traveling along the tracks of the subway system. It worked efficiently until, in 1913, the newspaper moved its presses to the current building occupying the slice of real estate between 43rd and 44th Streets. Now, One Times Square houses the *Times's* pressroom and administrative offices, but is best known and used as a gigantic advertising billboard towering over the square. And just before midnight on December 31, it is the tower from which a ball descends, marking the beginning of a new year.

We looked around at the ghostly, barren loading platforms, saw the closing of the huge double doors, and followed in through them to the cement room in the foundation of the building. There was no escape but by the freight elevator or a stairway, and from the hum of pulleys and wheels it appeared that our man was taking the easy way up. All that was left for us to do was to travel the hard way. We climbed the stairs.

"Fred," I whined, "what are we doing?"

"Going up to the roof."

"It's too many flights, I'm all rung out."

"But, the thrill of the hunt!"

"My dogs are spent!"

"Then, stay here!"

"I will not! I'm coming with you, soon as I get these shoes off."

The T-straps had to be unbuckled, and by the time I got them off my feet Mr. Benchley was already at the top of the first landing. The icy-cold cement was heavenly on my feet, and I was able to sprint up the first two flights with new ease. But by the time I started on the third flight, it felt like Everest would be easier to scale. And finally on the roof level, where twenty years ago extravagant New Year's Eve parties were held with fireworks that threatened to repeat the San Francisco fire in this East Coast city, I was so breathless that I couldn't speak at all.

The roof was ablaze with electric lights. A party was going on under stars outshone by the great expansive fields of electric lights that swept the distance beyond and below us, known as the Great White Way: swells and gals and a band tooting out *Sweet Georgia Brown*; champagne glasses raised and spilled. Mr. Benchley was at the roof's railing, one of many men shouting down into the crowd through the lofty night sky. The sound of a hundred thousand or more drunken fools pressing forth to fill Times Square, like a Texas cattle roundup, rose up in hissing whines. So extraordinary and infectious was the sound of cheers rising from the cavernous space formed by the surrounding buildings that I was overcome, startled by the effect. In a city where, surrounded by millions of people, one can wither from lonesomeness, it is at times like this, times of celebration, like the Armistice celebration in '18, when citizens come together with camaraderie and renewed hope for a better future.

"The assassin," I choked out to the policeman, "where'd he go?"

"Over the top," he replied, and then tried to prevent my progress.

Suddenly, a fight broke out between a couple of drunks and soon spread like a disease to the party guests. Hair was pulled, a dress torn, beads scattered as three women engaged in a cat fight. As the officer holding me was suddenly distracted by an elderly matron's elbow to his ribs as she attempted to back away from a flying punch, I broke free, ducked a right hook, took a splash of champagne in the face, and made it through the obstacle course to Mr. Benchley's side.

I wedged myself in between him and a policeman, and looked down into the crowd, expecting to see a dead man fallen down into the street.

The glow of the brilliantly lit ball obscured the view of the undulating mass of humanity below. The sight of the killer standing on the ball, light bulbs rupturing from his weight and sparking in bursts of cinders as he gripped the connecting rod that was suspended over the street, sent my stomach to my knees.

The crowds were chanting something in a sing-song rhythm, and I realized they were counting down the seconds: "—eight, seven, six—"

If he fell or was electrocuted, how many people would he kill or injure other than himself?

"—four, three, two—"

The ball stopped on its track.

"—one!"

It was like having your ear at the track of a speeding freight train. The mindboggling roar from below was the emanation from the throats of a hundred thousand children behaving badly. Confetti and streamers and tickertape rained down from the windows and rooftops of the buildings lining Broadway and Seventh Avenue. Noisemakers cranked, tambourines rattled, paper whistles shrieked, streetcar bells rang, and every automobile horn in the city honked—it was loud enough to awaken the dead. The people of New York City were celebrating in toto voce their mantra: *Live for today, for tomorrow we will all be dead.*

There was nowhere for him to go. If he thought that ball would carry him down into the crowd and then into freedom, he miscalculated. The ball stops two stories above the street, and a fall would kill him.

As the crowd continued rejoicing, and the pickpockets made hay before the pickin's grew slim, the lights on the ball were extinguished and the engineers were ordered to bring the ball back up to its container, suspended off the edge of the roof. In less than a minute, "Timothy Morgan," the imposter priest and murdering assassin, was properly ensconced in a metal cage.

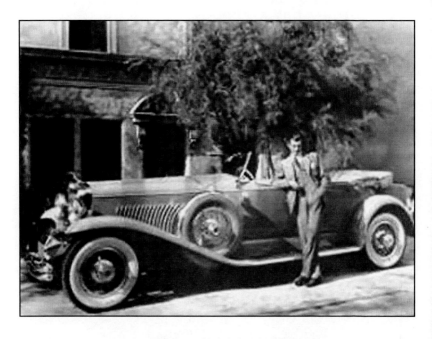

**The real Pinchus Seymour Pinkelton
standing alongside his Doozie**

That's Father Tim (a.k.a. Rowdy Healy) next to the Reynolds woman in the white hat just below Clarence Darrow's raised hand!

Boaters appeared to float along Times Square in the daytime as we awaited news of winner of the Dempsey-Carpentier fight.

The Final Chapter

André Peer and his ten-man Cotton Club Orchestra were really cookin' tonight, and as usual, by two o'clock in the morning the musicians were caught up in their hypnotic jazz reverie. The atmosphere had turned from red-hot and pulsing to blue and sultry.

But the party was far from over, although its remnants lay crushed on the floor beneath our feet, the dots of confetti and curling streamers brushed off the dance floor and gathered aside like old memories in corners and under tables and chairs.

Mr. Benchley and I missed the midnight show—Earl "Snakehips" Tucker and Evelyn Welsh burning up the stage with their new dance routine.

But, as we sat at the big round table surrounded by our friends, we rather enjoyed the somber blues ballads weeping softly from the bandstand.

When we arrived at the club half an hour before, the celebratory spirit was still high. We were greeted by Aleck and Edna, FPA with a little chorine he'd picked up at the Friars Club, and Jane and Ross, who were bored at the party they'd attended and decided to take up the standing invitation to join us. George and Ira and Irving rounded out the table. Arthur Garfield Hays, his wife, and Clarence Darrow decided not to join the midnight soireé. Darrow was leaving on an early train; he was tired after the lecture, and the Hayses took him home for a late dinner. But, the tab was on Hays, anything we wanted, and that meant that the champagne flowed and several good, genuinely imported bottles of scotch poured freely.

"Looks like you've been dragged through the city, Dot," came the strident tones of Edna Ferber. She ended her observation with a chuckle, which did nothing to endear her to me. But, she had been a sport yesterday, during our foray as Marx Brothers at the University Club. I think she was flattered that I had asked her to help, and I knew she'd had fun playing Zeppo for a day.

"I *have* been dragged through the city, Edna," I said.

My satin coat and dress had not faired all that well; there were streaks of soot I hoped the cleaners might remove. My hose was snagged and a run ran up from my right foot, the look reminiscent of a Hell's Kitchen hooker. I'd managed to comb my hair and apply lipstick after wiping off the smudges from my face. I figured everyone was, by that time, so very sloshed that no one would notice I'd been ravaged in my adventures.

Mr. Benchley, on the other hand, looked fresh as the morning dew, the rat!

There were questions after questions: To where had we run off from the Friars Club affair? Were we frightened? What did they do with the monster when they brought him up in the cage?

Frank told us he'd called the city desk with his comments for his morning column about the goings-on at the Friars Club party, and then had spoken to the crime reporter who scooped the story that Hermione Reynolds, the girl in the Scopes Trial photo, had been caught with her mother, Winnie Winkle, as they were leaving their apartment across from St. Agatha's, toting luggage. Left behind in the apartment was the leg-cast she wore to make her appear an invalid. Found inside one valise was a book with the names of her criminal contacts. She did break down and tell the police that she was the girlfriend of Rowdy Healy, a.k.a. "Father Timothy Morgan," the man who killed both Father John O'Hara and Father Michael Murphy when the latter discovered the real Father Tim, the godson of his friend John, had never left Grosse Pointe, according to a letter the Jesuit priest had sent a few days before Christmas after hearing of his godfather's murder. That letter prompted Father Michael to call us for help, soon after he realized the man posing as Father Timothy was an imposter. Timothy, I mean Rowdy, suspected Father Michael was onto him; something was fishy, and after he pretended to leave town, he snuck back in through the back garden door, killed the priest, and destroyed the incriminating letter.

"But he didn't kill Father John," I said. "I saw who did it. It was the Wild-Haired Man."

"*The Wild-Haired Man was a good guy!* He was Rowdy's older brother, Harlow," said Frank. "Harlow tried to stop his brother and the conspiracy to kill the lawyers. He was chasing his brother Rowdy *with* Father John when John was murdered by Rowdy in the crowd on Thanksgiving morning."

"Why didn't Harlow go to the police?"

"The killer was his little brother, and killer or not, he wanted to stop his brother, not turn him in."

"But who fired the shot at Mrs. Parker?"

"Rowdy."

"He could have done it, of course. Remember Father Michael told us that Father John's godson would be arriving shortly? The day we went to speak with him that first time?"

"He, Rowdy Healy, was waiting for us to come out of the rectory! The shot was fired from across the street in the apartment taken by Hermione Reynolds."

"Rowdy was out to kill you. Harlow was not the shooter, but he was trying to get us out of harm's way, not lead us into it! But, he ran right into the street and got struck by a car."

"How did Father John get involved in all of this?"

"He knew Rowdy was one of the men who set the darktown fire, but he must have suspected there were other plans brewing. Then he found out about the Klan's plan to kill Darrow from a parishioner in the confessional. One can only suspect that the parishioner was Harlow, converted to Catholicism several years earlier for his marriage to a young woman who died a year later in childbirth. Whichever it was that set them in motion, Father John and Harlow joined forces to track down Rowdy and stop the assassination. John went to Detroit, trying to see Darrow there, and when he found out he was out on a lecture tour, he followed him to New York. A letter was found among the young Jesuit's things—the real Father Tim—from Father John, to be opened in the event of his death. Timothy thought the envelope contained John's will, and when he heard that his godfather had been murdered he opened it and found, not a last will and testament, but Father John's confession in handwriting: He was disgusted by the hatred he'd witnessed during his years in the small Southern town, and a crisis of faith had made him reluctant to stand up, if only in his pulpit, against the prejudice he abhorred. Finally, he could stand by no longer. The first-hand knowledge of the arson and the planned assassination made him culpable if he did not take action. Thus the trip to Grosse Pointe, where he knew plans were shaping up, the hatred for Darrow brewing because of the upcoming Sweet Trial. Harlow was close by, in Detroit, hoping to find and convince his brother, Rowdy, to stop the madness. The priest and Harlow left for New York together. The letter to his godson was insurance that if anything happened to him Timothy should call in the authorities."

"Who killed the godson?"

"A Klansman, probably; I don't know if we'll ever know who actually sabotaged the Jesuit's automobile or what was in the letter that the real Father Tim wrote to Father Michael, when he heard about his godfather's murder. That letter is probably what got them both killed," said Frank.

"Why didn't Timothy call the Detroit Police?" I asked.

"He did. Problem is, the department is pretty corrupt, and it's suspected the Klan has a number of members on the force. Going to them probably was the worst thing he could have done. It brought Timothy his death sentence."

"And the guy with the Duesenberg?" added Frank. "The true identity of the man posing as Pinchus Seymour Pinkleton?"

"Yeah, and the creep who had me kidnapped!"

"That's right; he's a Detroit businessman, Lionel

Struthers, who went to the University of Michigan with the real Pinny, and he's a member of the Detroit chapter of the KKK. Outraged that Negros are moving into his neighborhood. Wanted justice."

"He'll certainly get justice."

"He was running things from the University Club where the real Pinny has a membership."

"Did he kill the real Pinny?"

"*Nahh*, the *real* Pinny is shacked up with his mistress in Canada. Told his wife he was off for a few weeks alone fishing at his lodge on the lake. He's got some explaining to do...."

"And the goons who kidnapped me?"

"Amateurs. White-trash country boys, do anything they're told. Rowdy brought them in. Seems Rowdy liked to run around his hometown with his lackeys at his heels, but made the mistake of giving them something to do, 'sides minding the still. The flunkies were picked up by the sheriff when they got off the train in Dayton."

I had no more questions, only regrets. The man I believed was trying to kill me had been trying to protect me, and he ran to his death on the streets of New York. I saw Mr. Benchley's somber expression, and I knew he felt in some way responsible for the fellow's death.

It was all over now; time to get back to our normal lives of sleeping 'til noon, lunching from one 'til three, cocktails at five at my place or at Neysa's, dropping by my favorite speak, Tony Soma's, shopping and gossiping with Tallulah and Jane, five nights a week at the Theatre, and when there was time, writing an article or story or two. Most of all, I missed my little man, Woodrow Wilson, and I promised myself that tomorrow we'd take a nice long walk together up Fifth Avenue and into Central Park.

Aleck, who'd been unusually quiet, said: "You haven't noticed!"

"What's that?" I asked, still deep within my own thoughts.

"My opera cape and top hat!"

"Oh, I see they've been returned."

"Scavenger hunt! Those naughty boys on break from Columbia, same ones stole the turkeys last month and freed them on Sheep Meadow? They done the dastardly deed. Came by messenger this afternoon with a note from Mrs. Sidney Snodgrass, apologizing for her son, who took the evening clothes. She saw my advertisement in the paper and instantly knew they belonged to me. Had them cleaned and sent off immediately with her note, begging me not to press charges, and saying that she would not accept the reward." Aleck sat back with a smile on his face. "It's been a very good day."

André Peer came over to our table to say "hello" and to meet George, Ira, and Irving. "Could we have the pleasure of your sitting in with us, Mr. Gershwin?"

he asked George, who perked up and beamed out a huge grin.

"If the fellows will have me, it'd be an honor to play a little of your kind of jazz."

A young, light-skinned Negro man came up to our table and placed a little red-covered book in George's hand: "I just read this fine little novel that came out a couple months ago, and the more I think about it, I feel you've got to read it too, to see what I mean. Du Bose Heyward is the author."

"What about Du Bose Heyward?" asked Edna, looking up from her cup. "Anybody read his book, *Porgy?*"

Everybody laughed.

"It was one of the most compelling books I've ever read," I said. "My heart breaks for Porgy and his Bess."

George clutched at the book, and it looked like he was anxious to start reading. "Thanks, I'll read it tonight. I always like a good book."

He looked questioningly at the young man. "Have we met?"

A shy smile, and then, "My name's Langston Hughes, Mr. Gershwin. I'm up for the holiday from Lincoln College. I write poetry, too."

"Oh, yes, I know who you are, and I've a feeling this story is the ticket, all right! Sit down and join us, Langston, meet my friends while I'm gone."

"Now, what do you want to play," asked the orchestra leader as he walked George over to the piano. The audience saw who was walking to the bandstand and broke out in applause.

Mr. Benchley smiled at me, refilled my champagne, and then lit my cigarette.

The New Year had gotten off to a shaky start, but here we all were, with laughter, great music, rivers of booze, and friendship.

The End

Mr. Benchley and I missed the New Year's party, but, ain't we got fun?

Poetic License

I have taken poetic license in the *Mrs. Parker Mysteries* quite often, but with great care. I have tried to be historically accurate with dates and times when my characters were really roaming the streets, theatres, and speakeasies of Manhattan during the 1920s. I've taken a few liberties, which will, no doubt, raise the proverbial red flags before the eyes of the purists and Round Table devotees. For instance, Dorothy Parker's rooms at the Algonquin did not face the 44th Street front entrance of the hotel as I have placed them, but toward the back of the building on the eleventh floor, overlooking the rear facades of buildings along the south side of 45th Street. At one time, she had a room on the second floor. So it is, too, with Robert Benchley's rooms at the Royalton, the bachelor residence directly across the street from the Algonquin. His rooms were at the rear, not facing 44th Street. He kept those rooms for sixteen years, but for some time lived on Madison Avenue with Charles MacArthur, as well as at the Algonquin. He did not take the Royalton rooms until 1929. Aleck Woollcott did share a residence on West 47th street with Jane Grant and Harold Ross, but that situation lasted only a few years. He bought an apartment on 52nd Street facing the East River, dubbed "Wit's End" by Dottie Parker.

And for the sake of action, I have occasionally

placed an alleyway where there never was one, or invented a church or a theatre that never existed, that sort of thing.

Officer Joe Woollcott of the NYPD is a figment of my imagination. But it is not unlikely that Aleck would have had such a down-to-earth cousin. Aleck was his family's anomaly.

At different times throughout the 1920s, Alexander Woollcott, Robert Benchley, Heywood Broun, Marc Connolly, and Robert Sherwood wrote for, or were editors of, many different publications. To avoid confusion, and finding the changes in employment of no consequence to the storylines of my books, I have kept them on the staffs of only one or two papers or magazines.

Woodrow Wilson, our lovable Boston terrier, was one of a long line of dogs embraced by Dorothy Parker, including Robinson, a dachshund, and two poodles, each named Cliché. But, I chose Woodrow, and have kept him alive years longer than was actually the case.

I do not refer to Dorothy Parker's real-life romantic attachments, nor include those gentlemen in any of my stories, except for her husband, Eddie, and he is mentioned only to give the reader an understanding of her circumstances and the effects of World War I on her life and times.

While researching, I have encountered many

conflicting accounts of events involving my leading characters. It usually has to do with who said/did what to whom, and as these biographers/sources are sincere and unquestionably creditable, and as most of the stories in question are hearsay, or second- or third-generation accounts that these sources are retelling, situations that might not even have happened, these differences are of little importance, really, so forgive me my trespasses, please. First-hand accounts might have been embellished to enhance entertainment effect. (For example, Hemingway credited himself with several clever lines that were quipped by others, but were good enough for him to claim as his own.) I still cannot definitely attribute the line, "Let's get out of these wet clothes and into a dry martini," to Robert Benchley. Some suggest it was a press agent or Aleck Woollcott who actually said the words. Lots of people claim credit. As nearly a century has passed, these retold events might be assigned to folklore. (I wasn't there; you weren't there; so we'll never know for sure what really occurred.) Also, famous quotes once spoken by these famous people were not always spoken at the time and place at which I have put them in my novels.

Praise for *Dorothy Parker Mysteries*

Those of us who since childhood had wished there was a time machine that could let us experience and enjoy life in other periods, should read Agata Stanford's "Dorothy Parker Mysteries" series. They wonderfully recreate the atmosphere and spirit of the literary and artistic crowd at the Algonquin Round Table in the 1920s, and bring back to life the wit, habits, foibles, and escapades of Dorothy Parker, Robert Benchley, and Alexander Woollcott, as well as of the multitude of their friends and even their pets, both human and animal.

—*Anatole Konstantin*
  Author of *A Red Boyhood: Growing Up under Stalin*

Agata Stanford's "Dorothy Parker Mysteries" is destined to become a classic series. It's an addictive cocktail for the avid mystery reader. It has it all: murder, mystery, and Marx Brothers' mayhem. You'll see, once you've taken Manhattan with the Parker/Benchley crowd. Dorothy Parker wins! Move over Nick and Nora.

—*Elizabeth Fuller*
  Author of *Me and Jezebel*

About the Author

Agata Stanford is an actress, director, and playwright who grew up in New York City. While attending the School of Performing Arts, she'd often walk past the Algonquin Hotel, which sparked her early interest in the legendary Algonquin Round Table.

Printed by BoD in Norderstedt, Germany